THE ABBERLEY BEACH MURDERS

An addictive crime thriller with a fiendish twist

D.E. WHITE

Detective Dove Milson Book 3

JOFFE BOOKS

Joffe Books, London
www.joffebooks.com

First published in Great Britain in 2021

Cover art by Nebojsa Zorić

ISBN: 978-1-78931-896-8

PROLOGUE

Did you notice me, from across the road?

I might have missed you if I hadn't turned quickly to sidestep the little girl. She was skipping along beside her mother, long, curly red hair flying out behind her in the summer breeze, a yellow balloon dancing above her head, the ribbon clutched tightly in her hand.

I saw you then. I saw you looking at her from the dusty pavement, just as all those years ago I watched you hungering after the others. You wanted them but you couldn't touch them. Something changed, and nobody could figure out why, certainly not the police. You're smart, I respect that, but I think it's true to say I'm smarter.

It was over in an instant, that moment of gut-tearing recognition. You were swallowed up by traffic, throngs of tourists and locals enjoying the sticky, throbbing heat of summer. I don't think you saw me. Our eyes never met. My heart beat painfully fast. My head felt as if it was swelling, floating away like the balloon. Bloody sparks danced in front of my eyes and my chest rose and fell way too fast. I blinked hard. My vision cleared again. I was calmer.

Did I want you to see me? A part of me did. A part of me wanted you to register that I know what you did, that I know you're walking around as though none of it ever happened. Another part of me knows I need to let it go — let you go, and get on with my life.

1

I stood there at the light, fixed, unmoving, and for a while it was almost as though I was the only person standing still in the entire universe. People jostled, pushed impatiently past, their hot bodies briefly touching mine. The smell of sweat and that sugar-sweet scent of summer mingled unpleasantly, hot and heavy, overpowering.

But I was almost afraid to break the spell, to step out from my memories, from the person I once was. When I did force one foot in front of the other, pushing my way across the road, you were long gone.

Perhaps you never existed at all.

CHAPTER ONE

It was almost dark when she finally jogged back up the beach, the fine shingle crunching under her bare feet, struggling a little with the weight of her board. Shadows steadily lengthened and merged as the sun dipped behind the headland, and a cool breeze lifting her long, damp hair was a welcome respite from the sticky heat of the day.

She had deliberately driven further west to the rockier, harder-to-access coastline. Claw Beach was for the surfers and adventurers, not the candyfloss-devourers and sun-worshippers who flocked to the sandy strips nearer the town centre.

Tonight, she was the only person here. It was perfect. The dying light, the loneliness, sharpened her senses. The taste of salt on her lips, the tiny movement and murmur of nesting seabirds in the cliffs to her left . . .

And the stealthy crunch of other footsteps. Light, hardly detectable, and moving slowly ahead of her, on the other side of the rocks in the car park.

Dove paused on the footpath that led to the car park, breathing hard after her exertions, listening harder, feeling her muscles tense. Her car key was in her right hand, her board under her left arm. She could see her car now, could see part of the car park even. To get to it, she needed to go ten metres up the narrow chalky path, which was cut deep in the dry turf and jumbled rocks.

Probably just another person in search of solitude, she told herself. But bitter experience had taught her always to react as though danger was present. It was hardwired into her soul, the instinctive muscle memory and the checklist flicking methodically through her brain.

Shadows moved across the ground as the moon slid out from behind the clouds, and her breathing slowed. Footsteps still ahead, soft and light, moving on the other side of the cut-through. Dove carefully placed her board on the ground, shifting her weight silently as she pulled her phone from its waterproof belt pouch.

She waited a heartbeat, holding her breath, straining her senses, but the only sound now was the waves behind her. Before she could take another step, a yell of fear and pain lashed through the night, like a whip-crack echoing across the beach, bouncing off the cliffs.

A car door slamming, raised voices, exclamations and the thump of flesh on flesh. A new yell of pain and fear . . . Dove punched out triple-nine, phone at her ear, and ran straight towards the sounds. She arrived in the car park in time to see two shadowy figures fighting on the ground, and a third emerging from behind a green camper van, which was parked next to the black BMW she had noticed when she pulled in an hour ago.

Her call connected. "This is DC Dove Milson. I'm at Claw Beach," she spoke quickly, "there's a fight in progress. One person's down. I need back-up and an ambulance immediately."

Leaving the line open, phone in hand, she approached the three figures. The larger of the aggressors was kicking the one lying on the ground. The fallen seemed to have given up the fight, curled into a ball to deflect the blows, grunting with pain. The third person hovered uncertainly in the background, hunched into a dark-red hoodie as though afraid.

"Stop, I'm a police officer and I have back-up on the way!" she shouted. This was always a risk: disclosing you were a police officer could either make you an instant target or have a miraculous calming effect.

For a moment it seemed to be the latter. The fight now appeared to be over. The victim was lying on the ground moaning, and both attackers were backing quickly away towards their vehicle. They exchanged a few urgent words that Dove couldn't catch.

Suddenly the main aggressor pushed his accomplice out of the way, and lurched towards Dove, shoulders hunched, breathing heavily. She checked the call was still open, then shoved her phone back in the pouch and faced him.

"Just calm down, okay?" she told him, palms facing out, showing him she had no intention of fighting.

The third person circled, moving behind Dove, out of her line of vision. Dove had just enough time to decide they were female, before the man bunched his fists in a boxing stance and came straight at her.

"I'm a police officer, don't do anything stupid. I've got back-up on the way," she repeated, dodging a punch, weaving on the balls of her feet. Clearly the de-escalation approach wasn't working. She dodged another blow. "Look, cool it, this isn't going to do any good."

He was big, muscular, with his hood pulled down over his forehead. There was blood on his lip, a slick of wetness on his skin, his uneven teeth gleaming as he launched into his next attack in a rush.

Where the hell was the back-up? Dove sidestepped again, and twisted so that his grasping fingers slipped off her arm. He swore and grabbed for her again, this time successfully. With a rip her wetsuit came away at her shoulder, and a sudden coolness as her skin was exposed.

A quick elbow jab to his throat, a swift knee in the groin and she was free, just as a crashing blow came down behind her left ear, sending her spinning to the ground, tiny shards of light clouding her vision, the pain sharp and all-encompassing.

She tried to bunch and roll away, but she was kicked hard in the ribs. The larger attacker bent down beside her, his breathing ragged. She squinted at him, but his face was distorted, his eyes glittering black with menace.

The sound of the emergency dispatcher on the open line asking anxiously if she was okay came out in tinny bursts from her phone. The man cocked his head to one side, listening. He grinned, cracking his knuckles, clearly thinking he was the big man.

Sweat poured down his cheek now — his T-shirt, a flash of white under his unzipped hoody, was soaked with it. The heat from his body burned against hers, just for a second, as he leaned over her. The stench of his strong aftershave, mixed with the sourness of his sweat, made her want to gag. The thick knuckles, which were currently angled close to her face, were bloody. He touched a gold signet ring on his little finger to her cheek, then reared his hand back to resume the attack.

Suddenly the female figure scuttled forward and pulled Dove's attacker away. Dove could hear them hissing something in the big man's ear, then a quickly smothered bark of laughter, before they both came back and stared down at her.

Why were they just staring at her? Her past contained many people who might recognise her, want to hurt her . . . Perhaps this wasn't a carjacking as she had assumed, but some kind of organised crime?

It was unnerving, like being a mouse waiting to see if the cat would keep it alive a little while longer to prolong the pleasure, or kill it quickly. Her vision was clearing, and to her left, Dove could sense the other victim lying motionless. She continued to play dead, eyes half-closed, head and ribs throbbing painfully, muscles tense, waiting for their next move, assessing her chances of escaping a further beating. If she had to, she would fight again.

Just as she was wondering how long this stalemate could continue, Dove finally heard the welcome wail of sirens in the distance. The two assailants reacted quickly enough now. Abandoning their victims, they ran towards their vehicle, gunning the engine as they slammed the doors, before lurching out of the car park, turning left down the coast road across the cliffs.

CHAPTER TWO

Clutching her head, Dove came to her knees, then staggered to her feet. She explored beneath her hair with shaking fingers, her left hand coming away sticky with blood. The flashing blue lights in the distance spun crazily like disco balls before her vision cleared.

She hauled out her phone, hands slippery with blood and sweat, and spoke again to the emergency dispatcher, updating her, trying to remember the registration number, reassuring her she was fine, that the cars were approaching, she could see them, they were less than half a mile away.

"All right, I'll leave you now then. We've got an ambulance on the way too," the dispatcher said.

Dove thanked her and ended the call. She took a couple of careful breaths, aware of a sharp pain in her side, hoping there was nothing broken.

Picking her way slowly and unsteadily across the stony surface, Dove approached the other victim. "Are you okay?"

He muttered something and spat out blood and a tooth, but she felt a flood of relief. He was at least breathing and conscious. Her own ribs were sore and the attacker had only delivered a few kicks. This man had been on the ground when she interrupted his attack, and the sickening sound of boots and fists on flesh was fresh in her mind. The smell of blood filled her nostrils. It was a scent she associated with violence, and with work. She could almost taste it. She coughed, which made her head spin again.

Dove put her hand to her injured side, pressing gently but firmly on her ribcage. No cracking, hopefully that meant it was just bruised. She focused on the victim again.

"Just stay still. Listen, I've got help on the way. What's your name? Do you know who attacked you?"

He just grunted in response, and his outstretched fingers scrabbled on the stony ground as though he was looking for a handhold to push himself upright.

"It's okay, stay still if you can."

She was still kneeling beside the injured man when her uniformed colleagues arrived, shining powerful torches and illuminating the crime scene with their headlights. The man was still curled on the ground, his face turned to the right, a mess of blood, and what looked like a broken nose. He was still groaning, but Dove hadn't been able to pick out any actual words.

He was a large, overweight man, with close-cropped brown hair and a bloody moustache. His navy suit was torn, tie askew, and his white shirt was stained with blood. One shoe was missing. Dove spotted it underneath his car. Shiny brown shoes. The foot without the shoe was misshapen and swollen, and she guessed from the sizable boot print that the attacker had stamped on it.

"DC Milson? PC Jack Goss. Can you tell me what happened?"

He was young and smart in his uniform, and he had a worried expression on his face. At least she thought he did. Her vision kept swimming in and out of focus and those damned bright lights weren't helping. She mentally hauled herself together, and quickly repeated the description of the attackers, the van and the registration number she had relayed earlier.

"We've got two cars out on the road right now, so if the perps are still around, we'll get them. How much of a head start would you say they had?"

"Taking into account the back roads across the downland, five, maybe eight minutes max. They took off when they heard the sirens, but it's wide-open country until you get to the river."

"Ambulance is on the way." Another uniformed officer shone a torch at the side of her head. "They should be here any minute now that we know the scene is safe."

"I'm okay," Dove told him, wincing as his torchlight hit her full in the face again. "Might need a few stitches but he's in a far worse mess." She waved an arm towards the man on the ground. He was making no effort get up, and she hoped his injuries weren't even worse than she feared.

The remote clifftop car park was now alive with the static of radio calls, shouts from those securing the area, and engine noise from the approaching ambulance. A herd of sheep, which usually grazed the short turf along the downland, was huddled fearfully in their shelter, eyes gleaming brightly when the lights caught them.

The paramedics jumped down, hauling essential kit from their vehicle, as a fluorescent-coated senior officer briefed them.

Dove, who was by now sitting on one of the huge chalk rocks that lined the perimeter of the car park, recognised one of the paramedics as Sarah, a friend and colleague of her fiancé, Quinn.

Sarah stopped dead at the sight of Dove. "Dove! Shit, you look a mess. Garry, you start on the other patient."

Her colleague nodded and walked over to the man on the ground.

"Come and sit over here so I can take a look at you." Sarah led Dove to the ambulance. "What the hell happened?"

"I interrupted something. I'm okay. If you could just patch me up, I'll get someone to drop me down at A&E for stitches or whatever."

Dove sighed, furious at the complications this would cause. She would have to get one of her colleagues to bring her car home as well. What a pain in the arse. What had these three been up to in a remote car park? Drugs? A carjacking? A mugging perhaps . . .

Sarah's colleague returned as Dove was being patched up. "We'll need to get the stretcher for him and strap him up before we go. Query broken ankle on the left and a lot of bruising to his abdomen. Obs are fine but his face is a mess. He took a right beating, didn't he?"

"Okay, thanks, Garry. I'll be with you in a minute," Sarah replied.

"You're Quinn's other half, aren't you?" Garry asked Dove, rummaging in the lockers for splints and extra equipment, as Sarah gently swabbed the blood away.

Dove clutched the side of the seat as the pain triggered a wave of nausea. "Yeah."

"I remember seeing you at the Christmas party. You had your arm in a sling. Gunshot wound then, wasn't it?" Garry tucked the splints under one arm.

"It was." She blinked up at him as the nausea passed. "This was just bad luck. Whatever was going on in this car park, I was just coming back from surfing. Shit, I need to remember to get my board!"

"I'm sure someone will find it for you." He squinted at her head. "You need an X-ray and stitches on this one, mate."

"Just what I said," Sarah agreed. "But she's getting a lift with one of her colleagues."

Dove scowled in pain and frustration. "Bloody hell, and that bastard tore my suit. That's a few hundred quid down the drain . . . Okay, I'll go and find a car now, and that leaves you with the one victim. No point in any more wasting resources on me."

"If you're absolutely sure?" Sarah looked worried.

Dove reassured her, stepping carefully out of the vehicle and into the floodlit car park. Once again the harsh artificial light made her wince, but she felt steadier on her feet.

Sarah and Garry soon finished preliminaries on the injured man, and Dove watched him sit up, tentatively touching his battered face, trying to answer questions. They supported him carefully, manoeuvring him on to the stretcher with the help of several police colleagues.

"You sure you'll be all right, Dove?" Sarah checked again, as they eventually passed with the patient.

"Sure. Did he say what happened?"

Sarah shook her head. "As far as he can talk, with all those broken teeth, he seems to think it was an opportunist mugging, but I'm not sure your colleagues agree. He's hardly dressed for a walk on the beach, is he?"

"Not really, no," Dove agreed thoughtfully. The road to Claw Beach was way off any of the main routes in and out of town. "Did you get a name?"

"Alex Harbor. His wallet, watch and some other bits have been stolen, and like I said, the poor guy can hardly speak." She changed tack. "Quinn's going to go crazy when he sees your head. You gonna ring him now?"

"On my way to the hospital," Dove told her. She hated disturbing Quinn at work, hated ringing any of her family to tell them she was hurt. It made her feel weak. Which, as her sister Ren was always lecturing her, was ridiculous.

Sarah shrugged. "Your call. Take care."

PC Goss was back, his quick gaze taking in Dove's bandaged head. "Your surfboard is propped against your car. Paramedics say you want a lift to the hospital?"

"Oh, thanks for that and yes, please, for a lift. I'm all patched up but I just need to get myself checked out by a doctor." Dove was looking at the injured man, who was now being loaded into the back of the ambulance. Sarah was right. With his dark suit, shirt and polished shoes, he looked ready for a day at the office. Or a date, maybe?

"No worries," PC Goss told her. "Let us know when you're ready and I'll let the boss know." He indicated a short woman with cropped brown hair, who was in deep conversation with another officer. "We've got your statement, so just give us a call if you think of anything else. I guess you won't be at work tomorrow!"

Dove said nothing but smiled gratefully at him. She walked carefully over to her car and slowly and painfully loaded her precious board on to the roof rack. It had cost her a load of money, her board, and according to Quinn, she loved it more than him. A hybrid soft-top, it was a go-to for advanced riders in smaller waves, and this particular board was from South Bay Board Company in California. A little bit of childhood nostalgia, she had thought, when she ordered it.

Gingerly, because sudden movements were still making her head spin, she secured the board with straps and chucked her waterproof kitbag into the boot.

"Hey, I'm going to drive you to hospital and someone else will bring your car." It was PC Goss, indicating his vehicle. "Cool board, by the way. I'm more of a paddleboarder myself."

"Thanks, yeah I like a bit of SUP too. Got a couple of boards at home." Dove settled into the passenger seat of the police car, squinting at her head wound in the visor mirror. A little blood had soaked through the bandage, but the pain was definitely easing, and her vision was fine now. She was pretty sure she would be able to drive home from hospital. If not, she'd get a taxi or something. "Have you got the perps yet?"

"No sign of them," he said, "but that's a pretty distinctive vehicle and they haven't exactly got speed on their side."

She called her fiancé on the way, relieved when his phone went straight to voicemail. "Hi, Quinn. Just wanted to let you know I was involved in a minor scuffle in the car park off Claw Beach. I am honestly fine, but getting a lift to the hospital to get checked out just to be on the safe side. Love you."

From the driving seat, PC Goss gave a conspiratorial smirk, and Dove shrugged. "No point in worrying him."

The drive to Abberley General took twenty minutes, and within ten Quinn was on the phone.

"How hurt are you? Did someone actually attack you?" His voice was sharp.

She gave a brief recap, adding, "It's just a few bruises and a cut. I'll ring and let you know what they say after I'm seen."

"Do you want me to come and get you, babe? I can clear it with dispatch and take an hour out, or longer if I need to?" Quinn's voice was heavy with concern.

"No, my car is being brought down, so I'll either drive home or get a taxi."

There was a brief silence. "Did they catch the guy who did it?"

"No, not yet, but it shouldn't be too hard. The first responders were only a few minutes behind the getaway vehicle."

"All right, babe, we've got a job coming through, so I'd better go. Seriously though, call me if you need. I can ditch everything to come and pick you up."

"I know. Love you." Dove had always had problems expressing her emotions, but because Quinn was so open in that respect, and so often finished their conversations with a term of endearment, she had found herself doing the same, and she knew it made him happy too.

The radio call came in just as they arrived at the hospital. The suspects from the Claw Beach attack had not been caught, but their distinctive green camper van had just been spotted on a beach five miles away. It appeared to have driven straight across the grassy downland and off the cliff edge.

"Bloody hell," PC Goss commented, as a load of static and sharp voices followed. "I'd better get back out there. What the hell did you interrupt in the car park, DC Milson?"

Dove found her fingers tightening on the door frame as another wave of nausea hit her. She was just as shocked. "Clearly it was something worth fighting for."

CHAPTER THREE

Dove's phone buzzed at 4.40 a.m. She blinked, confused, wondering why she seemed to have the worst hangover ever. Recollection of the previous evening's events hit hard as she propped herself upright on one elbow and grabbed her phone. Naturally she hadn't rung in sick — had decided, as the X-rays were clear, she would be fine. After a few painkillers and a bowl of soup, she had crawled gratefully into bed.

It seemed fairly inevitable she would get called out after that rather rash decision, she thought now. She groaned loudly as there was nobody else to hear. Layla, her grey cat, was stretched out at the bottom of the bed, regarding Dove with narrowed green-gold eyes, disapproving of the early-morning disturbance.

The text was brief, summoning the Major Crimes Team to a murder scene. Four bodies. The address was the Beach Escape Rooms down on the pier. Intriguing. Dove took all of ten seconds to decide she *was* fit enough to report, stood up too quickly, and felt her head spin and her ribs ache. *Shit.*

It was a good thing Quinn wasn't yet back from work. He was doing a long shift and wouldn't finish until half six. Dove, having already had a lengthy phone conversation with her fiancé after the A&E doctor discharged her, now sent him a hasty text to let him know she had been called out.

A hot shower made her feel better, but also revealed several angry blue-and-red bruises around her ribcage. For a second, as soap cascaded down her naked body, Dove ran her fingers lightly over the scars on her abdomen. She had once been stabbed by a gangland criminal, who was holding her hostage after a police operation went badly wrong. The near-fatal experience and subsequent injury had changed the course of her life. So much so that she was now able to brush off mere bruising and a headache. Nothing would ever compare to nearly losing everything.

* * *

Despite her slow start, Dove arrived on the scene within half an hour of the team text. The rendezvous point was in a large car park above the beach, just twenty yards from the pier, and the dirty red entrance barriers were wide open. The pay-and-display machine was decorated with colourful graffiti, and shingle from the beach had pushed its way on to the concrete, mingling with the litter.

It could have been a depressing scene, but the early-morning sun and clear skies promised another scorcher of a day, and the thought raised her spirits. She glanced quickly in the driving mirror before she got out. Her injury was *almost* covered by her wavy black hair, and in her crisp white shirt and grey suit she certainly didn't look like someone who should have called in sick. But she knew that her amber-brown eyes looked tired and bloodshot, so she slipped on her sunglasses.

Her long-time work partner, DS Steve Parker, and their immediate boss, DI Jon Blackman, were just getting out of their respective vehicles. They exchanged quick greetings.

"What happened to your head?" her boss asked. He was frowning at her injury, stepping closer.

"Minor accident in a car park yesterday," Dove told him airily, pulling her plait further forward over her shoulder to hide the white patch covering her wound. "What have we got?"

"Four bodies were discovered in one of the escape rooms under the pier. Looks like the room flooded at high tide, so possible drownings. Signs of a break-in near the main gate to the premises, and also the door to the escape room." He had been reading the information from his phone, but now looked up, his serious grey gaze moving from person to person. "Preserving any evidence is going to be a nightmare with water involved. The paramedics were first on scene and managed to liaise with the fire service and the coastguard to get the victims out, just in case. Hard to say but if we could have left them in situ it might have made our lives a little easier . . ."

Dove nodded. As ever, for all the emergency services, the main aim was to preserve life, even at a potential murder scene. She always remembered the story of the newbie PC who was first on scene at a stabbing and panicked, pulled a knife from the victim's ribcage, only to realise he had screwed up, and hastily reinserted it.

According to the story, the coroner had been most confused to find the body had two stab wounds, which might have suggested murder, when actually it turned out to have been a suicide.

DI Blackman continued, glancing round, raising a hand in greeting as other members of the on-call Major Crimes Team arrived in the car park. "The owners, Jamie Delaney and Caz Liffey, are now on site. They live just up the road. I'm going to liaise with the incident commanders, find out who's taking the lead on this one and get an up-to-date report. Lindsey and Josh, see what's happening down by the water over there." He indicated the beach area directly below the long, narrow car park, and slightly to the right of the pier structure. "Looks like a dog walkers' party. Maybe they saw something or have found something. Take some

16

of our uniform colleagues with you if you think it might be trouble."

Dove nodded at the other members of the team. Only DS Lindsey Allerton looked bright-eyed and alert. Her short, curly hair was held back by a bright green headband, and her round cheeks were rosy.

"Preliminaries, people, and then straight back to the office, where we'll collate and split up FLOs and teams," the DI announced. He was tall and thin, an avid marathon runner with a shaved head and a poker face. "I don't need to remind you it will be all hands on deck with this one. Four victims says anything from accident to serial killer, so I'll get the DCI to drag in as many extra officers as he can."

Dove could see the small gathering directly under the pier, down near the water's edge. The tide was on the way out, beginning to expose streaks of sand and stones. She checked an app on her phone. High tide had been at 00.52, and low tide would be at 07.09 today.

As well as a few people in gym gear and the dog walkers, pets barking excitedly, she could see what looked like the group of rough sleepers who congregated under the pier in the warmer weather. In her experience, these people saw everything, but often went unnoticed, so she hoped they would be able to provide some leads.

"The rest of you come with me and we'll get the scene set up, make sure the cordons are as far out as we can get them. Jess is Crime Scene Manager and should be here any minute. I've asked the council to lower the bollards so she can drive straight through the pedestrianised area on to the pier," the DI added, striding away now, boots crunching in the pebbles as he jumped down on to the beach from the car park.

Dove and Steve walked towards the pier, following the concrete path that briefly gave out on to wide pavement next to the busy coastal road, before they arrived at the pier entrance.

Here the pavement widened into a large arc to take in the pedestrianised area. On a normal day, it was busy with pop-up kiosks selling popcorn and candyfloss, and packed with milling tourists. Now, police tape fluttered in the breeze, and emergency service vehicles blocked the road in either direction.

Jess Meadows and her team were unloading the van, which had been parked close to the pier. Plastic boxes of equipment were being piled up neatly and white suits were being donned.

"Four bodies, and it isn't even six in the morning yet," Jess greeted Dove. Her shiny blonde hair was tied up in a knot on the top of her head and she wore large designer sunglasses, giving her petite face an almost alien appearance.

"Lucky us," Dove replied to her friend, glancing over the side of the pier at the rapidly increasing crowd of bystanders. Most were snapping photos on their mobile phones. A couple of others had larger, more professional equipment and were taking photographs or videoing with tripods and cameras. The press.

"I know, and I only saw you last week for dinner. Normally we get at least a month before we have to meet up again," Jess quipped, while she quickly and efficiently suited and booted up in the regulation white plastic gear. "Yet here we are and . . ." She dropped her sunglasses down her nose and peered at Dove's head. "What have you been up to?"

Dove waved her comments away. "Tell you later, it's not important." She grinned reassuringly in the face of Jess's piercing stare, then followed Steve and their uniformed colleagues down the wide wooden pier towards the escape rooms. Her boots echoed on the wooden boarding, and she could see the beach below through the gaps in the structure.

The Beach Escape Rooms was a fairly new venture, less than a year old. She vaguely recalled reading in the news that it had caused a sensation when it was first installed, with lots of planning permission objections from locals who feared the new buildings would ruin the look of the old pier.

The funfair, fish-and-chip kiosks and slot machines were still in situ, but it was true these now looked drab and old-fashioned compared to the glass and chrome of the creation at the end of the pier.

As soon as you passed the halfway point, you left the traditional seaside attractions behind and were confronted with high metal gates underneath a neon sign proclaiming:

Beach Escape Rooms. The ultimate adult entertainment.

"Makes it sound like a brothel or some kind of dodgy sex shop," Steve commented.

"No under-eighteens. I expect the insurance is too expensive," Dove surmised, looking at a smaller notice filled with disclaimers underneath the main sign. It directed potential customers to a website and gave mobile phone numbers for both the owners.

Members of Jess's team were already carefully examining what appeared to be the remains of a padlock and chain. Others were dusting for prints and putting scattered debris into neatly labelled plastic bags.

Dove and Steve signed the log and pulled on gloves and plastic boots to avoid evidence contamination. The morning sun cast a pleasant warmth across the proceedings, and the sea glittered enticingly, but Dove could already feel sweat under her jacket. Her head was aching, and she was glad she had thought to slip a packet of painkillers into her pocket, just in case.

The central office was square, with a domed glass roof. On either side, six glass escape rooms staircased down into the sea (when the tide was in), the lower rooms disappearing under the pier. Dove's youngest niece, Delta, had already been with friends on a night out, and raved about the adrenalin-pumping addition of cold seawater seeping into the game, and the added thrill of watching and being watched by anyone on the beach while you tried to solve the puzzle and beat the clock.

DI Blackman was walking towards the office next to a tall man with close-shaven hair bleached white-blonde and a shorter, muscular woman wearing a blue vest top. The long hair piled on top of her head was a dirty yellow colour.

The pair were holding hands, their shoulders sagging, whispering to one another. As they turned to look towards the main gate, Dove could see both were wearing appropriate expressions of shock and horror. She guessed these were the owners, Jamie Delaney and Caz Liffey.

The trio vanished inside the office as Dove and Steve looked over the rail at Escape Room Six. It was one of the lower rooms, and was currently half underwater. At high tide, as Delta airily had informed Dove, the lower rooms were completely submerged, but due to a pipe and pump system, combined with a vented roof, completely safe. Dove remembered expressing concerns about air supply and Delta brushing her comments aside, telling her not to be so boring.

Behind them, white tents numbered one to four had been erected over the wooden boards of the pier to protect the four bodies within, and the vital evidence they contained. The bodies had been laid on their backs on to plastic sheeting, which was stretched in a large square. Dove and Steve took turns to edge into the tents and peer carefully at the victims, avoiding the photographers and evidence collectors.

"Two men, two women," Dove commented, taking in the attire. "Dressed for a night out?" One of the women was wearing a short black dress, the other a long, fitted, floral number, and the two men were in shirts and trousers. Their shoes were lined up neatly next to the bodies, awaiting the bagging and tagging procedure. High heels and shiny lace-ups, Dove noted.

"Looks like a broken nose and bruising on the male in tent three," Steve commented, as they backed out of the tents and walked towards the main office to get to Room Six, careful to tread on the metal plates that had been laid across the pier, following the yellow arrowed route.

"No obvious fatal injuries," Dove said. "I think there are scratch marks to the face on the woman in tent one."

"Do you want to see the footage?" One of the first responders stepped forward and offered his iPad.

"Thanks, that would be good." Everything was always carefully documented, and with so many teams responding to a shout like this one, it was almost always possible to take photographic and video evidence of the immediate scene as it was initially presented.

The footage had been taken using a long shot from above, before slowly panning down one side of the escape room. It was brief, showing only the rescue operation, but Steve asked the officer to pause the video on the initial scene.

Two men and two women. They bobbed gently in their watery tomb, giving a macabre illusion of life. The water was a little over three-quarters of the way to the roof of the escape room. Dove frowned at her watch. High tide would have been about four hours before they started fishing the bodies out. But why then had the water not emptied by then, draining out of the escape room with the tidal flow?

The water was grey-green and discoloured with sand, sediment, small pieces of seaweed and bits of debris. Dove could also see a couple of food wrappers and a juice carton.

"Can you rewind just a bit? Looks like the woman on the far left, with the long dark hair and black dress, has cuts on her face." Steve was peering intently, shoving his sunglasses on to the top of his head in an attempt to aid his vision. "She was in tent one, wasn't she? You thought she had scratches."

"Maybe they got into a fight? Or possibly even self-inflicted?" Dove narrowed her own eyes, squinting at the video, trying to see through the glass and seawater. Flotsam and jetsam from the escape room bobbed in the water, obscuring the view. She reached over and pressed play, watching as the video footage showed a difficult extraction made to look smooth and swift. The victims were passed up out of the flooded room through the escape hatch, laid out on to the hard surface of the pier and assessed by the medical teams.

"The water could have almost filled the room completely, then, at high tide?" Steve checked, as the video finished.

"From the marks on the walls, yes, taking into account tides and air pressure inside the room," the uniformed officer agreed. "The metal ladder you would use to climb down into the room was laid on the roof outside, and the air vents you can see over there were closed, but if they could swim, there would have been enough of a gap between water and roof to get some breathing space."

"I suppose it depends how long they were in there," Dove commented, thinking how easy it was to get exhausted even treading water if you weren't an experienced swimmer. "Although the question for me is, even supposing the water somehow almost filled the room, which is weird because I know from my niece it fills to around a foot high or less, why has it not drained away with the tide?"

The officer nodded in agreement. "There must be a safety mechanism on these rooms. Maybe it was faulty?" He looked over his shoulder towards the sea. "Tide's well out now, and the other escape rooms at sea level are all empty, as you would expect them to be.

"Thanks, we'll take a look at the room now," Steve said thoughtfully.

They moved on, Dove taking in the details of the other escape rooms, impressed by the solid, almost futuristic glass pod-like structures. The lower rooms were accessed via roof hatches and ladders, while the two rooms on the same level as the pier had normal doors. There wasn't as much litter down this end of the pier either. Even the wooden boards of the pier looked freshly scrubbed. She mentioned this to Steve, who nodded.

"It does all look practically sterilised. Either the owners are clean freaks, or someone has done a good job of getting rid of any evidence." He paused and looked out to sea, where a coastguard vessel was slowly tacking back and forth, searching in a wide radius of the crime scene. "I'm guessing there was no sign of any other victims, or anyone doing a runner from the scene."

Dove pushed her sunglasses back down on her nose to shield her eyes from the brilliant mirror-flash of sun and sea. "Perhaps the victims were already dead when they went in. It would take a lot of manpower, but you could bring a boat in, tie up and drop them down the hatch."

"The main gate showed signs of a break-in, though," her partner reminded her.

"Could have been faked?"

"True," Steve said soberly, gaze still fixed on the gentle swell and dip of the waves. "Just because it looks like they drowned, doesn't mean to say they drowned *here*."

CHAPTER FOUR

Seeing him has brought it all back — the pain, the loss and that agonising tearing feeling in my chest.

In times of stress there is only one place to go, one person to visit. Nobody tries to stop me, and after I dropped the conversational bombshell, I know they would rather discuss things alone.

Before I pick up my car keys, I check the baby one last time, even though I know my mum will sit watching her until she wakes. She won't let this one go; she's already told me many times.

It doesn't help, hearing her say that, but I know she thinks she has failed one child already. My dad too. As the years have gone by, he has retreated into his shell, smoking and drinking too much, losing weight until his arms are half the width of mine. In a way I completely agree that they did fail, but I keep this thought locked deep inside my heart.

The baby is asleep, her tiny face oblivious to the confusion in the world around her. The hurt and the hate, it doesn't touch her world, and my heart fills with something that could be love. I'm wary of emotions, because they can hurt you, betray you, when you least expect it.

But she is mine and she is perfect. I drop a kiss on her brow, because I know it is expected of me, and my mum beams. The baby has made my parents a little happier, given them some hope, and time away from their grief.

I drive slowly, shock making my reflexes slow, my mind sluggish. Almost against my will I find myself remembering eighteen years ago, and another birth. I remember so clearly the time when she was born. She came home from the hospital so small and helpless and I was fascinated, the bond forming almost instantly as I held her, felt her warmth and stared deep into her innocent eyes. A tiny brand-new living person. Light-headed and almost giddy, I laughed. The sun was shining and I felt like the luckiest person ever to be given such a gift.

When I arrive, I get out of my car slowly, like an old person, almost struggling for breath. Am I having a panic attack, or is this it, and my heart is finally giving up? I'm too young to die, surely, at twenty-five? Ironic, a voice in my head chides, you can die any time. It only takes one person to push you over the edge and life is over.

My heart rate accelerates painfully and my chest is tight, like someone is pulling a band around my ribcage, squeezing my life away. For a few moments I teeter, before my shoulders sag and my breathing begins to slow.

I'm okay, I really am. In fact, I've been more than okay for years, but now one man is ruining my new life, kicking my legs from under me and trying to destroy it once again. I can't allow that to happen.

The door is closed, and as I push it open I inhale the smell of her, her room, her life. It is cooler in here, bright and peaceful without the distractions of real life. It is a room for meditation or contemplation.

Her face is so serene, so different from the film reel in my head, and when I take her hand it feels both warm and cool at the same time. But my usual contentment eludes me.

She's alive, but she is not, imprisoned in this room, this bed . . . in her own body.

And it is all his fault.

CHAPTER FIVE

Because it was on the lowest level, the access route to Escape Room Six was down a flight of metal steps, which clung tightly to the struts of the pier. Dove and Steve climbed carefully down and edged on to the wooden platform that ran around the perimeter of the room, presumably for maintenance purposes. Towering above, just behind them on pier level and in no danger from the tides, was Room Two. The water level in Escape Room Six was still high, it had fallen to just a little less than three-quarters full.

Dove could now see how the video footage so easily encompassed the whole scene from above. From where she stood, she could look down into the room. She glanced to her right. To access the room, customers had to climb through the large square hatch and down the metal ladder. The hatch was currently open and the ladder in place, reaching solidly right down to the glass floor of the room. Although the escape rooms looked enormous from a distance, close-up she could imagine it would be fairly claustrophobic once you were shut inside. Perhaps five or six large adults could fit comfortably in the room, but with precious little space between them.

Steve was studying the inside of the room. "Looks a bit sci-fi, doesn't it? I mean, it's not as tacky as I imagined."

"I told you, Delta said it was great, and she's normally very condescending about the entertainment around here," Dove said, also absorbing the complexities and slick design features. "It must have cost a hell of a lot to set this all up, though."

Set along the glass wall on the pier side was a complex-looking control panel with various dials, screens and coloured buttons. A large red sticker above this read *Game on . . . Are you ready?*

The wooden platform was easily big enough to accommodate ten or so people spaced around the edge, but it was clearly not built for teams of emergency services, plus all the usual paraphernalia that accompanied them. Steve, who wasn't keen on heights, held on to the metal handrail, affecting a casual stance while his fingers gripped so tightly his knuckles showed white.

"Shall we walk round the edge, along the platform?" Dove suggested, noticing her partner's discomfort. She squinted at the glass chamber. "We might get a better view?" The four bodies had been floating near the ceiling, face down, and she pictured the scene again.

It was the most bizarre set-up. Short of being murdered in some kind of crazy futuristic theme park, she couldn't think of any comparisons. The only way in and out was via the escape hatch in the roof, with a metal ladder. The ladder had been moved out of the way to allow the rescue team to retrieve the bodies and must have been put back into position after the initial photographs, to allow easier access to the room.

It would have been physically possible, following her earlier theory, for someone to have dropped each body down through the roof hatch, but that would have taken time, even with several perpetrators. She considered this.

It would be more for display and effect than an actual way of committing the murder — a revoltingly sensational way of showing off the four victims, and ensuring maximum press coverage. Sometimes these points were important to a perpetrator.

27

A police officer was leaning into the tank, dipping a long rod-and-bottle contraption in, carefully taking water samples, plastic gloves and boots squeaking on the hot metal and glass. "Jeez, it must be like an oven in here on a hot day, even with the air-conditioning system," he commented. "And why *would* you pay to get locked in a glass box under the water?" The man raised his eyebrows, sweat dripping down his nose. "What's wrong with going to a bar, for God's sake?"

"A bar would be my choice too. I wouldn't personally enjoy this kind of thing, but seems like the business does well. Every time I've driven past in the daytime, there've been queues at the gates," Steve said. Having examined the hatch, he inched reluctantly off the platform and stepped on to the walkway. "I kind of like the escape-room idea in theory — it's basically puzzle-solving, isn't it? But when you get wet, that's where it would end for me. You might as well just go swimming. "

Dove was leaning over the platform, one latex-gloved hand resting lightly on the glass wall to steady herself, peering inside at the murky water. "There should be plenty of prints, with all this glass and metal around . . . Anyway, Delta said it was cool. And you don't get completely submerged, that's the whole point. If you go into one of these undersea chambers, Room Six and Room Three, the water only rises to your knees *inside,* and you get loads of klaxons and alarms going off . . . But it's a game, so there isn't any real danger. Or there shouldn't be anyway. There are probably videos on the website on how it's supposed to work."

Steve jabbed a thumb towards the pier, where the tents covering the four bodies lay, stark and alien in the bright morning sunlight. "Tell them it only goes up to your knees. Did someone forget to turn the tap off?"

Dove stared at the scene, committing each detail to memory. From the video, the escape room had been almost completely full of water. Now the water level had dropped a little, probably from displacement when the bodies were removed. And yet the majority of the water had stayed in the room, looking grey and sluggish, and out of place among the other five pristine escape rooms.

Dove swung her gaze out to sea, before dropping it to her watch. Just over an hour and a half until low tide. "Is the roof hatch damaged?" she asked the officer taking water samples.

He nodded, squinting as he checked glass tubes of water before adding stoppers and placing them carefully in a plastic rack. "There's a simple bolt mechanism that shuts each one, and they are then secured by a padlock. Same MO as the main gate, and it looks like the bolt cutters were used to get inside."

"But if this *was* a break-in and they all went down into the escape room for a laugh, why didn't they just climb out when the water started rising? Even without the ladder surely you could float on top of the water, swim to the hatch and push it open. It wouldn't be easy, but surely possible . . ." She tried to imagine the sequence of events leading to the deaths. "Unless they couldn't swim? The escape rooms close at eleven. The opening hours are listed on the sign. We might get some CCTV on the victims' arrival if we're lucky."

"Perhaps the victims were incapacitated in some way before the water started to rise?" her colleague suggested. He snapped his case shut and transferred the racks of samples to a plastic box. "In theory, the escape route, the roof hatch, was there all the time, so I would say it's more a question of why didn't they take it?" He nodded at them both, and headed back up from the escape-room platform on to the main pier.

Dove and Steve followed him, and while Steve added to his notes, Dove watched the man walk briskly towards Jess, pause briefly to speak to her, and move onwards down the pier. Jess was standing near the far end of the pier now, next to the wooden ladder that led to the sea. She was talking urgently to a couple of police divers, who were pulling on fins and checking their equipment. "Who knows what the hell happened, but the DI's right, this is going to be a nightmare of a scene to get evidence from. I wonder if the coastguard has found something worth diving for?"

Dove glanced at her watch. "I suppose there might be evidence under the pier, or maybe they're going into Room Six now to collect any evidence, before it's drained."

"Perhaps. Bloody hell, we'll have to pinch more than just some FLOs for this one. This is going to be overtime for a month," Steve said as they clambered back on to the main pier structure.

"I'm sure I can see two mobile phones at the bottom of the tank, some loose change and . . ." Dove was looking back down at Room Six. "It's easier to see from this angle, without the sun in your eyes. A black wheel thing on the floor, and is that two panels on the pier-side wall? But they must already be in situ and part of the game, I guess. Nobody's going to bring a steering wheel on a night out, are they?"

"Beats a traffic cone," Steve answered. "If they had phones, and they were initially conscious, why didn't they call for help if something went wrong? And does that look like a possible emergency exit door to you?" He was pointing to the far corner of the nearest escape room, which was on a level with the pier and labelled 'Room Two'.

Dove followed his gaze, and saw one of the glass walls appeared to have *push to break* instructions on the inside, and the outline of a square door.

"Maybe." Dove walked over and tapped the glass with her gloved hand. "For fire regs and health and safety I suppose there has to be an alternative exit, although I didn't see this in the wall of Room Six . . . Unless it's fake and that's part of the game too?"

They began to walk slowly back towards the middle of the pier and the white-tented area, before heading towards the sea end. Dove gazed down again at the sand and shingle between the wooden boards of the pier which stretched until around a metre from the end, where she knew there was a steep drop from the sandbank at the low tidemark. The grey-green water swirled and sucked beneath, just audible over the thud of many boots, and the brisk conversation above.

Jess was still talking intently with the divers, pointing at the escape room, and back towards the office building. Metal stepping plates had now been extended, stretching like shiny mushrooms all the way from the main gates, round the office and further down to the end of the pier.

"Hey, Jess, bloody weird one, isn't it? What do you think?" Dove asked when her friend had finished her conversation and the divers had climbed down from the end of the pier into the waiting police launch. She peered over the edge. "Did they find anything out there?"

"Not sure. Possibly just debris, but possibly not. I'll let you know." She bit her lip, turning to stare out to sea, before she spoke again. "I'm thinking, how the hell am I going to preserve evidence at this scene? Were they dead when they went into the escape room? Or did they drown in situ? And if it was the latter, why the fuck didn't they just get out of the hatch when they realised there had been a malfunction and the waters were rising?" Jess said smartly, snapping her folder of notes shut and pocketing her pen. "You?"

"Pretty much the same. In addition, hoping it was an accident? Maybe a malfunctioning drainage system, and they were all pissed from partying so they couldn't find the door?" Dove suggested.

"All of them? Nice try," DS Lindsey Allerton said from behind them. "But we just checked out the outlets from the lower rooms. On Room Six, it's been completely blocked and the pump mechanism jammed."

"Shit. Anything from the group under the pier?" Dove asked. She hadn't clocked any regulars she recognised earlier.

"Well, opinion differs from a boat arriving after midnight, and tying up to the end of the pier, to a swimmer messing around under the pier struts around the same time, to a purple unicorn galloping along the beach." Lindsey sighed. "Having said that, they are not keen to talk to us, and will not stand up to being any kind of reliable witnesses, due to a fair amount of drug and alcohol use last night, which

31

may or may not have impaired their vision and general perspective on life."

DC Josh Conrad, who was in his early twenties, tall with curly black hair and dimples, agreed. "There was some kind of rubber bung fitted to the end of the drainage pipe . . . Here, take a look . . ." He proffered his phone and Dove leaned in to check out the tampered-with pipe. "The one on the left is where the water goes in, and I assume there is some kind of ballcock system that kicks in, with a shut-off valve, when the water rises to the correct level. The pipe on the right, as you can also see, is where the water should flow out to clear the room. In addition there is a pump system to push water in and help it out during the game."

"There you go," Jess added. "Once the water started coming in, if there *was* an automatic shut-off that was messed with, *and* the drainage outlet was blocked, the water would just keep on rising and fill the room like a goldfish bowl."

"I hope they were dead when they went in," Steve said soberly. "Because that is a hell of a way to die if they weren't."

CHAPTER SIX

The office was buzzing by six thirty when Dove and Steve joined the queue for coffee, before heading in for the briefing.

DI Blackman was writing quickly and clearly on the whiteboard, and shoved the pen in his pocket before he turned and addressed the team. "DCI Franklin is unfortunately off sick today, but with four victims this morning, plus the stabbing from last Monday as an ongoing case downstairs, we have decided to divide this particular case between myself and DI Lincoln. DCI Franklin reckons he'll be back in two days but we can check in with DCI Colburn if we need her."

He sighed, and Dove could almost feel his entire team silently sympathising. Everyone knew that funding cuts meant fewer and fewer officers, with specialities often shared between cases and area forces. This made every murder investigation a competition to get ahead of the queue for the pathologist, the forensic lab testing, or to get as many officers as they could assign to one team.

Drooping, grey-haired DI George Lincoln, nicknamed 'Vampire', normally volunteered for the night shift, but was just now gamely gulping his coffee and tucking into a box of doughnuts to boost his energy levels.

His morose expression rarely changed, and was enhanced by a sparse grey moustache. The only passions he appeared to harbour were for the job, and for tropical fish. He was divorced, but according to gossip he had profiles on several dating sites. Dove could only imagine it would take a fairly unique person to be interested in him.

DI Blackman was tapping the whiteboard with an impatient finger now, cutting through the murmurs as DC Maya Amin carefully pinned up photos of the victims. "Four victims. From early information we are working on the assumption that they drowned, but obviously this is pending PM reports and further evidence from our Crime Scene Manager."

Here, he glanced at his colleague to take over. DI Lincoln sighed heavily and waved a hand towards the photographs. "Victims are Oscar Wilding, twenty-six." He paused for a moment, in apparent sympathy for the dead man. Dove always thought he sounded like he'd been chewing on gravel for breakfast, and his voice grated on her nerves, but there was no doubt he was a shrewd investigator.

"Aileen Jackson, forty-two, Dionne Radley, thirty-nine and one as yet unidentified male, who appears to be in his mid- to late forties. The owners of Beach Escape Rooms, Jamie Delaney and Caz Liffey, state Jamie locked up as usual after their last customers and left the premises at around midnight last night. They have a four-month-old baby, and apparently Jamie has been working the late shifts recently."

"CCTV appears to have been intentionally damaged during the break-in, and in addition to this we also have padlocks cut at the main gate and the hatch leading down into Room Six, which suggests the four victims may have entered illegally." He paused to study the photographs of the four victims, which were now up on screen next to the whiteboard. "Looks like a neat job and some kind of bolt cutters were used, but these are yet to be recovered."

"What about the video from the first responders?" DC Josh Conrad asked.

DI Blackman bent over the laptop on the table in front of him and clicked to bring the video up on the big screen. "As you can see, the padlock securing the hatch was cut, presumably to allow illegal entry." He rewound the video to show the bodies in situ. "First question for me is, when the water started rising, why the hell didn't they just exit the way they came in? The current answer, until we have more evidence, is that the ladder was removed to prevent them doing so, and the water never rose high enough for them to reach the hatch without it."

"Witnesses reported seeing a swimmer near the escape room at around midnight. Presumably, whoever the swimmer was, they blocked the outflow pipe, and locked the emergency valve to ensure the water flooded the room, but never drained," DC Amin volunteered.

When Dove first joined the MCT, Maya's twin brother, also a DC, had been working on the team. But he had transferred the previous year, joining the Cybercrimes Unit, and his sister had taken his place on Major Crimes.

"Four victims — so was the perpetrator wanting to kill all of them, or was he after one, and the others were just collateral damage? The former says serial killer, the latter could be harder to trace," DI Lincoln added, stroking his moustache thoughtfully with one nicotine-stained finger.

Dove was chewing a thumbnail as she viewed the video for the second time. Floating bodies, a locked room. "Did the coastguard find anything?" she asked eventually.

"No sign at all of any other victims or possible perpetrators, and no evidence a boat was around the pier last night, apart from the suggestion from one of the rough sleepers on the beach." The DI shook his head. "But he started talking about mermaids and a purple unicorn right after he gave out that little gem. From the state of him, it's unlikely he saw anything but the bottom of a bottle last night."

"The water sports place next to the marina has jet-skis and various craft for hire, so we need to keep an open mind about a possible escape route for our attackers or attacker,"

DC Amin commented, pushing her short, dark hair away from her face.

DS Lindsey Allerton was making quick notes as she watched the video. "What if the perpetrator broke in with the other four, got in the escape room with them and then exited? Maybe he or she left, sealing the others inside, sliding the bolt on the hatch, removing the ladder, etcetera? The tox reports aren't back yet, but the victims could have been drugged? Or perhaps we're looking at a suicide pact?"

"Excellent thought, and another angle to consider." DI Blackman took a gulp of coffee from his huge mug. He never relied on the paper cups from the machine, preferring to use his hefty *Go fast or go home* relic of some gruelling mountain-range marathon he had taken part in.

"Timeline as we know it so far starts at 4.15 a.m. when a dog walker spotted the bodies and called 999," DI Lincoln continued. "But Jess said in her preliminaries she expected time of death ranged between 1 a.m. and 3 a.m. It'll be virtually impossible to work out who died first, but if anyone can, it's Jess. Even so, accuracy is going to continue to be an issue, especially factoring in the saltwater and the warmth of the night."

Dove glanced through her notes so far, listening intently to the flow of conversation. She was impatient to get out and start piecing together the victims' last movements, but she knew these briefings were vital. Every single member of the team needed to be working from the same information. Cock-ups occurred when people went off and did their own thing. She herself — paying attention to lessons learned the hard way — was methodical and meticulous when it came to the tedious paperwork.

"We are currently working on the assumption all four were alive and walked in of their own accord, but again, we may find this was not the case," DI Lincoln continued slowly and carefully, as he worked his way down his own notes, tracing items with a finger, pausing to put various relevant items up on screen. "As we mentioned earlier, CCTV was damaged during the break-in but the camera above the escape room was partially working. Technical Support have already recovered some footage showing the bodies were present and the room was filled with water by at least 2 a.m. this morning, which coincides with the tide times."

"Thank you, George. One last thing before we start to crack this case." DI Blackman held up a hand, briskly interrupting the murmurs from around the room, and read from an email on his iPad. "Independent experts have now confirmed what we suspected initially — that particular escape room was tampered with. The outlet pipe was blocked with a rubber bung, and the emergency shut-off was disabled, probably using a knife or chisel to prise the valve away from the wall connection."

"There will be massive press interest, naturally," DI Lincoln added before everyone started gathering their things, "and we really need the support of our community on this one, so we will be scheduling a press conference for later this afternoon to appeal for witnesses. Let's get going."

DI Blackman started pairing off the members of the MCT, before splitting the whole team in half. Numbers had been swelled by another five officers who had been drafted in, but it was still a small number for such a large investigation.

Dove and Steve were initially assigned to the team investigating the two female victims, and immediately began gathering up their notes, heading for the computers. They would report directly to DI Blackman.

Lindsey, assisted by Josh, was FLO, or Family Liaison Officer, for the relatives of Aileen Jackson, while DS Pete Wyndham, nicknamed 'Donkey' for his rather unfortunate dentistry and braying laugh, was assigned to the family of Oscar Wilding. Pending identification of the second man, Dove supposed the DI would have to pull at least two more FLOs out of the hat. Ideally there should be two FLOs per family, but logistically this often created problems when there were multiple cases ongoing and multiple victims to be considered.

FLOs were hugely important, not only as primary family support, but also as excellent detectives themselves, embedded among the relatives and friends of the deceased, teasing out threads of information that people were often unaware they had.

* * *

"So what really happened to your head?" Steve queried as they sat down at their computers and pulled up the case files for an update.

"I got into a fight," Dove told him evasively, before seeing he wasn't going to give up. She sighed and enlarged on the events of the previous night, while she sipped her second coffee. "Rankin's team has taken the investigation."

"Ouch. You were lucky to get off so lightly. Probably a drugs drop or something," Steve suggested.

Dove considered the Claw Beach attack. "Maybe. It just felt odd. You know, like why beat the hell out of the victim when they'd already taken his stuff? The bloke who went for me seemed like he could have been off his head on something." Dove watched as DI Blackman headed out of the door with DC Maya Amin to check back in with the escape-room owners.

She switched her mind back to the task in hand. "Something else has been bugging me. The name Jamie Delaney seems kind of familiar, and I can't work out why. I suppose I've seen something about the escape rooms on social media, or in the newspapers . . ." Discovering a packet of salt-and-vinegar crisps in her desk drawer, she pulled a face and dropped them on her desk for later.

"Or maybe your photographic memory has been damaged by the rock thrown at your head?" Steve suggested helpfully, and laughed as she threw the bag of crisps at him. "Sorry. The name doesn't ring any bells with me, and anyway the DI's taking the lead on that."

Dove took off her grey jacket and slung it over the back of her chair. The air conditioning in the office was as erratic as the heating system, and today it seemed to be barely functioning. "It'll come to me . . ."

"I can't believe you're working and Quinn hasn't got you tucked up in bed at home, or at least taking the day off," Steve added, looking at her closely. "You did tell him, didn't you, Milson?"

"Of course I did, Parker," Dove said briskly, attacking her keyboard and gulping her coffee, "but he was working the night shift and he wasn't home by the time I was called out this morning. We had a brief conversation after it happened and a longer one after I got the all-clear from the doctor. He knows I can take care of myself. Now shut up, and get on with solving this investigation."

Steve raised his eyebrows and pulled up some of the witness statements on his computer, speed-reading as he spoke. "There isn't any new info in this lot, although the stuff about the person swimming in the sea around 1 a.m. is interesting. Lots of sleepers under the pier in this weather, so if this person is linked to our case, they must have known they risked having an audience. You got anything?"

"Nope. Jess must be tearing her hair out with vanloads of evidence to trawl through," Dove replied. "Oh, wait — the bloods are back. Shit, look at this!"

Those left in the office glanced over at her exclamation, and Steve read over her shoulder: "Blood-alcohol levels were through the roof on all four, and the tox screen shows presence of zopiclone, a nonbenzodiazepine-related sleeping tablet. It is classed as a cyclopyrrolone, and molecularly distinct from benzodiazepine drugs. Drug names always get me. How do they even make these up?"

Dove, ignoring his banter, was skimming the lab report with intense interest. "So either they were drugged, or they voluntarily took the pills before they went in." She was picturing the victims, mentally assessing each victim's body weight, wondering how long the zopiclone would take to react.

"Different weights, different heights, tolerance to alcohol, impaired liver function," Steve reeled off. "Lots of factors.

They wouldn't all necessarily have just keeled over, and certainly not at the exact same time. Maybe they take drugs on a regular basis and it was used as an alcohol enhancement?"

Dove frowned. "It's not really a street drug, is it? Maybe we really are looking at a suicide pact."

CHAPTER SEVEN

Preliminaries and paperwork completed, an hour later they headed out to speak to Dionne Radley's husband, Tomas. Pausing by the coffee machine, Dove snagged two takeaway cups but the machine only half-filled the second. She frowned in exasperation and gave the machine a kick.

"I came up to check you were all right after last night, but I guess you're feeling fine." It was Jack Goss, the young PC who had been one of the first responders to the Claw Beach incident and later given her a lift to the hospital. He was grinning, having clearly seen her kicking the coffee machine.

"Oh, thanks. I'm fine. I was going to pop down and see you anyway, but we just landed a case. Any updates on last night?" Dove asked him.

"Camper van was empty. Looks like the driver and passenger set it in motion, jumped out at the last minute and scarpered over the hill into the Seaview Estate." He pulled a face.

"At least they aren't dead. I was a bit freaked when I heard the vehicle had gone off the cliff last night. What about the victim?" Dove asked, having already decided not to tell him she had a sneaked a look at the case file earlier. She had her own case and nosing in on someone else's was considered bad form, not to mention a pain in the arse.

"Changed his story a few times, but now claims he was just coming home from working late at the office, and decided to sit and chill out somewhere nice and quiet before he went home to the wife."

Dove raised an eyebrow, and immediately wished she hadn't — although hidden by her hair, the head wound was still sore. "You don't sound convinced."

"CCTV shows he left the office at 6.30 p.m. He works in the centre of Abberley for a very respectable solicitors' firm, Pearce and Partners. Our vic lives out towards Stollyton village, which as I'm sure you know means he was geographically taking a big detour if he is telling the truth. If it was a straightforward case of carjacking or an opportunist mugging, why would he lie?" PC Goss said. "You did say in your statement you thought the attackers were an older man and a younger boy . . ."

"I really didn't get a look at the second attacker, so it is just an impression." Dove leaned back against the wall, going over the events of the night before in her head. "It could have been a woman, I guess?"

"But you can't be sure?"

"No," she said regretfully. "Shame we lost them, but keep me posted, won't you? I wish I could have been more help, or at least hung on to one of them," Dove said, suddenly aware Steve was at the door to the stairwell, making impatient noises. "Gotta go, my partner gets grumpy if he doesn't get his caffeine fix."

"Let me know if you remember anything else or want to add to your statement. DI Rankin is going to be running with this one. Hey, I don't suppose it's worth doing a photofit for the first man, the one who attacked you?" he called after her.

She considered for a brief second, memory flashing back. "Not really, I only got a look at his mouth and a rough outline of the lower part of his face."

"No worries!"

Dove caught up with Steve as they finally emerged into bright sunlight, and quickly updated him on the Claw Beach attack. "No joy from last night on a perp either. It's all going well this morning . . . Also, the machine is screwed again, but you can have this one." She handed him the full cup.

"There are reasons I like having you as a partner." Steve grinned as she started the car. "God, this seat is boiling — it's going to be another scorcher today. Zara's got the day off, and is taking Grace to the beach with some of her friends," he added. "She loves the water."

"A little wannabe surfer," Dove suggested. Steve's baby daughter was gorgeous, even if, as he frequently commented, she still hadn't discovered the joys of sleeping through the night.

The sky stretched a glorious vivid blue over the town, and the dusty streets were already busy with tourists and day-trippers. Quaintly historical Abberley, with its ancient church and cobbled streets, coupled with Lymington-on-Sea with its full deck of modern conveniences, made the two-town coastal sprawl a must-stop for beach-lovers in search of a day out. The two towns, after forty years of infill building and new developments devouring the green downland above the coast, were now joined, although still referred to by their separate names. There had been an outcry when the county council suggested renaming the fast-growing area to create a new "super-town".

Dove, ignoring Steve's comments about the perfectly efficient air conditioning, wound her window down and let the familiar smells of dust, fast food, sweat and summer pour in, cooling her hot face and ruffling her hair.

Tomas Radley was working on a building site just to the north of Lymington-on-Sea, and according to the site manager Steve had called earlier, had taken the news of his wife's death without visible emotion and then insisted he wanted to carry on at work.

"I told him to take time off, or at least to sit in one of the spare offices in the show home for a bit. Took no notice of me.

43

He's Latvian," the manager added, as though that explained things. "Angelicized his name when he moved here. Radovic or something originally." The manager's tanned face, just slightly too orange, was puckered with worry and shiny with beads of sweat, and his elegant silver-grey hair combed down across a lined forehead. "He's the one with the orange vest over on site four." He pointed, before retreating thankfully into the air-conditioned show home.

Dove and Steve picked their way past noisy machinery, stacks of tiles, bricks and other building supplies, all caked with a thick layer of dust.

"Mr Radley?" Steve called. "Can we talk to you for a few minutes, please? DS Steve Parker and DC Dove Milson."

Tomas Radley straightened and looked hard at them. He had just picked up a massive load of bricks, and was standing with them hoisted over one shoulder. "Need to drop these off," he told them, before walking in the opposite direction.

"I thought Lindsey would be over here by now," Dove said, and she and Steve followed, feeling rather stupid and conspicuous in their suits, among the hard hats and fluorescent jackets.

"Maybe she got caught up with our other vic's husband instead," Steve suggested.

"Wait! Who the hell are you? You haven't got any safety gear on," another man was shouting from the scaffolding of a half-built house.

"Bloody hell," Dove muttered, before raising her voice, "Police. Major Crimes Team. We are just borrowing Mr Radley for a little while, and we're going straight back to the office."

"Are we?" Steve queried.

"No, but we haven't got time to faff around looking for safety equipment," Dove said, as the man dumped his heavy load and stomped slowly towards them.

"God, you're bossy," Steve complained.

Tomas Radley was a powerfully built man, probably in his late forties, with dark hair and eyes, and a solemn unsmiling face. "What do you want?"

"Mr Radley? We are very sorry to hear of your wife's death, but could we please have a quick word?" Steve asked respectfully. Most people liked Steve on sight. With his messy brown hair framing his face in random spikes, small glasses and slight tummy bulge, he was deferential, genuinely interested and compassionate. It was a winning combination, coupled with a sharp brain. Perpetrators were often fooled into thinking he was a bumbling cliché of a policeman, but were then trapped by their mistake as surely as ants in honey.

"It's Tomas, call me Tomas." The victim's husband looked hard at them, bloodshot eyes travelling slowly across first Dove's then Steve's face, before he spoke again. "Why do you need to talk to me? She is dead, and she died doing something stupid. I don't need to know any more. I already said this to the other police officers."

He made as if to walk off but Dove delayed him with a gentle hand, while Steve continued talking. "We are detectives from the Major Crimes Team, and it will be our job to discover exactly what happened and why. Come and sit over here. We just have a few questions, and I promise we won't keep you for any longer than we have to."

Dionne Radley's husband looked exhausted, grief-stricken and everything in between, Dove thought, with a wave of sympathy for the man.

He seemed to dither, before sighing heavily and allowing Dove to shepherd him towards a wooden bench just outside the site boundary. He pulled out a packet of cigarettes but didn't offer them around.

"I told you, I already spoke to the police. They came earlier to tell me Dionne was dead. They told me where it happened and who she was with." He blew out a long breath of smoke, and tapped a muscular knee with his free hand. "I had no idea she was out, no idea she was breaking in, playing games in an escape room with friends I don't know, but Dionne, she did her own thing. I thought she was working last night."

"Were you at home all evening?" Steve asked casually.

"No, I was with my brother from seven thirty. He lives on Sands Park in one of the static homes. I sometimes go and spend an evening, stay the night if we have a beer. Last night we sat outside on the deck, watched the sun go down, and talked about things, while I thought Dionne was out working until at least midnight, maybe later. Dionne knew where I was, and what I was doing."

Tomas' voice was bitter and sad. "She could have called me at any time if she needed help, if she was in danger. Even with everything that has happened between us, I would have always helped her, and she knew it."

"Do you recognise any of these people?" Steve flipped his iPad round to show Tomas headshots of the deceased.

"No, I don't know her friends, her men, anything about her anymore," Tomas said. "She has been this way for a couple of years now, saying she wanted a new life, she hated her job, hated my job. Last month I said we should get a divorce."

"What did she say to that?" Dove asked.

Tomas met her eyes, his own dark and pain-filled. "She agreed that we should. She was going to deal with it because she said she knew a solicitor in town but nothing has happened yet." He wiped a hand across his sweaty brow, and took a bottle of water from his tool belt. His fingers shook slightly as he unscrewed the cap.

"Where did Dionne work?" Dove asked, feeling sweat drip down her back, wriggling her shoulder blades with discomfort. The heatwave was really only glorious if you were on a beach somewhere.

"She's a cleaner for an agency, Camillo's. They clean offices, many businesses, including the solicitors'. Pearce and Partners, it's called. I used to pick her up sometimes after work, but now she gets her own rides home." Again a shrug of the massive shoulders. "Apparently these law people often work late. The cleaners come in later so as not to disturb them, but they meet anyway. She got talking to one man." He shrugged his vast shoulders. "I suppose that is who she was asking about our divorce, I don't know. She said she was going to be working there last night, this Pearce and Partners, before going on to do some offices in Lymington-on-Sea. It's a regular gig for Camillo's."

"Sorry to have to ask, but did Dionne ever have affairs?" Steve asked carefully.

He nodded sadly, a giant of a man, with all his bluster gone. "Of course. She had many. Our children had left home. My brother says we married too young, had our children too young. Two girls we have, both now living and working abroad. They are devastated about their mother. I rang them just after the other police officers left. They couldn't believe it at first . . ."

"Did Dionne ever take sleeping tablets?" Dove asked carefully.

"No, never. She was always a heavy drinker, more than me even." He gave a faint smile. "But never any drugs. She hated to even take antibiotics when she was sick."

"How was she recently? It must have been a shock when you suggested a divorce?"

"I think not really," Tomas paused. "She has not been happy for a long time, as I told you. One thing she said the other day, which was painful to hear . . . She said, 'Now I'm free I'll go crazy and do whatever the hell I want with my life.'" He nodded, face sombre again. "I felt very sad after hearing that, as you can imagine. Now she is dead."

"We are doing all we can to find out what happened . . ." Steve began, but the man stopped him, holding up a massive rough hand.

"I don't want to know. She is dead. Something went wrong and accidents happen . . ."

"This wasn't an accident," Steve said.

"Someone killed her? Killed them all?" He appeared to consider this, shaken and pale under the tan and the dust. Tomas moistened his lips, clearing his throat before he spoke again. "You are saying she was murdered?"

"We are investigating all possible leads," Dove told him smoothly, inwardly cursing the cliché. "When your wife

47

died she had a lot of alcohol in her system, which from what you've told us, doesn't seem to be unusual?"

He nodded, eyes wide and fixed on her face, hands fidgeting with the cigarette packet, turning it over and over in his massive palms.

"She had also taken a drug called zopiclone, which is prescribed as a sleeping drug or for anxiety."

"Never, she would never have taken drugs." He lit another cigarette from his first, before shoving the lighter and packet back in his pocket. "But, I suppose, whatever. Who am I to say this now? It was those people she hung out with. Maybe they pushed her into this? Or spiked her drink?"

"People?"

His shadowed, red-rimmed eyes were wary. "I told you, men, and I don't know them. I don't think she did really, I just heard gossip. I have no names that will help you, it was idle gossip. And now I must get on. I will help, of course, if you need to ask more questions, but for me it is over. I will be staying with my brother. 204 Sands Park. It's off the Cliffacre Road."

"I know it," Dove said. "One of our colleagues will be over later just to see if you need anything. Thank you for your time, Mr Radley."

"Tomas," he repeated, and shambled away, shoulders sagging under an invisible weight, even though he no longer carried a load of bricks.

CHAPTER EIGHT

"What do you think?" Steve asked as they made their way back to the car, waving at the anxious-looking site manager, who appeared at the door of the smart red-brick show home.

"Not sure. I mean, he's clearly devastated, but he also admits knowing his wife was having affairs," Dove said as they drove out of the building site. "He has an alibi, assuming it checks out."

"Sands Park is pretty busy this time of year, maybe one of the other homeowners saw Radley and his brother sitting outside on the deck with their beers," Steve suggested. "We can easily swing by and ask around, once we've seen Aileen's husband. The site manager will have security cameras too." He checked his watch. "Plenty of time. Tomas Radley certainly has a motive."

Dove agreed. "Let's stop at Ren's for some takeaway coffee and cake. We have to go right past to get up to Junction Road, and the husband of victim number two, Aileen Jackson, lives at the top. He should be waiting for us."

"You need a sugar fix. You really should eat breakfast," Steve told her, pressing the button to send the windows up again.

"Can't. I feel sick if I eat breakfast," Dove said. "But I can easily sink a bacon sandwich with brown sauce by ten, especially if I've been out on the water."

"Ketchup," her partner corrected. "Brown sauce is disgusting."

"It's luscious. There's something else I thought of while Tomas was talking . . . Might just be a coincidence, but the victim from the Claw Beach incident last night is a solicitor at Pearce and Partners. Alex Harbor." Dove had been mulling this over in the back of her mind ever since Tomas Radley had mentioned his wife worked there.

"I wonder if the man from last night is the solicitor Dionne Radley was going to talk to about her divorce?" Steve suggested. "I guess it would be too much to hope for that we could hit two cases at once. Worth a visit, I think, even if just to follow up on Dionne's movements."

"DI Blackman will go nuts if both cases *are* entangled," Dove commented, "especially as I'm a Sig Wit for the Claw Beach attack. Look, if I pull over behind that delivery lorry, I'll run in to Ren's place. What do you want?" Dove neatly manoeuvred through the busy street.

"Large latte and a slice of carrot cake, thanks. I'll ring Camillo's and see if I can ask a few questions about Dionne. Her employers might be able to give a little more insight into last night."

"Okay, cool." She left him and wove her way through the traffic to Ren's coffee shop. It was situated in one of the older town buildings, and the warm brick and red-painted signage drew people in. They stayed when faced with the luscious baking smells and promise of iced coffee. This summer, Ren had an ice cream counter too. Dove was partial to the blue bubblegum flavour, which made her sister laugh.

Today, Dove joined the queue impatiently, waved at her elder niece, Eden, who was serving, and smiled as she heard Ren singing along to the radio out the back.

Eden had always said she enjoyed the homely atmosphere of the family coffee shop, and now her little son, Elan,

50

had started nursery, she was helping out more often, even trying her hand at some baking.

"Hi, Dove, what can I get you?" Her niece was smiling at her, long brown hair caught up in a high ponytail, blue eyes sparkling with well-being. There were still times when she was sad and silent, but these were getting less and less, Dove thought, smiling back.

"Large latte, iced coffee with hazelnut syrup and two slices of carrot cake, please," Dove said, moving along the counter as her order was collected.

Her mobile rang as she paid and gathered everything up, and she swore under her breath, put everything back down on the counter, fumbling for her phone.

"Yes, boss?"

"You two still on your way to see Billy Jackson?"

"We are."

"Updates for you from the first post-mortems. Aileen was pregnant, about seven weeks."

"Oh my god," Dove said softly, horrified. She found her hand was clenched on the phone, shoulders tensed, and deliberately relaxed them. It was an instinctive reaction, she thought, to such news, and nothing to do with her personal issues.

"Exactly. And we have an ID for our fourth victim: Ellis Bravery. He's forty-seven, with no record apart from a couple of parking tickets. I've sent Maya and Josh straight over to his place with the SOCO team. He's an IT consultant, and a whizz-kid entrepreneur. Lives next to the marina in one of those new apartment blocks with his girlfriend," the DI said briskly.

"Big difference in social demographic for all four of them," Dove commented, recovering quickly.

"Right. Let me know if you get anything. Be back for the briefing at six. And tell Steve to switch his bloody phone on!" the DI said sharply.

Dove staggered back to the car and relayed the information to her partner. "Oh, and Steve, the DI wants to know why your phone is switched off?"

"It isn't, I just used it . . ." Steve yanked it out of his trouser pocket. "Shit, the battery's dead now. Grace was up at midnight and I was on it then. I must have forgotten to charge it."

The drive to the Jacksons' home took fifteen minutes, and by the time they arrived snacks and coffee were gone, and Dove's energy was back to sky-high.

The house was a neat red-brick affair on a housing estate. The windows all had white lace curtains and the perfect square of green lawn at the front of the building was made of artificial turf. A sad-looking ornamental tree grew right in the middle of the lawn, leaves wilting in the heatwave.

"No cars on the drive," Steve noted, wiping sweat off his forehead.

The sun was approaching midday heat, and Dove's shirt already felt damp, clinging uncomfortably to her body. Her trousers felt as if they had shrunk two sizes, but like most of her female colleagues she would never have dreamt of wearing a skirt or dress to work. As her MCT colleague DS Lindsey Allerton had once summed it up, "Those kinds of clothes are a liability out in the field. You need to be able to run away and kick the shit out of someone if they go for you, so trousers are the only option."

Steve knocked on the smart glass-panelled front door and they waited. He rang the bell. "Maybe he's gone out?"

"He knew we were coming," Dove said, pulling her sunglasses back on. "Let's try round the back. Perhaps he's in the garden?"

Although they rang the doorbell numerous times, peered through the neatly cut shrubbery at the lounge window, tramped round the back and leaned over the fence, and called the number they had been given, Aileen's husband was definitely not at home.

Dove called Lindsey. "How was Billy Jackson when you saw him?"

"Took it quite well, considering he was clearly blind-sided by whatever she had been up to. He works nights stacking shelves at Tesco's, and as far as he was concerned they were quite happy and she was at home all evening. No kids . . . He was staying at home and he was going to call his neighbour to come over and be with him. Devastated, but coping, I'd say. Why?" Her voice was sharp.

"We think he might have done a bunk," Dove told her. "Did he have a car on the drive?"

"Red Vauxhall Astra . . ."

"Well it's not there now."

"Shit. Well, there was no sign of him about to pull a fast one when I left him. Sorry, mate."

"Yeah, okay, we'll call it in. Thanks, Lindsey. Oh, hang on, there's a car pulling into the driveway now. Looks like him." Dove hastily rang off and she and Steve went to greet the man, who was now slowly getting out of his car.

Aileen Jackson's husband was small and round. His receding grey hairline and lined face suggested a man far older than his fifty-odd years, Dove thought. Despite the hot weather, Billy Jackson was dressed in grey trousers, a pink shirt and a long beige cardigan. The clothes were all carefully ironed and the creases sharp.

"Sorry, I went to get some shopping but I forgot my list . . ." he said vaguely, without asking who they were. He was waving an empty shopping bag. "Aileen always likes to do the grocery shopping in the morning . . ."

"Mr Jackson? We're with the Major Crimes Team — DS Steve Parker and DC Dove Milson," Steve explained. "Can we talk inside?"

"Call me Billy, and of course, come this way." He walked very slowly to the front door, fumbled with his key for a few minutes and finally led them into an immaculate house. Dove, greeted by a waft of lemon-scented disinfectant, coughed, feeling her eyes water. She could smell bleach and furniture polish so strongly she could almost taste them.

Billy Jackson's eyes were faded grey and bloodshot, and his glasses kept slipping down his large nose. He kept pushing them back up with a quick nervous flick of his hand.

Within minutes in his company, Dove was desperate to rip the glasses off his face and get him a new pair that fitted.

"We are so sorry for your loss," she told him.

"Thank you," Billy said, smiling weakly. "It's all been such a shock. I came home this morning to find Aileen not here, and then got a visit from your colleagues telling me Aileen was dead. It was . . ." Tears started sliding down his cheeks and he gulped, fumbling in his cardigan pocket and pulling out a piece of carefully folded kitchen roll. "It was a terrible shock, and we were so happy. Everything was going right for once."

"Billy, I'm sorry, but we are doing everything we can to find out what happened," Steve told him. "Can you tell us where you were last night?"

"I was working the night shift at Tesco's. I generally do nights. It's far more peaceful . . . Around 1 a.m. I received a call from the nursing home, informing me my mother had had another fall and was asking for me." He sighed. "She has dementia and sometimes nothing will calm her except a visit. I'm always happy to do that, of course, and my manager is good about it. I sent Aileen a text, because I knew she would be asleep and I didn't want to wake her, and drove down to East Dean."

"That's about an hour's drive?" Dove queried.

"It is." Billy nodded. "I was able to calm my mother down. She didn't have any injuries, and once she was asleep the staff offered me a bed for the remainder of the night."

"When did you drive home?"

"I was back here by seven. Why?" His face was suddenly flushed, cheeks and the tip of his rather bulbous nose turning red. "You can't possibly think any of this was down to me? Her own husband? I would never . . ." He caught himself, almost choking on the words.

"We just need to eliminate people from our enquiries," Dove told him soothingly. "It's standard protocol and nobody is accusing you of any wrongdoing."

Billy dried his eyes and sat staring owlishly at them from behind his thick lenses. "But I thought you knew what happened? It's obvious, isn't it?"

"Is it?" Dove was taken aback by his sudden intensity.

"Aileen was obviously forced to take part in something against her will. She may even have been kidnapped, and these others she was with were obviously criminals. My poor wife was murdered by a gang!"

CHAPTER NINE

"There is no evidence of that at the moment," Steve replied gently. "Unless you have anything to tell us? Is there something in Aileen's background that might suggest she has links to organised crime?"

Billy sat back, lips pursed, clearly confused. "Oh . . . well I don't have details but I know she . . ." He broke off, pressing his fingers to his thin lips. "But what else could possibly have happened? Do you mean it might have been an accident after all?" His voice was tinged with doubt, and possibly hope.

"This is a complex investigation, as I'm sure you will appreciate," Steve told him, "and anything you can tell us may help us to find out what really happened."

Billy switched off the kettle before it boiled, caught himself and switched it back on again, before dropping teabags into three mugs. "We were very happy. As least I thought we were. Aileen was working part time in a charity shop when we first met." He turned to them, and Dove saw the colour had completely washed away, leaving his cheeks deathly pale. "We met online, and we married four months later."

"How long have you been married?" Dove asked, glancing at the two framed photographs on the wall in the living room. Both were wedding shots. Aileen had been very pretty, with curly dark hair framing a round face, and sparkling brown eyes with a hint of mischief. Billy didn't look any younger, Dove thought, and was a little shorter than his bride, but was looking at her with such an expression of love and pride it made him almost handsome.

"Three years. I was able to buy this house with some inheritance. Aileen was a quiet soul, she just liked to sit reading books on her laptop in the garden, do some crochet, and she loved baking too." He stopped, pouring far too much milk into the mugs, and stirred them all slowly with a teaspoon. When he passed them over, Dove saw the teabags were still floating in the top.

"Aileen told me she had a troubled past." Billy sat with his mug of tea in his hands, shaking slightly, not drinking, but staring down at the liquid as though it might reveal the answers to his wife's murder. "She said she had been with an abusive partner, and done things she shouldn't have done."

"Like what?" Dove made another note to dig into Aileen Jackson's background.

"Well I never pushed her to talk about it but she said she was a party girl when she was younger and got into a bad crowd." He put his mug down, and slopped hot liquid over the glass coffee table, without appearing to notice. "Aileen said with me it was a fresh start and the only true romance she had ever had. She was happy; we both were."

Wincing, Dove asked about the pregnancy, and Billy Jackson, surprisingly, after the initial shock had crossed his face, smiled. "Don't be silly. Your police doctors would have got that wrong. Aileen couldn't have children, and I had a vasectomy for health reasons many years ago. It was another reason we were meant to be together, I always thought." His absolute certainty was almost eerie, and his eyes were wide and vacant now as he nodded at them both. "It will be a mistake. Everyone makes mistakes sometimes, don't they?"

"All right, thank you." Steve paused, and then smiled reassuringly. "Can we get you anything before we leave?"

Billy was shaking his head as he carefully gathered up the teacups, spilling more on to the table. "No, thank you. I'm honestly better on my own. I just want to sit and remember the good times. I do have a friend popping over later. She's my neighbour Caroline, and she's always been so kind to both of us since we moved in."

"Thank you, Billy. You've been very helpful, and do call us if there is anything else you think of." Dove stashed the signed statement in her folder and smiled kindly at the devastated man.

He smiled weakly back. "I don't think I've really taken it in . . . I keep expecting her to be in the house, or reading in the garden. She loved to read, did I tell you? Oh, I did, didn't I? Sorry . . ." His eyes were wet and he blew his nose loudly on the piece of kitchen roll.

"Was your neighbour going to come over?" Dove asked, lingering at the door, thinking he really shouldn't be alone.

"Oh, yes. Caroline is going to make us both some lunch. I must go shopping . . ." He stood up, and picked up his bags again. "I might get some cheese and ham, but where did I put my list?" He began to look frantically around the small downstairs area, dropping his wallet.

"Billy?" Dove exchanged glances with Steve, went back inside and laid a gentle hand on the man's arm. The cardigan was thick and woolly under her fingers, but his arm was thin and frail. He stopped his searching and just stared at her. "Billy, would you like us to wait until Caroline arrives? Or is there someone else we could call?"

"No, thank you." He smiled bravely at them, but his gaze was still far away, almost trancelike. "Caroline will come. She had to take her cat to the vet, but she'll be back soon. It's all arranged. Everything is arranged as it should be."

* * *

Dove glanced nervously at Steve as they slid into the car. "What do you think? I reckon we should see if Lindsey could come back over here."

"Assuming the alibi checks out, I guess he is in the clear. He's certainly not what I was expecting," Steve said, pulling out his sunglasses. "But he and Aileen have only been together three years, so how much does he know about her? He may have a bit of a Cinderella complex, and feel like he rescued Aileen, but I don't see anything else."

"I don't think he should be on his own," Dove reiterated, and Steve agreed.

"Let's just hang around for ten minutes. He said he was going shopping, so if he makes it out of the house at least we know he's okay."

Dove rang DI Blackman to update him, but his phone was off, so she left a succinct voicemail instead, and followed it up with a quick text to Lindsey.

"Billy Jackson seems hardly capable of making a cup of tea," she added, turning back to Steve. "And certainly there's nothing to suggest he's capable of killing four people including his own wife. He clearly had no idea what she was up to last night." She unscrewed her water bottle and took a swig. The contents were warm and tasted faintly metallic but she was so thirsty she didn't care. "Interesting, his comments about her links with organised crime, though, and worth checking out. He also said she didn't drink or take drugs, but perhaps she has in the past?"

"It's a lead," Steve admitted. "I can see the workload getting bigger by the minute, with four backgrounds to dig into and a whole load of skeletons probably poised to fall out of the closet. Amazing the secrets that come out after people die."

She sighed, winding down the window, letting the breeze cool her hot skin and tease strands of her long dark hair. "I don't think anyone would discover any dark secrets after my death. My caffeine and sugar addiction are fairly well known."

DI Blackman called back as she and Steve were still waiting in the car, watching Billy Jackson emerge from his house and walk slowly up the hill, inevitable shopping bags dangling from his right hand. Dove felt another pang of concern.

He was on the edge, she could tell, but you couldn't force people to stay at home after they had lost a loved one, even though her instinct was always to tell them to stay on home territory, to surround themselves with friends and family. But it seemed the Jacksons had nobody but themselves.

The DI sounded brisk and efficient as ever. "Good work. Okay, change of plan. Can you go and get a statement from Ellis Bravery's girlfriend? Pete's got a bloody car problem and they're waiting for the tow truck now on Camber Road."

* * *

"Let's go back through Abberley, past the market square," Dove suggested as she started the engine. "We could also pay a quick visit to Pearce and Partners, the solicitors Dionne Radley cleaned for last night."

"Done," Steve agreed. "I think the connection between Dionne Radley and your Claw Beach victim must be a coincidence, though. This town isn't that big."

"Mmmm . . ." Dove slowed the car down to a crawl and edged past a big crowd of families and toddlers who were gathered on the picturesque cobbled bridge, spilling over the narrow pavement, chucking sticks into the river. "Do you think they've forgotten they're on a road or what?"

"On holiday," Steve said, who was checking his phone, fiddling with the charging lead. "Hey, more reports from the lab . . ."

"Go on then!" Dove said impatiently.

"I'm reading. Blah . . . blah . . . all four drowned, and there's saltwater present in their lungs, so either in the escape room, or maybe in the sea itself? Oscar Wilding and Dionne Radley both have facial bruising consistent with a punch or a slap. Her nose was actually broken."

Dove nodded, listening intently.

"Oh, this is interesting — Aileen Jackson has a number of historical injuries . . . fractures to ribs, left tibia, fingers on her right hand, right fibula. Bloody hell, that's a list!

Pathologist, not surprisingly, has queried possible historical abuse."

"Would that fit with what her husband told us? Suddenly Billy doesn't seem quite so way out after all," Dove said softly. "What if Aileen was running away from her past and somehow it's caught up with her?"

CHAPTER TEN

I tried to kill him once before, when I was a skinny seventeen-year-old.

I saw him outside his house when I came back late after an evening out. He was standing there, texting, as I walked along the road towards him. The estate was quiet and nobody else was around.

I could hear music from radios, the murmurs of TV shows through the soft summer darkness.

In my hand, I was swinging an empty beer bottle, and in my mind, I could see her dancing. He was startled when I appeared round the hedge, the recognition bright in his face. There was fear in his eyes which made my heart sing and my breath come in sharp bursts.

But I was too pissed, too angry and I missed when I swung the empty bottle at him. My fist connected with his face, and the satisfying thump of bone and skin, the subsequent trickle of blood from his nose, sated me for all of twenty-four hours.

He never reported me, never reproached me, just carried on with his life. To me, that was proof of guilt, and in my head over the next few years, I killed him a million times.

CHAPTER ELEVEN

Steve was flicking through the documents on his iPad. "Perhaps Billy Jackson found out his wife was having an affair, or at least on a night out without him? Ellis Bravery, victim number four, whose girlfriend we are supposed to be visiting now, was the eldest, and he had scratch marks down his back, but no other injuries. All in good health. Oh, and signs of sexual activity. Trace evidence of semen present inside the vagina of both women. I'm amazed it didn't get washed away."

"Harry's pulled it out of the bag to get preliminaries so quickly, especially considering so much evidence must have literally been washed away." Dove admired Dr Harry Iziah, the lead pathologist, even though she was also slightly intimidated by the cool, sour-smelling morgue. "Anything from Jess?"

"Nope, and waiting on all the tech stuff from the lab. I reckon that will shed a whole load of light on our foursome. They must have communicated about the meet-up last night . . . I wonder how they all met in the first place? They seem like they were from very different backgrounds, and the only common denominator is geographical at the moment."

"You think they were having some kind of orgy in the escape room?" Dove pulled a face. She was no prude, but she couldn't imagine how it would be fun being locked in a glass room with three other people to have sex.

"Takes all sorts," Steve said, as Dove finally escaped the holiday traffic and pulled up outside the imposing stone building that housed the solicitors. His phone rang just as they were about to get out. "It's the wife. I'll just quickly take this, if you don't mind. She's picked up some bug and been feeling sick on and off for a couple of weeks now. Not serious, but she had a doctor's appointment booked in . . ."

Dove waved in agreement and left him leaning against the car in the shade, while she ran lightly up the stone steps and into the blessed cool interior of the building. It smelled of paper and whatever rather strong scent was in the reed diffuser on the reception desk. Roses and lavender, she thought, politely approaching the desk. It was more like the foyer of a luxury hotel.

"Good afternoon, ma'am. Can I help you?" The immaculate young man had such perfect polished teeth and shiny blonde hair that Dove felt sure he was judging her sweaty, slightly bedraggled appearance. She squared her shoulders. At times like this she blessed the fact that she was tall, and could look rather imposing when she felt like it.

"Yes, please," she peered at his name badge, "Donald. Nice to meet you. I'm DC Dove Milson. I just have a few questions, if you have a moment?" She flashed her ID but he reached out and studied it closely, before pushing it back across the desk to her.

"Just a second, if you don't mind." He tapped importantly at his keyboard, frowning, and finally nodded. Clearly it must be important business, although he couldn't disguise the glint of eagerness in his eyes as he gave Dove his full attention. "Sorry about that, and of course I'm happy to help in any way I can. Is this about Mr Harbor? Your colleagues came round this morning and told us he was in hospital. Shocking! He's such a nice man. I was so sorry to hear he had been attacked."

The vast marble hallway was empty, and full of whispering echoes. Dove leaned a little closer. "I'm actually with the Major

Crimes Team and I'm investigating another case. Can you tell me anything about Camillo's? The cleaning service you use."

The young man's eyes opened wide in surprise. "The cleaners? Sure, if you like." Donald pursed his lips, rattled through his keyboard with precise, pale fingers. "We've used them for eleven years. Very reliable. The owner is Mr Herbert Gunter, but you probably know that already." Another flashing smile.

"Do you have any direct contact with the cleaning staff? I mean, after hours or anything?"

"Like all-nighters? Oh no. This isn't a New York law firm, Detective. This is a respectable family solicitors'." He smiled, slightly condescendingly. "Sometimes one of the partners might work late, but that would only be until about seven or eight. It would be unheard of for anyone to be here any later, and the cleaners come in at nine."

"But if someone wanted to stay later, they could?" Dove persisted.

"Well yes. Access and egress is by swipe card and keypad."

He was loving this, Dove could tell, waiting expectantly for each new question, eager to impart information. Well that was fine by her. In her experience it was unusual to have people willing to talk to the police. Most people didn't want to get involved. "So you have a record of everyone leaving and arriving?"

"Of course." Another rattle of keys. "I can tell you for the last month everyone has been out by seven . . ."

"Can you go back to June?" Dove asked.

"Sure. Sooooo . . . Ah. Two late departures in June. Neither of them from Mr Harbor." He shot her a look from under his lashes.

Dove kept her face expressionless. "Can I have the names of the two who worked late in June, and a printout for June, July and August, please?"

"I can . . . what was the investigation you said you are working on?" He paused suddenly, as a door opened and two men walked quickly down the hallway towards the reception desk.

Dove could tell anything she said would be relayed, probably with embellishments, to everyone in the firm. No harm in rattling a few cages, and she felt strongly that there was something here. Unlike Steve, she didn't believe in coincidences.

The two men, both wearing dark suits and with shiny polished shoes, turned left and opened the door to another room. Dove watched as they vanished inside, but they barely gave her a glance. Out of uniform, she probably looked like just another harassed client, she thought. She turned back to Donald, mindful of Steve still sitting in the car. Why hadn't he joined her? Hopefully there wasn't anything wrong with his wife. "It would be very helpful if you could do that. We are investigating the death of several people, including Mrs Dionne Radley."

The look of surprise, shock and something else didn't escape Dove's sharp eyes. "Do you know the name?"

"No, doesn't ring any bells, I'm afraid. She doesn't work here, you know."

"She worked for your contract cleaners, and was part of the team who cleaned your offices last night. It's very important we try to trace her recent movements."

"Oh. I see." He relaxed a little, hit another button with a flourish and the printer spat out the documents she needed. "Glad I could be of help, Detective. Here you are."

"One other thing. I see you have CCTV. Can I see the footage from last night?"

"You can. I already showed it to your colleagues earlier this morning. They said they were tracing Mr Harbor's movements from yesterday evening." He peered at her, eyes bright with speculation. "Goodness, do you think Mr Harbor's attack could be related to your investigation?"

"There is no indication at the moment that the two cases are linked." She smiled. "Sorry, but as this is a separate investigation I do need to have a quick look at the CCTV as well."

He smiled back, but Dove thought she detected a trace of worry returning. "Look: this is the footage of last night from 5 p.m."

She walked around his desk, noting the immaculate state of his computer, the single white lily in a blue vase complemented by a royal blue notebook and gold pen. This close, the floral scent from the reed diffuser made her feel sick.

The footage was good, as she had expected from a solicitors', and they watched in silence as people came and went. The mass exodus slowed at six, and Donald started to name-check the employees.

Last person out was Alex Harbor, the Claw Beach victim. He left at seven. Donald went to stop the film, but Dove make a dissenting sound. She wanted to see when the cleaners arrived.

They came in a group. Five women and one man, dressed in blue overalls, carrying cleaning equipment and cloths. Dionne Radley. She was there, dressed for work at nine o' clock that evening, long black ponytail swinging as she walked with a sure, confident stride.

The man swiped the cleaners in and after that Donald was able to switch to footage from various cameras in hallways and rooms, which showed them working quickly and efficiently.

"Fast forward slowly," Dove said.

The cleaners left promptly at ten thirty. All of them, including Dionne.

"Have you got outside footage?" Dove asked.

He pulled it up. "Here you go."

Five people got into the logoed Camillo's van, leaving one person to walk away alone. She had not taken the transport, been safe with her colleagues on her way to another job. Three hours before her estimated time of death, Dionne Radley had walked briskly towards the Bond Road, dressed in her blue cleaner's overall and baggy trousers, a large white bag over her shoulder. Her long dark ponytail bounced in time with her strides.

The last frame of footage showed her turn the corner, still alone, into the alleyway that linked Bond Road with Cliffacre road. Had she been making her way to see her husband and brother-in-law after her shift?

CHAPTER TWELVE

"You've been ages. The DI was on the phone again."

"You all right?" Dove stared at him. He seemed a little pale and she was still wondering why he hadn't followed her into Pearce and Partners. "You look like you're going to throw up."

"Yes . . . I mean no, I'm not going to vomit." He laughed and rubbed his cheeks with both hands. "Zara said she had done a test and . . . Shit, Dove, she's pregnant again." He peered at her anxiously, suddenly mindful of her recent history. "Sorry, I wasn't sure whether to tell you or not."

Dove slapped him on the back, grinning, thankful to be feeling genuine pleasure for the couple. "Why would you not tell me, idiot? That's great news! A bit quick after Grace . . . You won't be getting any decent nights' sleep for a while. Congratulations to you both. When's the baby due?"

"February." Steve's voice was warming back to naturalness. "I'm just a bit shocked, I guess . . . We weren't trying or anything and suddenly Zara says she's pregnant again and do I like the name Michaela for a girl, or Joseph for a boy. Jeez!"

As Steve was still trying to absorb the fact he was going to be a dad of two, Dove read through the notes on Ellis Bravery, the third victim from Escape Room Six.

"Steve, you need to focus. Get some beer in on the way home and celebrate properly, but get your head back in the case for now." But Dove was smiling at his evident pleasure at the news. "Recap for your scrambled brain: Ellis Bravery, forty-seven, with no previous convictions. Divorced, owns an IT company. His ex-wife lives in Edinburgh, no kids, but he does have a girlfriend. She's at his place now and waiting for our visit."

Steve's phone pinged and he scrolled down, checking his emails. "Aileen Jackson, née Boyle, has previous convictions for prostitution and possession of amphetamines, intent to deal, etcetera." Apparently sufficiently recovered, he tapped the screen. "No evidence of links to organised crime, but certainly an interesting rap sheet. I can see why she might have brushed it off to her new husband as being a party girl. He doesn't seem the type to have ever set foot in a nightclub."

"Maybe she wasn't hiding out from any dealers or pimps she might have grassed up or owed, perhaps she really did just decide to change her life and go straight," Dove mused, indicating right at the junction, swearing at a kid on a moped zipping through the traffic at high speed. "That's an accident waiting to happen."

Steve agreed, "He's right next to that HGV. There's no way the driver can see the little idiot." He paused. "I think Aileen's worth pursuing. If she started a new life with Billy, and settled down to play housewife, why was she out partying again? Because there is nothing to suggest she wasn't a willing participant at the moment. And if he found out about the baby, knowing of course that it wasn't his, it gives him even more of a motive to kill."

* * *

They left the vehicle in the dim coolness of the underground car park and took the lift up to the ground floor. Ellis lived in one of the newer apartment blocks near the marina. His place was on the top floor, and the whole building was a luxury development that spoke of money. A smiling, efficient concierge with quick, darting eyes, sent them straight up when they showed their ID.

"I thought hotels had concierges, not flats," Steve muttered, as they got back in the lift and rode to the eighth floor.

"This place has a pool in the basement too." Dove pointed at the lift buttons. Not only was there one marked '*swimming pool*', but also '*spa*' and '*gym*'.

"I'm in the wrong job." Steve shook his head. "Grace or the next baby had better turn out to be some kind of genius city trader or something, because if I have to rely on my pension, I'll be down on the Seaview Estate."

Dove rolled her eyes at the mention of the notorious housing estate further down the coast. "Don't worry, I'm sure Zara will be able to keep you in the manner to which you could clearly become accustomed. Didn't you say she had two new clients already this month?"

"True, her graphic design business is going great." He glanced at Dove. "I suppose you and Quinn would be happier with a beach hut than a penthouse."

The lift stopped and the doors slid smoothly open to a marble hallway with discreet lighting and oak panelled walls. Dove grinned and turned back to her partner. "You suppose right, but we're thinking somewhere a bit hotter, and preferably with palm trees, so it will have to be a damn small hut."

Ellis Bravery's girlfriend, Ally, a skinny redhead, opened the door as soon as they pressed the buzzer. Her face was a mask of make-up so thick Dove found it hard to detect any expression whatsoever, and her long red-gold hair fell in a ponytail to her waist.

"I can't believe he's gone." Ally led them through the apartment after they had introduced themselves, and indicated white leather sofas for them to sit. "He was going to propose and we were so happy together . . ." She dabbed at her eyes with a tissue, but Dove noticed no tears streaked her thick black lashes.

"Can you tell us when you last saw him?" Steve asked.

Ally smiled at him. She had very small, even teeth. Feline-like, her green gaze was calculating, the weight of her false lashes narrowing her gaze to mere slits. "Last night he came home as usual and we went out to dinner. We eat out a lot, and Ellis hosts a lot of parties," she added with apparent satisfaction.

"What happened after dinner?" Steve asked.

"Well he quite often has meetings late at night, or very early in the morning, and when he does we sleep in separate rooms. He has properties all over the world, you know." She half-smiled, but paused again as her face clouded with genuine grief. Dove suddenly realised just how young Ally was and how possibly unprepared she was for this situation. "He was very successful, but it came later in life. He always said he was just starting to enjoy his money, and now it's been taken away from him . . ." She buried her face in her hands for a moment, taking quick shuddering breaths. "I honestly can't bear it. Do you think he . . . suffered?"

"We are so sorry for your loss," Dove repeated. How old was Ally? Maybe twenty-one? And Ellis had been forty-seven. That was a big age gap . . . "But we need any information you might have to try to catch whoever did this to Ellis." She paused to allow the girl time to compose herself. "I thought he had an IT business?"

"Oh, he does—" She stopped abruptly. "He did . . . But he started investing in property in Florida, and he also bought some flats in Tobago in a holiday complex. It's just gone from there. It's just a side project, but it's made a lot of money."

"How long have you been together?" Steve asked.

"Six months." It came out quick, defensive. "But it's been long enough for us to know we were meant to be together. People think it's his money, you know, and they can be quite mean. Older people think that . . ." She ground to a halt, clearly realising she was giving an explanation when none had been asked for.

Disregarding this, Dove prodded her with the same question. "We aren't here to judge, we just need to find out

71

what happened. Going back to last night, you came back from dinner, and then what?"

The girl tapped manicured fingers on the coffee table, apparently thinking. "We had a nightcap, and he said he had some business to take care of, so he would see me in the morning."

"Did he say he was going out?" Dove was finding it very hard to believe Ally wouldn't notice her boyfriend leaving the apartment. The floor was wooden, and everything else seemed to be marble and glass. Footsteps anywhere would surely echo around the place. The apartment reminded her of Pearce and Partners, the solicitors.

"No." Again that flash of guarded annoyance from under the thick lashes. "I don't know . . . I don't remember. This place is huge and if he said he was doing business I usually assumed it was in his office, which is at the opposite end of the apartment to the bedrooms."

"Surely he would have told you if he was going out?" Steve pressed.

"He was very considerate, and perhaps he didn't want to disturb me," Ally said. "I went to bed around eleven and he was sitting on the sofa right where you are now, with his iPad and a glass of wine. When I got up at nine, he wasn't here. I made a coffee and got on with my day, thinking he'd probably text or something . . ."

"You know Ellis met with Oscar Wilding and two other women for a night at the Beach Escape Rooms?" Steve prodded.

The woman shrugged, dismissing the other women with a wave of her hand. "I don't know anything about that. Our relationship was based on trust. I was shocked when I found out how he had died, but . . ."

Dove and Steve waited, but she shook her head. "I don't know what he was doing down on the pier, and I've never heard of those other people, the ones who died with him. He meets a lot of people in business, and I don't pay much attention."

Steve turned his iPad round and showed her photographs of Aileen, Dionne and Oscar. "Have you ever seen these three? Out socialising with Ellis, or maybe to do with a business transaction?"

She peered intently at the photos, and to Dove's surprise she tapped Dionne's photograph. "Her. I've seen her somewhere but I can't think . . ." She frowned and brought her hand to her forehead. "I know! It was at Blue Domino's. You know, the nightclub on Broad Street. Ellis and I were there with some of his friends and she was part of another group he seemed to know. They were wild, and almost got thrown out of the VIP area because they were that pissed. We weren't actually introduced but we got talking at the bar later."

Suddenly Ally's face was bright with the memory, long nails tapping her slim thigh, leaning towards them in her eagerness, and making Dove feel guilty for doubting her. On first impressions Ally had seemed a little vapid and shallow, but suddenly a keen intelligence was showing through the doll-like exterior.

"Go on. When was this? What did you talk about?"

"Oh, the usual . . . Music, the vibe that night. She said she was starting a new career in interior design. I asked how she knew Ellis and she said she had a friend who did business with him . . . I guess it would have been last month, because Ellis and I were just back from his villa on the Costa del Sol. June eighteenth, but I'll double-check the calendar." The flood of information halted abruptly. "That was all. She wasn't with him, though." The sharp pink nails tapped Oscar's picture before going back to her phone. "I would have remembered him because of his red hair. You always remember a fellow redhead." She smiled prettily, the bland little doll again, raking a hand through her own glossy mane. "Yes, I was right . . . Look." A moment later she showed Steve and Dove the packed calendar on her phone.

So Dionne had been drinking in a rather upmarket nightclub with her friends at the same time as Ellis Bravery and his girlfriend last month. Dove was very keen to see the tech report on the phones back from forensics, and find out what kind of contact all these people had. Glancing at Steve, she could tell he was thinking the same thing.

"Are you sure you didn't hear any phone calls, any late-night visitors from last night?" Steve asked now.

But the girl shook her head. "I sleep really soundly, and I trust Ellis a hundred per cent." The tears started again, and she rubbed her eyes, sniffing, smearing black make-up across her face. "He always said I slept like a child and laid in like an adult."

Ally seemed to find this comment sweet, but to Dove it sounded more than a little creepy and she felt herself wondering again about their relationship.

"I can't think of anything else. He was just normal, just Ellis. He was so busy and smart but really caring too, you know?" Ally said now. "My friends said we were made for each other, with our names and everything. You know, Ally and Elly . . . That's what he liked me to call him, Elly. He was so supportive of me building my career as a model and influencer, and told me how much he believed in me."

"Yes, we understand. I'm really sorry, Ally, but are you happy to sign a statement based on what you've just told us?" Dove felt she might need a motion sickness bag if the girl gushed about her relationship any more. Ally and Elly.

A sideways glance at Steve showed her he was holding in laughter and she deliberately avoided catching his eye. It might even be true, all these hearts and flowers, Dove supposed, but Ellis's girlfriend certainly seemed to have no idea what he got up to. Although she had lit up at the memory of Dionne, perhaps that had just been a safe path for her to travel down, to show the police how helpful she was being.

Dove turned at the door as Ally showed them out. "Just one last question . . . Do you have a cleaner, or a housekeeper?"

"Of course. We have a cleaner." She waved a slender arm. "I couldn't possibly clean all this myself and work on creating new content." The half-smile again, quickly followed by the sad little glance from under her lashes.

"What's your cleaner's name?" Dove asked casually, but her heart rate was accelerating. There was something here, she could feel it. Connections being made, almost invisible threads weaving the victims' lives together . . .

"Oh, I don't know, sorry, the firm sends different people every time, and I'm often out shopping or at the gym at the time they arrive." She smiled. "I prefer not to be around to watch them work. It makes me feel a bit guilty. I do have a card for the firm, though. Hang on a sec . . ." She headed for the vast marble kitchen and rummaged around on the magnetic whiteboard on the wall, before passing a card to Dove.

Dove took it with thanks and glanced at the details:

Camillo's, for all your cleaning needs.
Industrial and domestic contracts undertaken.

CHAPTER THIRTEEN

After talking to Ellis Bravery's girlfriend and taking her statement, Steve and Dove had made it back to the station with half an hour to spare and were hastily using the time to collate their notes before the evening briefing.

The two DIs were already back and most of the team were now filing in, sweaty, exhausted and carrying takeaways and iced drinks. Clearly nobody imagined work was over for the day.

"Ally, Ellis Bravery's girlfriend, was arrested for shoplifting last year, but the store dropped the charges. Looks like it was the wine store on North Street, and she was laying in supplies." Steve was reading out loud. "Says she was going through a bad patch and was going to get help for her drinking."

Dove thought back to the perfect and polished girl in the gleaming apartment. The flashes of personality beneath the painted exterior. Had she just been playing a part for Ellis? "I reckon she's a lot smarter than she gives out . . . She seemed a bit disdainful that Dionne and her friends were drinking heavily at the club. If she had a drinking problem previously it might mean a lot to her that she's kicked it?"

"Right, and if she *hasn't* managed to kick the habit, she might be extra careful about her pristine reputation. Maybe

Ellis didn't know she'd had any alcohol problems?" Steve pulled a face. "If you must eat those disgusting things, please keep them away from me. They smell of plastic."

Dove swept her packet of jelly sweets off his workspace but planted her elbows next to his keyboard, studying the statement they had just taken from Ally. "And what would she have done if she found out he was out playing games with other women, and therefore perhaps not quite the perfect fiancé she thought he was?"

"If she's turning a blind eye to his activities maybe that extends to illicit meet-ups?" Steve suggested. "She mentioned the money a few times and seemed a bit defensive about it. Perhaps it was worth putting up with his quirks to stay as the live-in girlfriend?"

"Let's send the whole lot over to the DI." Dove pushed herself upright, tipped the packet and poured the last of her sugar rush straight into her mouth.

"You are a class act, DC Dove Milson," Josh said, catching her stuffing her face as he walked past with Lindsey, laughing.

She stuck a middle finger up at him and followed Steve out to the briefing room.

DI Lincoln kicked off the briefing, methodically running through his notes, including the information that had already been sent to the entire team during the day.

"He reminds me of my year-eight history teacher," Steve muttered to Dove.

"Is that a good thing?" she murmured back, eyes on the whiteboard, tracing the tangled lines relating to the last movements of all their victims. There were a lot of blanks still left to fill in.

"I failed history GCSE, so probably not," Steve admitted.

"Thanks, George. A quick summary is now up on the board and circulating via emails, so I won't bore you with the whole update now," DI Blackman interjected, jumping in as his colleague stopped to take a sip of his tea. Clearly seeing the team had switched off, he continued. "Main points being, as DI Lincoln has just mentioned, none of the relatives, other halves, friends we know of, have so far admitted to knowing where the four victims were last night. Lindsey?"

She nodded in agreement. "Both female victims had husbands, and they claim to have had no idea the women were out last night. Dionne's husband, Tomas, has an alibi, which checks out, and we are still confirming Aileen's husband, Billy, who says he had started off working the night shift at the local Tesco's before being called to check on his mother."

"Maya. Did you get anything?"

"Oscar Wilding seems to have been a bit of a loner, keeping himself to himself. Can't find any family, friends, etcetera, but his neighbours say he's . . ." she looked down at his notes to quote, ". . . a nice polite man. He always helps with the bins and chucks the kids' football back when it goes over his garden fence. Works as an odd-job man, and does deliveries in his van. You know, man with van for hire."

"Got it. Steve?"

"Ellis Bravery's girlfriend says she was asleep in their apartment, that Ellis often worked late and she didn't notice him go out," Steve said. "And we have a link between Dionne Radley and Ellis. They were both out at the same club last month, and the cleaning firm she works for, Camillo's, also cleans his apartment." Steve shuffled his notes. "Kind of a weird set-up, and it seems like she just turns a blind eye to everything apart from their relationship."

"Good. Dig a bit more on that one," DI Blackman told him. "Great work in general, everyone. Email is just in with a report from the lab on mobiles and other tech devices. Mobile phone records were expedited, so there will be more to come, but . . ." He clicked the mouse and various text messages appeared on the drop-down screen. "So, three of our victims look to have had two phones each. Dionne Radley just had the one phone, a burner, on her. But they all had a burner and a normal phone that contains pretty much their whole lives. It is possible, and hopefully probable, that Dionne's other phone will turn up during our searches."

"Secret phones?" Josh winked at Maya, "How original."

Ignoring him, the DI continued, "As you can see from the screen up here, text conversations between them suggest this was a planned meet-up, and they all knew exactly what they were getting into. There are a lot of conversations to pick through, but these are from last night. Hang on, I'll put them up on the screen . . ."

Dove studied the copy of the transcript of the recent group chat on WhatsApp:

> *Oscar: You gonna be late again E?*
> *Ellis: Just gotta make a call & wait till baby is asleep. It's all good. Meet you there.*
> *Aileen: OK.*
> *Dionne: On my way. Wearing the black dress ;-)*

"Just before midnight," DI Lincoln added, "Oscar and Aileen, from the mobile triangulation, were on the pier, and he sent this." He clicked through to another message.

Oscar: We've just arrived. This is gonna be best yet!

"Finally, all four were on the pier by twenty past midnight. None of them used their everyday phones during this period, although Aileen Jackson's phone has an answerphone message from her husband, left at 1 a.m., saying his mother has had a fall and he's going to leave work and drive straight over to her nursing home." DI Blackman raised an eyebrow at Dove and Steve.

Steve nodded. "Corroborates his statement."

Josh was leaning back against the wall. "So from the group chat, this suggests clearly they all knew each other previously."

"Certainly well enough for this to be a prearranged meeting," DI Blackman agreed. "They were all headed for the escape rooms, not suggesting meet-ups in a bar or for dinner. Doesn't look like a spontaneous thing. I'll send you all copies, and trawl through the rest of the chat. Dionne's everyday mobile phone is currently switched off. Her husband says he called her twice last night to ask if she was working next Tuesday, as he wanted to make plans to have an estate agent visit."

"Ellis Bravery doesn't have a baby," Dove pointed out the obvious. "But his girlfriend did make a slightly odd comment about the fact he likes the fact she sleeps like a child . . ." Suddenly their slightly off-kilter relationship didn't seem that amusing after all.

"So he can go out swinging when she's tucked up past her bedtime, maybe?" Lindsey suggested sarcastically.

DI Lincoln's phone rang and he picked it up, turning away into the corridor to take the call.

"What about the owners of the escape room?" DC Maya Amin queried. "When we spoke to them they seemed really shocked, but I'm certain their CCTV would have captured any break-ins. They said they paid a lot for the system to be installed." She glanced at DI Blackman, who was now adding to the timelines on the whiteboard in his neat handwriting.

"Most of the CCTV is not going to be recoverable, unfortunately," the DI answered. "And the owners do seem more worried about their insurance than who killed four people on their premises last night. They are childhood sweethearts apparently, both originally from further along the coast in Salthaven. They've got a young baby, Lila, so are pretty distracted by her too."

The team began to disperse, chat volume levels rising as they compared notes and theories, Dove and Steve drifting with the tide. DS Pete Wyndham opened a packet of chocolate digestives, looking meditatively out of the window as he crunched the biscuits, staring at the timelines.

DI Lincoln finished his call and returned to the room, his expression sombre. "Extra update for you. Aileen Jackson's husband, Billy, has just been found dead at the train station. He jumped in front of the 8.07 Southam–London service. Never had a chance. Numerous witnesses say he was sitting on one of the benches drinking from a bottle of whisky, suddenly got up and took a running leap. He left his phone and wallet in a shopping bag on the bench." The DI paused and glanced around the room. "There's a suicide note, handwritten and taped to his phone, stating he's sorry for everything."

CHAPTER FOURTEEN

Quinn was eating pizza in the garden with a beer dangling from his hand when Dove finally arrived home. Nobody joined the police force expecting a nine-to-five job, but sometimes even she was exhausted by the seventeen- or eighteen-hour shifts they all put in at the start of a murder investigation.

Her fiancé called a greeting and she dumped her gear and went straight out into the sunny patch at the rear of the house. The late-evening light, gold stained with pink, cast a gentle glow around the small garden.

"Hi babe, how's your head?" He squinted up at her from the blue-striped sunlounger.

"It's fine." She kissed him. "Okay, it hurts a bit, but I'm okay. I feel like I haven't seen you for weeks."

It was always like that when Quinn had a run of shifts, especially nights. They could go days just communicating by texts and the occasional kiss hello and goodbye. Demanding jobs with stressful implications. Typical, Dove thought, perching on the end of his lounger and snagging a beer from the ice bucket, that her fiancé now had some days off and she had just started what was looking like one of the most complex MCT investigations she had worked on yet.

Quinn smiled lazily up at her. His messy black hair flopped across his forehead and his green eyes glittered in the late-evening sun. He had acquired freckles across the bridge of his nose along with his tan. Her heart, as always, gave a lurch of love for him. Her rock.

"Hey, let's go out on the water," she said now, forcing her mind away from the investigation. Her mind was exhausted and her body ached, but she was craving the best stress release she knew, and the one she could share with Quinn. It was tough, but she had been working extra hard on trying to switch off when she was at home with him. "Although on second thoughts, how many of those beers have you had?"

He sat up, sweeping his arms around her. "Just the one. You can have my last pizza slice before we go."

Half an hour later, marvelling at the warmth of the water at ten o'clock at night, they were jogging through the shallows with their paddleboards. Dove could feel her exhaustion washing away as they went further and further out. The sun was a fierce orange gold, blazing a trail across the sea, by the time they turned back to the beach, paddles dipping rhythmically, lazily, the gulls calling, soaring on huge wings overhead.

Afterwards they lay on the beach as darkness approached. Dove prodded Quinn's bare leg with her sandy toes. "Are you still awake?"

"Starving," he replied. "Let's get some food on the way home."

Dove dived into the corner shop at the end of their road, picked up snacks and some ready-made seafood salads. Her T-shirt clung to her damp body and her hair was still wet, hanging heavily across her shoulder blades. She could taste salt on her lips, feel the sand crunching inside her flip-flops, and the intermittent throb of her healing injury.

As she came out, she bumped straight into a man heading in the opposite direction. Hard. "Ouch! Sorry . . ."

He was wearing a red baseball cap pulled down over his eyes, but nodded, smiled and brushed her apology away, continuing into the shop, brown shoulder-length hair flopping around his face.

She looked after him for a moment, supposing she must be more tired than she thought to walk straight into someone.

* * *

Later, curled up on the sofa, with the glass doors to the tiny garden thrown open, despite her best efforts, Dove went back to pondering the case. Suspects galore, but nobody who stood out apart from Billy Jackson. Was his suicide as a result of trailing his cheating wife and causing the deaths of four innocent people, or had her death just hit him hard? She dipped back into the crisp packet, half watching the Netflix film they had chosen.

"I was thinking next June for our wedding date," Quinn said suddenly, dragging her mind away from murder.

"You were?" Dove smiled at him. They had batted dates around for a while, but so far not committed to anything. "How about exactly a year from now and we make it the twenty-sixth of July?"

"Church, and then a beach party?"

"Sorted. Hell, Quinn, we're in the wrong jobs. We should be wedding planners," Dove joked, as her fiancé rolled his eyes.

* * *

It wasn't until she had just settled down to sleep, begun shutting down her mind, finally submitting to weariness, that she thought of it.

Dove sighed. She hated it when this happened, but for her that moment between consciousness and sleep was often when her mind made connections she had been too busy to pursue in daytime.

For a few moments she tried to unfocus, to sleep, but the desire for knowledge, for a new lead, was too tempting. Carefully, so as not to wake Quinn, she slipped out of bed and stood up.

The cool night breeze floating in at the open window touched her naked body and she shivered. She picked up a discarded T-shirt from the floor and slipped it over her head, before padding carefully downstairs to the kitchen.

It was warmer and slightly stuffy down here. The windows were shut for security reasons but she had left the vent open at the top of the back door. Dove grabbed her laptop, jumped violently as Layla slid silently in from the living room, and sat down at the kitchen table.

The cat watched her with enquiring eyes, uttered a squeaky meow and started to purr. Clearly she approved of Dove's nocturnal wanderings.

Mickey Delaney.

Wide awake now, pushing her hair back from her eyes, Dove logged on to the internet. After a quick search, she found what she was looking for. Almost every story showed pictures of Mickey competing in sparkly leotards, her body stretching out into incredible poses, red ponytail flying out behind her, or standing in happy family snaps. Jamie had been a redhead then, just like his younger sister, and she noted a family photo, with him smiling proudly and protectively down at his little sibling.

Mickey had been a promising teenage gymnast, when she was severely beaten and left for dead "by assailants unknown", almost five years ago. She had been attacked in the woods above a derelict sandstone quarry, a popular hang-out area for the local teens, and miraculously survived a thirty-foot fall on to sharp rocks below. She was discovered by forestry workers. Mickey had suffered so many trauma injuries, including damage to her spleen and lungs, doctors had been certain she wouldn't survive. But she had been in a coma ever since.

This was what had dragged her from her bed. Steve had said earlier Zara wanted to call the baby Michaela if it was a girl, she recalled, and finally her brain had made the connection with what felt like a sharp click.

It must have been horrific for the family, especially as the case had never been solved. And now Jamie Delaney was involved in a murder inquiry, which was . . . interesting.

Dove had been in the closing stages of one of her under-cover operations when it had happened, but the case of fourteen-year-old gymnast Mickey Delaney had caught her attention, much as it had caught the attention of the press. Mickey's picture had been everywhere, and speculation had been rife as to who had been responsible for her attack.

She thought back, tapping a pen on her teeth, staring unseeingly at the ceiling. At the time, Dove had been infiltrating an organised crime gang with the aid of her CHIS (Covert Human Intelligence Source). She'd had a meeting behind a dive bar with her CHIS and his brothers. His brothers had no idea that every word they uttered that night was incriminating them, or that their brother was earning a nice amount for grassing up their illegal enterprise and bringing a copper into their midst.

The night she'd learned about Mickey Delaney, the meeting had finished, and Dove had hung around, nonchalantly in character, smoking a cigarette, laughing at something her CHIS said, but all the time aching for the close, the kill. The investigation had gone well, and everything was in place, according to the plans.

She remembered watching a few of the girls from the brothel sharing cigarettes and whispering in the corner of the yard. In was a hot summer night, but their cheap, skimpy clothing would have been the same if it had been freezing cold and snowing. One of the girls was swigging from a bottle, another passing round pills from a plastic bag.

Dove and her CHIS had just finished their cigarettes and were turning to go, when there was a noise from the girls' corner. One of them had swung herself up on to the high concrete ledge that surrounded the yard area on two sides.

Poised for a moment, barefoot and skinny in her thin blue dress, she calmly started to dance, turning cartwheels and doing backflips before finally landing in an easy handstand on the narrow crumbling ledge, dark hair tumbling around her face.

She could have been an Olympic gymnast — like Mickey — but then she jumped lightly down, slipped her heels back on and was just another skinny teenage prostitute in Ari's Bar.

"Does she do that a lot?" Dove had asked, impressed but hiding it. What a waste of talent.

Her CHIS shrugged, clearly not interested. The girls were money, not people, to him.

Dove feigned slight amusement, disdain even, and they went back through the scummy, smoky dive bar, and out on to the street. Next day the bar was raided by her colleagues. A large quantity of drugs and knives were seized, but the girls seemed to have vanished into the night — except for two.

Later, after a forensic search of Ari's Bar, two dead bodies were discovered in the cellar. They had been tortured before being shot. Two young girls. One of them was the gymnast in the blue dress.

It was one of those things that stayed with Dove, skittering in the far reaches of her memory, a sore place in her heart. It turned out some members of the criminal gang thought the girls were responsible for leaking information and therefore they had been punished.

Dove glanced up sharply at the window, half-imagining a shadow moving swiftly back in the darkness, a blurred face, a tall figure. She was still half lost in her own past, confused, heart beating hard and fast. A quick thud of footsteps on the pavement outside. She flew to the window, throwing it open, peering into the night. In just the T-shirt, she suddenly felt naked and vulnerable.

Her chest was tight, breathing quick and shallow. The hand clutching the catch on the window was sweaty. But the cool night breeze only threw back a distant echo of waves on the beach. She listened for a moment longer, but if there had been someone watching her, they were long gone now.

CHAPTER FIFTEEN

I'm not sure what really happened, how I managed to survive, to still be walking around sane today. To an outsider, nothing has changed, but to me, it feels like a hole has been torn in my heart. The pain is so bad I want to curl up in a corner and scream.

I watched them carefully at first, trying not to stare in the darkness. They looked happy, excited, like two normal couples out on a Friday night date. I could smell perfume and cigarettes and sweat. But they weren't couples. Not really.

I wondered for a few seconds about the others, about their pasts, and what led them to this moment. I didn't really care, because I was only focused on one person, but I needed to wait, to make the most of the opportunity fate had delivered to me.

Later that night it hit me for the first time. Perhaps she thought I didn't know! She may truly have had no idea how much it would hurt me, but it makes no difference, it's done now and nothing can change the past.

It can be hard when people try to hurt you, when they turn on you for no apparent reason, or when you are blamed for something that simply wasn't your fault.

I know this better than anyone.

CHAPTER SIXTEEN

Dove smiled at Quinn's sleeping form. His face was peaceful, one tanned arm flung over the thin sheet, and she longed to snuggle up for a much-needed lie-in. But work beckoned.

The parking was limited in her road, and she usually had to tuck in on the end, behind all the nine-to-fivers who arrived home before her. Today she jogged across the road in the sunshine, mind already on the case, turning over what she had learned last night about Jamie Delaney.

On the one hand, so what if the poor man's sister had been the victim of an attack? On the other hand, was it relevant to this case? In her job, true coincidences were rare. She pressed the button to unlock her car, and stopped dead.

"Fuck." The vehicle had long, deep scratches along the side, from the driver's door all the way to the rear wheel. The black paint was scarred with vicious silver claw marks. She traced them with her fingers, furious at the wanton vandalism. A key or screwdriver probably, and it would cost a lot to get it fixed.

"Fuck!" she said again, remembering her impression of someone outside last night. Normally, this was a quiet road.

She decided to get to work before she made any calls. Anger made her movements sharp, and adrenalin was still pumping around her body as she wrenched the car door open.

"Hello, Dove. What happened?" It was Mary, her next-door neighbour, calling from her front garden.

"Someone keyed my car," Dove explained, trying to calm herself.

Mary frowned. "Unusual for round here. Maybe someone couldn't find a parking space and took it out on your car."

"Can't see any other vehicles that have been damaged. Such a nuisance, but I'll sort it out later, or I'll be late for work." Dove liked Mary. She was an unobtrusive neighbour, dedicating her later years to her art, her garden, and indulging in her passion for football.

"Off you go then! I've recently had one of those doorbell cameras fitted. I'll check and see if it picked anything up from last night," Mary said, stepping on to the pavement with her shopping basket, latching the gate behind her.

Dove, already in the driver's seat, called her thanks, and with a pang of regret, remembered Aileen Jackson's husband walking away up the hill with his empty shopping bags.

* * *

Down at the police station, carefully parking in an end space, Dove encountered DI Rankin, the lead on the Claw Beach case.

"Morning, DC Milson. Can we have a quick word later? Shit, what the hell happened to your car?" He bent down and squinted at ragged scratch.

"Got keyed last night. It's fine, I'll sort it later, and sure . . ." Dove checked her watch. "We can have a word now if you like. I've got a few things to do, but if you need me . . ."

He led the way inside through the main entrance, to one of the downstairs offices. "The victim from the Claw Beach attack, Mr Harbor, isn't talking, and doesn't want to press charges."

"Really?" Dove was surprised. "Did he say why?"

"CCTV from his office shows he left work yesterday evening at . . ."

"Seven p.m. I know. One of the victims from our quadruple homicide worked as part of the cleaning team who has the Pearce and Partners contract." Dove couldn't yet see how those invisible threads might connect Alex Harbor and Dionne Radley, but she felt it was fair to give the DI a heads-up.

He was a short man, with a pouchy face and a mass of wrinkles collecting under his eyes. Like a cartoon bloodhound, Dove thought. But his brown eyes were kindly, and his smile wide, even if he did stink of fags and coffee.

"I heard a rumour about that. George Lincoln is on the case, isn't he? We go way back. I'll swing by for a chat, just in case we're missing something." He nodded slowly as though adjusting his thoughts, choosing his words. "For your information, we are aware of several other incidents similar to the Claw Beach attack, which could be the same perps. Stolen getaway car, remote location. All three of the robbery victims are exactly the same demographic: male, married, fairly wealthy. And all three claim not to have seen the attackers well enough to give a good description."

"Sounds like a scam," Dove said after a moment's hesitation. She was still having trouble getting her head around her own case, and if the Claw Beach attack was just one in a series, her colleagues could be looking at a serial offender, or offenders. "What if the second person *is* a woman? Easy bait for a certain kind of man."

"And she arranges the meet? Maybe a prostitute, and she and her pimp are working a classic pincer scam? Picking on victims who aren't likely to squeal. I'll look into it and keep you posted, like I said," he added. There was a yell from the custody suites next door and an increase in foot traffic through the open-plan office to their left.

"No worries. I wish I'd seen more or at least held on to him," Dove told him.

She jogged upstairs. It seemed likely DI Rankin and his team were correct. The scam was an old one, but a good one. If your victim had a lot to lose, they were more likely to give up their valuables and respond favourably to blackmail. Why the beatings, though? Were some of the victims trying to fight back, or were drugs involved after all?

Dove knew she needed to compartmentalise. Three cases were filling her mind now: Claw Beach, the Beach Escape Rooms murders, and the cold case of teenage gymnast Mickey Delaney, Jamie's little sister. It was enough to give her even more of a headache. She sighed, dumped her bag on her chair, and headed straight for the kitchen, beating Lindsey to the kettle.

"Make one for me, will you, Dove?" her colleague asked, as she rubbed her tired eyes. "Hey, you look like shit as well. That makes me feel better."

"Were you up by 3 a.m. trying to crack the case too?" Dove knew Lindsey's habits well and the two women were similar in their single-minded approach to their jobs.

"Don't think I even went to bed," Lindsey admitted. "This is a big old sprawling mess, isn't it?"

"Black with three?"

"Ta." Dove passed over the mug. Lindsey held the steaming brew up to her nose and inhaled deeply before taking a sip. "Thanks, I feel half-human again now. How's your head?"

"Bit sore." She told Lindsey briefly about the link to the Claw Beach attack and the Beach Escape Rooms investigation.

"I suppose it's a small town really, so coincidences do happen," her colleague said slowly. "You checking out Camillo's today?"

"My first stop after the briefing. I already rang the owner. Hey, did you ever hear of the Mickey Delaney case? Five years ago?"

"No. I wasn't here five years ago, was I?" It took Lindsey no more than a second to assimilate the information. "Any relation to Jamie?"

Dove had momentarily forgotten Lindsey transferred from Yorkshire a year before Dove herself joined the Major Crimes Team. Steve wouldn't have been in this area five years ago either, nor DI Blackman. "Actually, yes. I was looking into Jamie Delaney's family history last night — the name kept bugging me, until I remembered his sister, Mickey. She was brutally attacked five years ago. She's still in hospital. I wonder if there is anyone on the team who worked that case? It might be interesting to see the files."

As they walked down the corridor towards the morning briefing, DI Blackman called out to Dove, "Can I have a quick word?"

"You're probably in trouble now." Lindsey winked at her, but Dove ignored her colleague's good-natured jibe and went into the DI's office.

"Firstly, DC Milson, I didn't realise how serious the attack at Claw Beach on the twenty-fifth was. You certainly didn't mention you had hospital treatment."

Dove shifted uncomfortably as the grey eyes drilled into her brain. He was sitting perfectly still, waiting.

"DI Rankin spoke to you?" she asked.

"He just rang the office looking for George. By the book, you should be on sick leave," he told her sternly. "But leaving that aside for a moment, we are considering whether the cases are linked. I also got your email last night regarding Jamie Delaney. Did you have a reason for dredging it up, or is it just interesting background on our owners?"

"The latter, really." Dove explained about the gymnastic girl in the brothel and how the case of Mickey Delaney had caught her attention because of it. "I can't see how it could be related to our investigation, but I was wondering if anyone on the team had worked the case."

"I checked the files after I read your email, and DCI Franklin did indeed work that one as a DI. He was one of the leads, and he is fully recovered so I'm expecting him at the briefing today. He can let us know if he sees any red flags regarding the cold case and our current investigation." He

92

narrowed his eyes, studying her face. "But I did have a quick look and the main suspects were Mickey's gymnastics coach, 'Colly' Hawthorn, who is now deceased, and her best friend, Jenna Essex."

"Her best friend? Ouch," Dove said.

"Quite. Both suspects eventually scraped through with slightly questionable alibis. Colly Hawthorn was arrested but later released without charge."

"Okay, boss, it was just a thought," Dove told him.

"Fine, get on with it. Camillo's is your first point of call after the briefing, I presume?" He was picking up a pile of documents now, attention already moving towards the next job.

"Yes, boss," said Dove as they walked across to the group gathered for the morning briefing. "We're chasing up Dionne Radley's journey from Pearce and Partners to the Beach Escape Rooms."

The briefing centred on further information from the press appeal, which had gone out the previous afternoon, and later also featured in the local evening news. After choice details of the murders had been made public a flood of phone calls from the eagle-eyed general public had yielded a few leads.

This was fortunate as the Beach Escape Rooms CCTV cameras had been rendered almost useless during the break-in, so the only evidence from that source was the sketchy footage the tech team had managed to clean up, showing the bodies in situ at 2 a.m.

"A taxi driver brought Dionne and Ellis to the pier. He picked them up on the seafront opposite Kenny's Irish Bar at about 11.45 and dropped them off at the end of the pier. Said he remembers telling them the pier was all closed up for the night, but the woman said she wanted to walk along the beach towards White Cliffs or something," DI Lincoln said. "Traffic cam from across the road picked them up getting out of the taxi and walking down the pier at five past midnight. It isn't great but it is footage we can use."

He played the video, and Dove squinted to see the two figures. They were blurry but just about recognisable, and a thought occurred to her. "Dionne was carrying a large white bag over her shoulder, like a beach bag. When she left Pearce and Partners she was wearing her blue work overall. She must have stopped to change somewhere."

"Right, get on to that after you've seen the owner at Camillo's," DI Blackman told her. "As we know, mobile phone signals have pinged three of our four on the pier by half past twelve. We are still missing Dionne's day-to-day phone. If she stopped at a friend's place or something to get changed she may have left it there. And I want to know where she met Ellis. They were picked up together and they arrived together. Where was she between leaving work and her taxi ride?"

Josh, sitting next to Dove, was sipping his coffee and swiping through notes on his iPad. "Shame Billy Jackson topped himself, poor bloke."

Dove agreed and glanced at her watch. Steve was sometimes a couple of minutes late, but he was going to miss the briefing at this rate.

"Lindsey and I are going to meet with a bloke who claims to have known Aileen back in the day. He says she was an escort." Josh rolled his eyes. "But he could just be after a bit of the action, because he wanted to know if he was going to have to appear on the news or Crimewatch."

"Sounds flaky," Dove told him. "Even if she's been involved in crime in her past, it does seem like she cleaned up her act when she married Billy. He certainly thought so, anyway."

"And yet here she was back to her old ways, maybe, hooking up with Ellis Bravery and the others for a bit of sex in a glass box."

"It sounds far kinkier when you say it," Dove told him, pulling a face, as she texted Steve.

Josh grinned at her and went back to his notes.

DCI Franklin was sitting between the two DIs, dwarfing them both with his massive shoulders. He was similar in physique to Dionne's husband, Tomas, Dove thought, watching his quick eyes dart from one face to another, making the odd note, nodding at each piece of new information. His silver hair and shaggy eyebrows made him look like a genial giant, but the piercing blue eyes told another story.

"Thank you, George," the DCI said now. "I'm sorry to have missed the first day, and I can see it will take me a while to get up to speed." He indicated the incident board, which now covered two sections of wall, with green straggling lines and photographs on timelines stretching like spaghetti between scrawled updates and names. "This is a big case, and clearly it will take a while to untangle the links between our victims and the perpetrator, but the press are loving the novelty aspect, if you can call it that, so for our sake and the sake of the poor families waiting for answers, let's wrap this up as soon as we can."

DI Blackman ran through the various jobs and pairings for the day and released his team to work. Dove, unscrewing the lid on her water bottle to refill at the cooler, snagged Steve as he came in late.

"Bloody car broke down." His shirt was covered in sweat and he had an oil streak on his cheek. "It was only the filter but it took ages to sort out. I'd better go and make peace with the boss."

Dove slapped him on the back. "Bad luck, mate. Oh, and hurry up because we need to get across town to Camillo's by eight thirty."

Steve just groaned, so Dove, feeling she had been slightly unsympathetic, got him a takeaway coffee and a dubious-looking plastic-wrapped pastry from the machine. She presented these offerings with a flourish when he reappeared ten minutes later.

"Thanks, Milson, I needed that." He sank his teeth into the pastry, and it was gone before they left the building. "You can tell me what I've missed in the car."

"No worries, Parker. I'll drive so you can get your caffeine hit."

The car was sweltering inside already, so Dove wound her window down and dived straight into the rush-hour traffic, heading for the industrial estate. Steve for once said nothing as his hair was blown all over the place in the salty breeze.

Dove parked between two HGVs and turned to him. "So what do you think?"

"About Camillo's? We play it by ear. There's no evidence the cleaning firm is involved in any wrongdoing, is there? Dionne may have just been using her job as a way of, um . . . getting to know people?"

Dove agreed, pulled her hair back into a tight ponytail and exited the vehicle. "Let's do this."

CHAPTER SEVENTEEN

Herbert Gunter, the owner of Camillo's, was loading a van outside his unit when they walked over. "You must be the coppers. I'm bloody busy today so I've only got a few minutes." He scowled at them. "And don't come at me with invites for her funeral because I don't give a shit she's dead."

Ignoring the comment, Steve introduced himself and Dove, and the man paused in his work. He was big and flabby, with grey-flecked stubble and dark hair tied back in a lank ponytail. "I don't want any trouble. If Dionne's gone and got herself into shit, it was nothing to do with my business. Do you understand? No crime here at Camillo's. We're straight down the line and that's the truth." He fired the words at them, big hands resting on his hips, chest thrust aggressively forward.

Wow, Dove thought, *what's he hiding?* His eyes darted from one to the other of the police officers but never actually made eye-contact, just kept fidgeting with his pen and pad, before shoving it in his pocket and loading a few more boxes. He was acting as if he was wired. Maybe just too much coffee. Dove studied the boxes he was loading.

"There's nothing to suggest that would be the case, Mr Gunter," Steve reassured him. "We are just following up leads and exploring every avenue in the investigation. That's our job, to find out what happened to these victims and bring the perpetrator to justice."

"Dionne was a stroppy cow," the man said roughly. "Of course I'm sorry someone topped her, but to be fair she was probably asking for it."

"In what way?" Dove queried, leaning against the wall, notebook propped on one knee, scribbling quick sentences.

"She's been working for me for eight years without any hassle but this last few months she's missed shifts and . . ." He narrowed his eyes at them, considering. "She's bad news now. If you want the truth, I was going to sack her. My workers are honest and on time and she was neither by the end. I wouldn't be surprised to hear she was getting into drugs or something and we don't do any of that at Camillo's."

"Any examples you want to give regarding Dionne's recent behaviour? Presumably she has to clock in and out?" Dove asked.

"No examples, and yes they all do," Mr Gunter said curtly.

Various blue-uniformed staff were arriving or departing in other vans, and while he spoke to the police officers, Mr Gunter was signing dockets and time sheets, barking orders, and snapping his fingers rudely in the face of one worker. "Don't ask, just get the fucking work done!"

He turned back to Steve and Dove, an expression of exasperation on his large, square face, jowls wobbling as he shook his head. "Sometimes they need telling twenty times to do one thing. Good job they aren't all like that."

"Is there an office or somewhere quieter we could talk?" Dove suggested hopefully.

"No."

"Well perhaps you would be good enough to collect any paperwork you may have for Dionne? Her time sheet would be an excellent start . . ." Dove stared him down.

"Do you need a warrant to get stuff like that?"

Steve smiled pleasantly at the man, "No, but we could get one to search your entire premises, vehicles associated with the business . . ."

Mr Gunter cut him off. "Look, I can get her time sheet for you, her employment details and copies of the written warnings she had for being late. That's everything I've got on Dionne Radley, so you can take it and get out of my face."

"Did you know her husband Tomas, at all?" Steve asked, ignoring the aggression completely.

"Nope. I don't get into chit-chat. I work, my staff work, and that's why we're the best and the busiest cleaning service round here. Personal stuff fucks you up, so I never cross the line and I don't give a shit about anyone's home life as long as their work is good." He thrust out his jaw aggressively, scowling at them. "I gotta go." He turned and yelled at a tall, lanky young man who was walking quickly, head down, "You're late! Go and get Tracey and tell her to print out Dionne Radley's time sheets and any shit in her file."

The man nodded and disappeared quickly into the building.

"Did you notice anything different about Dionne last night?" Steve persisted.

"Nope." Mr Gunter turned away and picked up another cardboard box.

"Did she often make her own way home, not take the transport with her co-workers?" Dove asked.

"Sometimes." His lips closed tight and he seemed on the verge of saying more. But he merely shoved the box into the nearest van and picked up another. This time he paused, looked at them and added, "If I think of anything else, I'll call you. Where the fuck is Tracey with the paperwork?" He glared around the loading area.

Dove and Steve waited, both very aware he was holding something back, but he just shook his head. "Look, I do my duty and keep them safe. I like them to come back in the vans after a job, so they all sign out, but Dionne got one of the others to do her time sheet whenever she felt like it."

"Who?"

"Dunno. Anyone on the same shift."

"You clean for Mr Ellis Bravery at the Marina Apartments as well, don't you?"

He closed his eyes and tapped his forehead, before opening them and announcing, "Three-bed penthouse at the Marina, two bathrooms, every Thursday."

"Did Dionne ever clean that property?"

Something that might have been fear flashed across his face, and Dove hastily added, "It is extremely important we trace her movements from Thursday, so if she was working at that particular property, we need to know."

"Why?"

"Because Mr Ellis Bravery was *also* murdered that night, and there might be a connection," Dove informed him. There was no mistaking it now: although he was already sweaty from his work, the man was now agitated and trying to hide it. "Do *you* think there might be a connection, Mr Gunter?"

Herbert Gunter stared at them. "No," he said finally. "You check the rest of Dionne's time sheets if you like, see where she's been working. Tracey! Where the fuck have you been?" He yelled at his unfortunate employee, who had emerged from the building. She was wearing a blue-logoed Camillo's baseball cap pulled down over her nose. "Go and print off Dionne Radley's time sheets for the past twelve months and hurry up. These two police officers want to get going."

"Sorry. I already just did that. Alec told me you wanted the notes from her file too . . .," she held out a wad of paperwork, tentatively and at arm's length, as though her boss might bite.

Gunter snatched it from her trembling hands and handed it to Dove. "That's the rest of the paperwork."

The time sheets were slightly damp and the ink smudged slightly but they were legible. Dove hastily slipped them inside her notebook to study later.

Tracey, a skinny, stooping fifty-something with wispy hair half-hidden under her cap, waited. "Mr Gunter, did you want me for anything else?" Her voice was unexpectedly soft and gentle, and she spoke carefully, as though she was reading a bedtime story to a child. She stared at Dove and Steve, her huge overbite making her look like a frightened rabbit, before her employer curtly told her to get on with her work.

"Go and start looking over the delivery documents." He turned back to the police officers, "You can bugger off. I got a job on now, so I need to get moving." He nodded briskly at them both, then started yelling at his scurrying blue-overalled staff and leaped into one of the vans. A moment later doors slammed and he roared out of the industrial estate in a cloud of dust.

"I think he likes us," Steve commented, as they walked back to the car. Dove was frowning, looking back at the unit with its big blue and gold Camillo's logo above the door. "Give me a minute, Steve, I've got an idea."

He sighed, used to her sudden hunches. "Sure thing. I'll wait in the car. With the air conditioning on full."

Dove went back to the industrial unit. The doors were still wide open and she could hear activity inside, chatter and clatter from the vans being loaded and unloaded. The passageway was cool and dark. She blinked as her vision adjusted from the bright sunshine outside. Two huge fans in the roof whirred with an efficient humming noise, keeping the temperature down. She studied her surroundings carefully. Dionne's life, Dionne's work. After eight years, why had she suddenly had enough? In fact, why had she had put up with the boss from hell for those eight years?

Crates and boxes were piled either side of the passageway. Dove could smell bleach and furniture polish, mingling with sweat and fresh paint. A storage room marked with chemical symbols was firmly shut, but further on she could hear urgent voices. Tracey, her voice shaking, was talking shrilly to another woman. The softness and gentleness was gone. She was scared.

Dove paused again, aware anything she heard would be inadmissible in court, but she had seen Tracey's frightened glance when she handed over Dionne's time sheets. Frightened and knowledgeable. She knew something. The next comment seemed to confirm her hunch.

". . . the bloody police will find out!"

"They won't. The boss won't say anything and she's dead now. Why drag her name through the mud, and think of poor Tomas . . ."

"It might be important. Her and Ellis are *both* dead, don't forget. It's a murder enquiry!"

"Just keep calm. If you tell them, it will come out in the papers, hurt us, maybe hurt Camillo's. You say nothing and it's all good."

The other woman seemed to be winning the argument, and Dove waited in the shadows, listening to the clatter of mugs being washed, and finally the pad and squeak of trainers as someone exited the room.

Tracey turned up the passage and almost bumped right into Dove. Her hand went to her mouth and her eyes were wide with fear, but she didn't say a word.

CHAPTER EIGHTEEN

"Sorry to bother you again, I was just looking for a toilet?" Dove smiled at her reassuringly.

"I thought you'd gone," Tracey hissed, with a nervous glance back over her shoulder.

"Just about to head off now. Mr Gunter's just left for a job." Dove waited.

"The loo is down the end on the right . . ." Tracey was dithering.

"Thank you. Are you all right? It must have come as such a shock to hear Dionne was dead," Dove said gently, softly.

"It was . . . I . . ." She gave another quick furtive look around before she continued. "I'm not making a statement or anything but Dionne was my friend."

She stopped again, and Dove put a gentle hand on her arm. "Tracey, if you want to tell me something right now, it will be in complete confidence, okay?"

Tracey bit her lip, before her words tumbled out. "This never came from me, and if anyone asks I'll say I never told you, but Dionne's been kind of wild the last few months. She joined this online dating thing." Tracey paused and frowned. "I can't remember what it was called, but she said it was just about hooking up with people. She had this special phone she used . . . She said . . . she said it was her *play phone*." Tracey bit her lip, cheeks turning a rosy pink colour. "I caught her texting one time, by accident, and she told me she was having fun and it made her feel alive again."

"Did she say she was going to meet someone on the night of the twenty-fifth?" Dove asked, hardly daring to breathe in case they were interrupted. Her mind was spinning with possibilities. *Play phone.* What the hell was that? She had a sudden vision of her nephew Elan's plastic toy phone, and hastily dismissed it.

"There was a man she'd seen a couple of times, but I don't know his name. She said he was wild in bed." Tracey coloured up again and rubbed her cheek thoughtfully. "Yeah, she was going to get changed in the public toilets on the seafront, she said, like she usually did if she was off to party after work. She showed me her dress. It was black lace and very short, but she liked to show off what she had. Nothing wrong with that." Tracey stared at Dove. "She wasn't a bad person and whatever happened, she didn't deserve to die."

"Of course not." Dove's mind was replaying the events leading up to Dionne's death, adjusting the timeline to fit with Tracey's information. "Which toilets do you mean?"

"Opposite Kenny's Irish Bar. She used to leave her stuff there while she was out and then nip back and get changed before she went home. Just lately, sometimes she didn't bother, because she said Tomas knew, so she didn't care." Tracey picked nervously at a loose thread on her overall. "But she did care what this man thought. She didn't want him to see her in her work clothes, she said, or lugging a big bag around. It was part of the fantasy, that's another thing Dionne kept saying. It was all fantasy play or something."

"What did she mean?" Dove asked. DC Josh Conrad was going to love this spin on events, she thought wryly.

"I dunno, but Dionne did say last week she'd never felt more alive or more confident." Tracey's eyes grew moist, as she repeated urgently, "She wasn't a bad person, Detective."

A shout from the back of the unit made them both jump. "Tracey? What are you doing in there? I need two extra cartons of bleach for van six, love. Can you bring it over?"

"I've got to go." Panic flashed across Tracey's face, and she turned away.

Dove slipped a card from her pocket and passed it to Tracey. "Thank you, you've been really helpful, and if you remember anything else, you can ring me."

Tracey stuffed the card in her overall pocket, and called back, "On my way!"

Just before she disappeared, she turned back and whispered, "One last thing. Dionne hooked up with one of the solicitors at Pearce and Partners. He liked to do it in his office late at night. We'd all be working and she'd nip in for a quickie, and be out again in fifteen minutes."

"Did Dionne tell you that?"

Tracey rolled her eyes and huffed. "No, I caught them at it last week. Alex, his name is, Alex Harbor. But he's not the man she was meeting on the twenty-fifth, that was the fantasy man." She scurried off, grabbing a carton of bleach as she hurried down the passageway, grubby trainers squeaking on the sticky floor.

CHAPTER NINETEEN

I'm back at a different time of my life today. It's funny how random my dreams have been. Or are they memories?

Everything seems brighter, more intense, magnified. It's as if I can hear, can see, can feel, can join in conversations. Years or days or weeks pass in a haze . . . Was I ever real? Am I real now?

I can feel paper beneath my fingertips. A hard, glossy pink cover comes into my mind. And the heat. Sand stretching for miles. It's my diary in my hand.

I've never had a diary before. There's a pink flamingo pen decorated with feathers. To empty my mind on to the paper is . . . appealing. It's like a letter to me, from me . . .

That bleeping sound still. It's soothing. 1, 2, 3, 4, 5, 6. Six is my lucky number. Six is safe. Counting calms me I can write now, carefully, neatly, on the crisp cream pages.

My wrist still hurts. I turn it this way and that to ease the pain. But I keep forming words, pushing through the pain and the heat.

'No pain, no gain'. Who said that? Coach Hawthorn? The bars are my hardest event. Since I fell I'm scared to push myself. I won't get selected if I don't force through the fear. Mum won't mind. No more early mornings.

My competition leotard has blue sequins. It sparkles with dancing rainbows.

No mail today. No escape yet. I just need to hold on a little bit longer.

The beeping slows. The heat fades. I'm relaxed and cool again.

Everything will be okay, Mickey.
Everything will be okay, Mickey.
Everything will be okay, Mickey.
Everything will be okay, Mickey.
Everything will be okay, Mickey.
Everything will be okay, Mickey.

CHAPTER TWENTY

"So if the play phones are the burner phones and just used to arrange sex, who orchestrated it all? Ellis Bravery? How do you get from being strangers to distributing phones?" Steve queried, as he drove towards the public toilets on the seafront. "Did you say it was the one opposite Kenny's Irish Bar?"

"Yes, and I'm not sure. Billy Jackson said he met Aileen online. Maybe they met on a dating site?" Dove unscrewed her water bottle and drained the last drops, changing the subject. "The taxi driver picked up Dionne and Ellis there, so it's worth checking out."

"Agreed. The other possibility is her husband is lying and she went over to her brother-in-law's place to get changed for the night out," Steve said. "Although I can't see why she would want to wind him up. Everything so far points to secrecy from all four victims."

Dove was scrolling through her phone and tapping out an email to DI Blackman. "I wonder what dating app or site *Dionne* was using? Tracey seemed to imply it was just for sex more than actual dating. She didn't know what it was called, though . . ."

Stuck in the midday traffic on the one-way system, Dove called Jess and put her on speakerphone. "Hi Jess, I know you'll let me know when everything comes through, but I've got a specific lead I want to check out . . ."

"Hi love, it's fine, fire away," Jess said briskly.

Dove explained about the dating site. "Probably not a legit dating app or anything, but it would be a big lead if it comes up as a red flag on all four victims."

"Sure," Jess said slowly. "Let me check . . . Did you get the phone records through?"

"Yeah . . ."

"Let me make a call to a mate in the lab and I'll see if they've managed to lift anything from the search histories, or deleted emails," Jess said. "Looks like the report is due back by five today anyway, but I'll see if I can get any specific information expedited. Big suspect?"

"I wish," Dove told her. "Too many bloody suspects on this one. In fact, I feel like we've got so many extra leads it's almost taking us away from the main event."

"I know what you mean. It's a bit of a sprawler, isn't it?" Jess sympathised.

Dove grinned to herself. "That's what Lindsey said. Is that a technical term I missed in the training manual?"

"Very funny. Speak later, love." Jess ended the call.

Steve, after making several backstreet turns through the winding cobbled roads of Abberley, finally eased the car back on to the seafront and parked opposite the bandstand. "Let's go."

The Victorian toilet block was large, brick-built and known to be a hang-out for drug dealers and addicts by night. By day it was a gloomy, sour-smelling building populated by a stream of parents and children.

"I'll check out round the back," Steve said, as Dove began to politely push her way through the crowds around the Ladies' toilet.

At the sight of her ID, people began to whisper and stare. She ignored them, and gently pushed the main door, battered and heavy with metal reinforcements. It swung open. Her footsteps clattered on the grimy black-and-white chequered tiles. There were two rows of eight toilet cubicles and a line of enamel sinks, but Dove wasn't looking for somewhere the public had access to.

If Dionne had dumped her bag in here, in plain sight, someone would have reported it by now. The general public, primed by terrorist attacks, was excellent at reporting unattended packages and bags. Somebody would have found it. Were there lockers at the back of the building? That would have been a safer bet.

She walked past the cubicles to a line of filthy showers at the rear. These were hardly ever used, were cordoned off, and stank of damp and mould. But there was room to change if you had to, Dove thought. The end cubicle had the curtain pulled right across. She paused, listening, feeling the adrenalin flow as she caught sight of her reflection in a stained, black-spotted mirror above the grimy washbasin.

Dove slipped a pair of gloves on and walked down to the end cubicle. The floor was sticky and something crunched under her boot. She gently pulled the curtain back. The rings rattled along the metal rail, and the plastic sheeting crackled in her hand. "Shit!" She held her breath, heart thumping hard against her ribcage, palms sweating in the plastic gloves.

The smell hadn't just been damp and mould. A man's body stood upright, wedged between the shower and the wall. He was obviously dead, with a deep cut right across his neck, and blood spatters up the walls as far as the ceiling.

No other obvious wounds, so he must have bled out. How the hell was he still standing upright? Dove supposed rigor must have set in while he was wedged in that position. Had he realised the seriousness of his wound and tried to get help? At his feet there was an empty bottle of cheap white wine, and several of an equally substandard brandy. One was smashed into glittering shards, and the other showed a jagged edge at the neck of the bottle, where it had been broken. The top half was laying on the edge of the shower cubicle, close to the victim.

In the far-right corner was a white shoulder bag, also covered in blood, but partially unzipped to reveal a blue overall stuffed in the top.

The dead man stared sightlessly at Dove, and the smell was making her want to vomit now. He was wearing trousers and a shirt, and his shoes, from what she could see of them under the bloodstains, were black and shiny.

She couldn't stop staring. It was crazy, like a clip from a zombie movie. She half expected a practical joke, but the amount of blood and the horrible smell told a different story. Another victim, and it looked as though this one had had his throat cut.

CHAPTER TWENTY-ONE

"No fucking way. Seriously? You got another body?" DS Pete Wyndham was typing up his notes as Dove and Steve arrived back at the station and he looked at them in envy. "You get all the treats."

"We did, but I wouldn't call it a treat exactly," Dove confirmed. She was never quite sure about Pete. Sometimes he was friendly but other times quite sarcastic and sharp. Lindsey dismissed it as his Gemini split personality.

"Sounds like fun to me," Pete said, as he attacked his keyboard with vigour. "Well, you aren't the only ones who struck lucky. Ellis Bravery has form. Ten years ago he was questioned in connection with a Dark Web op focusing on a child-trafficking ring. Nothing ever came of it and he was cleared because although he had access, he and his solicitor argued that a work colleague also had access to the same computer. No charges were ever brought, and he has no record. Want to know what else, though?"

"What?" Steve was half listening, half checking his emails, but Dove was riveted by this extra information.

"He used to live next door to Jamie Delaney. In fact, he was their neighbour right up until a year after Mickey Delaney was attacked." Pete sat back in his chair and winked triumphantly. "I think that tops another body, doesn't it, kids?"

Ignoring his patronising use of the word 'kids', Dove was gripping the desk, her mind spinning. The invisible threads drawing their victims together were starting to get a whole lot more visible. "Was Ellis Bravery ever a suspect in the Mickey Delaney case?"

"No," Pete said regretfully. "He gave a statement, as did all the other neighbours, but he had an alibi for the entire evening. He was visiting his father in Kent the evening Jamie Delaney's sister was attacked. No question, solid alibis from his dad and stepmum, and motorway cameras picked him up on the way there and back."

Dove bit her thumbnail, considering this new evidence. It really came down to the problem she had expressed to Jess. The case was running off at different tangents, each seeming to lead to a different set of problems. She glanced towards the cluttered offices.

DCI Franklin was leafing through a mountainous stack of paperwork, when DI Blackman appeared from the corridor, followed by DC Amin, who was talking on her phone. She headed straight over to her desk and, wedging the phone between ear and chin, began typing furiously.

The DI beckoned Dove and Steve into his office. "This is starting to become a major headache," he began. "Firstly, though, great work with Camillo's and with tracing Dionne's bag. SOCO have already confirmed Dionne's phone *was* in the bag."

"Great," said Steve.

"We have an approximate time of death for the man in the shower of between 1 a.m. and 3 a.m. this morning, which means the bag was there the whole time."

"An execution, maybe?" Dove suggested. "I've never seen a dead person still standing up before, but if he was killed and then propped up as a warning, which might make it gang related . . ."

Steve agreed, "It makes more sense if his body was arranged once he was dead, but it looks like he just bled to death standing up. Weird."

The DI shook his head. "Hardly a good place to hang out at night, unless you're looking for drugs or sex. He could have been lured there with the promise of one or the other. We'll know whether he was a regular user after the PM, but it doesn't, at first glance, appear to have anything to do with our case. Dionne was long gone by the time this man showed up."

"Usually this is such a quiet town," Steve said sarcastically. "Must be because it's tourist season."

"Not funny, DS Parker. The council have confirmed the cleaning contract isn't currently fulfilled on that particular toilet block, due to cost-cutting, so they send someone over as and when to empty the bins, etcetera. They don't bother with the showers, which is why they were taped off." The DI was reading from his notes on the computer screen.

"The place is locked at dusk during the winter but not until midnight from April to September," Dove said. "Unless anyone went right down to the end cubicle and drew the curtain as I did, he wouldn't have been spotted."

"His wallet, ID and watch were all missing, but we have established from HOLMES that he was Mr Neil Ockley. Works in the local bank. They flagged his absence this morning." DI Jon Blackman ran his hands over his shaven head in a gesture of frustration. "You realise, of course, we are going to have to liaise with DI Rankin on this?"

"Really? Sorry, boss, you think this is something to do with the Claw Beach perps?" Dove was surprised. "But the MO is totally different."

DI Blackman nodded slowly. "Victimology is similar, and although this man died, it was another violent attack within the radius of the other four flagged by DI Rankin and his team."

"You mean they might have just gone too far this time?" Dove suggested. The DI was right, this case was huge, sprawling, and vital information was going to disappear down the cracks if they weren't careful, but she couldn't connect the dots on this one. It was a big step from robbery and beating to murder.

"Anyway, back to our own investigation. While we're waiting for the rest of the lab results on our Beach Escape Room victims, I want you and Steve to crack on with this dating-site lead. If that was how they hooked up, chances are they've done it before. It sounds like Dionne knew exactly what she was doing that night."

"Except for getting herself killed, obviously," Steve put in.

The DI gave him a look and opened the office door. "Evening briefing is at seven, and I want some concrete suspects. Naturally you will have heard about Ellis Bravery from Pete, which also puts our co-owner Jamie Delaney in the frame. I called Delaney, because I think we need him in for interview, but their baby is sick and they are currently at Abberley General waiting to be seen."

"We'll have to leave Delaney for a while then, but forty-eight hours in and we've got six bodies. Bloody marvellous." Steve sighed. "Want some coffee?"

"The usual, please," Dove replied, before her brain caught up. "Hang on, why six victims?"

"Neil Ockley from the toilets, even though it looks like he's going to be shunted over to DI Rankin's team, and Aileen Jackson's husband, Billy," Steve explained. "He won't ever be able to tell us what he was sorry for, will he?"

"Gotcha." Why was her brain so slow today? While Steve got the coffees in, Dove made a list of possible dating sites, keeping away from the obvious ones and concentrating on smaller chat rooms. Her head was aching but she couldn't tell if it was too much sun and stress, or her healing injury.

Her phone rang as time ticked towards the evening briefing time and she answered quickly. "Hey, Jess."

"I'm just sending the lab reports over ahead of the evening brief, but I pulled out a bit of info you might want right away. Dionne, Oscar and Ellis were regulars on a chat room called Fantasy Play."

"Sounds intriguing," Dove mused. "Or sleazy?"

"Considering your sister owns a perfectly respectable strip club, love, I don't think you should judge. Fantasy Play just made its first million and was set up by a tech entrepreneur. It's for anyone to chat fantasies, and the local hook-ups have separate rooms."

"Gaia owns two strip clubs, but you know what I mean. Creeping around on the web is different to blatantly flaunting it," Dove told her friend.

"Hmmm . . . Anyway, you've got it now so run with it, girl!"

Dove relayed this new information to Steve and pulled up the website. "You need to register and create an account to get on it," she said in disgust.

"Well, register under another name, brainless," he told her, grinning.

"Don't get smart, Parker," she retorted, and with a flurry of keys she soon had access to the site.

The graphics were smooth, and the site navigation was excellent. Partially dressed and carefully posed men and women featured in the header and sidebar adverts. She finally found the local chat room.

"Got it." She read rapidly through the last few posts and comments. "Who would have thought there were so many swingers round here?"

Steve sighed and shook his head. "What's wrong with just meeting people at a bar or a club?"

"Because it's easier online?" Dove suggested. "Easier to keep hidden if you have unusual preferences, or you want to keep it secret. Fantasy Play seems to be all about encouraging people to have affairs, from what I can see. All false names, too." She suddenly snorted with laughter. "Big Daddy . . . Now if that doesn't show a total lack of imagination. I wonder if that's Ellis or Oscar?" She scanned down, following the flirtatious banter. "Or neither? It's pretty popular and I'm on the local area hook-up bit."

Steve was leaning over her shoulder, and drawn to the screen. Other team members were soon joining the conversation.

"Aileen wasn't on the site, according to Jess," Steve pointed out. "But she did have a burner phone."

"But if the other three have all been active for a while they could have just asked her along? Or maybe she was seeing one of them on a regular basis," Dove said, still clicking on posts. "Look at Glamour Girl . . . Bloody hell, she's always asking for private chats . . ."

"Tech will be able to access those," Josh Conrad pointed out, who had done time with the Cybercrimes Unit before joining the MCT. "Maybe Dionne was friends with Aileen or something and, as you say, just took her along for the night?"

"No crossover with their work or friendship groups so far, though," Lindsey pointed out. "She's the odd one out. I don't imagine Dionne said 'Hey, let's go and have sex in a glass room on the pier at midnight' to someone she didn't know well, or who she didn't meet on Fantasy Play. It's pretty niche."

"I wonder if Alex Harbor is on here?" Dove said suddenly.

"Who?" Pete was leering at some of the photographs. "She's hot."

"She wouldn't have you, and she probably isn't even real. The man from the Claw Beach attack, aka the man who was also occasionally shagging Dionne in his office at Pearce and Partners," Dove told him.

"Are we having a party?" DI Lincoln tapped her shoulder.

"I think we might have just found what connects our four escape-room victims," Steve said. "No wonder Mr Harbor didn't want his wife to know what he'd been up to. If there is a crossover into that case there must be a lot more other halves about to get the shock of their lives. It's play time!"

CHAPTER TWENTY-TWO

"That sounds creepy, like a horror movie or something," Dove told Steve as they sat down in the incident room. She was instantly reminded of the dead man standing against the blood-spattered wall in the shower cubicle. "You would have thought it was bloody Halloween," she grumbled to Josh.

"I love a good horror movie," he told her. "A real classic like *The Birds*, *The Exorcist*."

The evening briefing was swift, and the two DIs had a lot of information to relay, ensuring everyone was up to speed with the latest happenings. With so much information to process, key points were analysed, theories were quickly discarded or added to, and the notes in the case file and the whiteboard scrawl grew larger.

"Fantasy Play looks legit. It's just that people on there are basically looking for extramarital sex, and a local search-and-hook-up function makes it easy for them," DI Blackman summarised. "Tomas Radley's alibi checks out. We don't know where Billy Jackson was for the four hours he said he was at work, before he got the call from the care home about his mother. His shift manager at Tesco's said he called in sick at the last minute, and added it was very out of character for him to do this."

"Did he suspect his wife was having an affair and follow her?" Lindsey suggested.

"Possibly. But he did indeed get a call about his mother and head over to East Dean at 1 a.m., so although chances are slim, he could still be in the frame." He glanced at the list of names up on screen. "Ellis Bravery's girlfriend was asleep. The CCTV from the building shows only Ellis exiting, and she doesn't leave until 6 a.m. the next morning, when she heads down to the gym, again caught on camera."

The briefing came to a close as Dove was still trying to work out if Billy Jackson might have followed his wife out for the night. She kept wondering what he was sorry for.

DI Blackman was speaking again, slightly wearily now, and she drew her thoughts back into the room. "Final sum-up for today then," DI Blackman said. "We are getting somewhere with our leads, so we just need to continue the process of elimination. Now go home, get some rest, and be back first thing tomorrow. Steve and Dove, you continue pursuing the Fantasy Play connection, but also bring Jamie Delaney in for a formal interview."

"I'll try him again before we leave it for the night," Dove suggested.

"Be careful," the DI said. "Check in on the baby before you do anything. He'll have massive public sympathy, and if he is the perpetrator, and it's because of the Ellis Bravery connection, lots of people will think 'good on him'. Plus, I checked dates and we are coming up to the fifth anniversary of his sister's coma, so it must be hard for him, whether he's innocent or not."

"Not to mention the press are going to love that angle," Steve said.

"If he did do it, he certainly had means and motive," Dove commented.

"With this rather unlikely connection with Ellis Bravery in mind, I don't want to spook Jamie, but I agree it gives him a powerful motive. I checked, and Mickey Delaney is still in a coma at Greenview Hospital, which is a private care facility,"

DI Blackman added, glancing down at his iPad as it pinged with incoming messages.

DCI Franklin nodded in agreement. "As you know, I worked the Mickey Delaney case, and it was frustrating not to be able to secure an arrest, but there was never a main suspect. If there was so much friction around her gymnastics prowess and team training that we were looking very hard at both her coach and one particular other team member, Jenna Essex, her supposed best friend. There was no evidence to tie them to the quarry where she was attacked, though." He sighed heavily.

Dove was thinking again about another teenage gymnast who would never have the chance to shine. She tried to put it out of her mind. This current investigation was complex enough without the ghosts of her past cases lurking in the background.

Dove noticed DI Lincoln was hanging back from the stampede to the door, chatting with the skeleton night crew DCI Franklin had managed to coax out of the budget. The night staff were invaluable, especially on a case this big. They would spend their shift sifting through the evidence, collating information coming in from the general public, and cross-checking witness statements.

Dove tried Jamie's mobile twice, and the second time he picked up. She asked carefully about the baby, putting the conversation on loudspeaker so Steve could hear.

"We think she's going to be okay." Relief was evident in Jamie's strained voice. "They want to keep her in overnight for some more tests and to make sure her temperature stays down, but they think it was probably a febrile convulsion. Caz and I will stay with her, of course."

"That's good news. We'll have a chat tomorrow. I just want to run a couple of pieces of information past you," Dove said easily.

Steve gave her the thumbs up.

"Is that the police? Have they found out who did it?" They could both hear Caz in the background, her voice shrill and anxious, half drowned out by a hospital tannoy calling patient numbers into triage, but Jamie answered without any hesitation. "Sure, if we can be of any further help, just call tomorrow."

Dove ended the call and could see Steve's frustration. "We could have pulled him in tonight, but at least the baby is okay. The boss said to go softly on this one, didn't he?"

Dove nodded as she swung her bag over her shoulder. "Let's call it a night. He won't be going anywhere because of the baby and has no idea we might even think he's in the frame for the murders."

* * *

It was already past eleven by the time Dove drove slowly home. This was partly due to the roadworks that had suddenly sprung up at the end of her road, and partly because she had a message from Quinn saying he had picked up the 4 p.m. till 12 p.m. shift as overtime, so he wouldn't be around tonight.

It was tough when their two worlds were out of kilter, and now Quinn was training as a Critical Care Paramedic, with a long-term view to applying for a secondment to the Air Ambulance Service, he was taking the chance to get any extra training and shifts he could manage.

Finally back home and restless, despite her exhaustion, Dove fed Layla and wandered out into the small back garden with an iced drink. An ancient lilac tree threw shadows across the grass, and the grey cat sprawled lazily underneath, purring as Dove sat down next to her. She closed her eyes, enjoying the soft saltiness of night-time on the coast.

As usual, she couldn't switch off. The various suspects and victims swirled around and around in her brain. After twenty minutes she was back at her computer, going through the files.

Did Jamie Delaney and Caz Liffey know more than they were letting on? What if, instead of innocent owners with what was effectively a glass tank of dead trespassers, they *were* somehow involved?

Dove swirled the remains of another orange juice, clinking the half-melted ice cubes against her glass. It spun the whole thing on its head. The information on Oscar Wilding seemed to be very sparse. As an odd-job man he could have access to all kinds of people.

It was strange too, Dove thought, as she clicked through another witness statement, that Aileen didn't seem to have been present in any form on Fantasy Play. From the current evidence gleaned, she had no job, apparently no friends and no life outside her home. It was almost as though she didn't exist at all, and yet she had wound up dying in some kind of sex play in a glass room. It didn't seem to fit. Billy had been insistent that her past had somehow caught up with her. Could she have been blackmailed into this?

Dove made a note to double-check the bank account details, but memory told her Billy and Aileen had just one joint account and a few savings accounts. Nothing had been red-flagged by Jess's team.

By the time Dove had made herself some cheese on toast, texted Quinn, who didn't reply, and rung her sister Gaia, who also didn't reply, she was so restless she decided to hit the beach. Not to take her board out, but just to walk along the shingle stretch through town.

She downed another glass of cold water, hearing the letterbox clank on the front door as something was posted through. *Probably another fast-food flyer.* Dove padded barefoot to the door. As she bent down to pull her trainers on, she picked up the single sheet of paper from the doormat.

It wasn't the usual glossy discount flyer, but a sheet of paper with a handwritten note:

Hello bitch,
You don't know me, but I know you, and I'm watching you.
Are you scared yet?
X

Dove's hand shook slightly as she reread the words. Scrawled handwriting, probably done with a cheap biro. In places, the ink looked as if it was running out. In others, where the writer had pressed extra hard, the paper was almost engraved with the words.

What the hell was going on now? She opened the door and looked out into the night, scanning the road. It was empty. A car drove slowly past, but she recognised the blue Renault as belonging to one of her neighbours, and sure enough it pulled into the driveway opposite.

It was nearly half past eleven now. The stars were out and the moon hung lazily over the sea. A prank? No, the note was too vicious in tone. The obvious answer was that this was related to a case, and the one that sprang to mind immediately was the Claw Beach attack.

The perpetrators had moved away, watched her, had whispered urgently to each other. The image of the night was vivid in her memory. She ran gentle fingertips across her healing wound, thinking hard. Her car, too. Was that also connected?

Someone who not only recognised her, but knew where she lived, what car she drove, was apparently following her, watching her, if the note was to be believed.

When her breathing had slowed, she called DI Rankin. He didn't pick up, so she left a message telling him about the note, suggesting the link was the case. Of course, in her job, and her previous one, lots of people might want to hurt her. But not many people knew where she lived. Did that mean at least one of the Claw Beach attackers was someone she knew fairly well?

She found a plastic bag in the kitchen drawer and slipped the note inside. It would be worth having that checked out tomorrow. Then she checked the windows were locked, and shut the vents on the back door. A stuffy house was better than inviting in a perp with a grudge.

Considering her options, she finally picked up her phone and her keys and slipped her personal alarm into the palm of one hand. Whoever it was might have gone after delivering the note, or they might be waiting in the shadows. She would show them she was not afraid.

Dove walked slowly along her road, glancing at her watch as she passed the shuttered grocery store on the corner. She was surprised to note it wasn't even midnight. Her heart was still pounding a little too fast. At every slight noise, her hand squeezed tighter on the alarm. The cooler night breeze lifted her hair, and she passed a few strolling couples, dressed up for a night out.

She went further into town, feeling safer among the crowded bars, tables spilling out on to the pavement, rowdy customers laughing, talking, enjoying the summer evening. Neon signs flashed above late-night fish-and-chip shops, kebab shops, and in the distance on the other side of the road she could hear the pumping beat of music from Stage 32, the three-storey nightclub. A group of girls staggered past her, one of them pausing to puke in the gutter, spattering her dress and sandals. Her friends were laughing, pulling her along, all of them clutching cans of lager.

Dove sidestepped the partygoers and walked across the promenade, down on to the beach. She could see the pier in the near distance. Several people had lit small fires on the beach, and music from their private parties drowned out the sound of the waves.

The sea was calm tonight, the waves just rippling on the surface of the water. It was high tide, so she didn't have to go far before she could kick off her shoes and paddle, wincing slightly as the sole of her foot made contact with a sharp stone. Allowing the ebb and flow of the saltwater to soothe her, she almost didn't hear the commotion to her left, just a couple of hundred metres to the east, near the old leisure centre.

The ugly Victorian building was a derelict mess of concrete, weeds and graffiti, boarded up and earmarked for housing development.

At high tide, the beach was narrow and steep here, and signs directed walkers back to the main coast road, to the safety of the pavement and shops, looping around the derelict estate.

It was on this stretch of beach that a man was pointing and shouting, but Dove couldn't hear what he was saying. Two more people joined him, adding to the clamour. Something was very wrong. Several people from the beach parties began to run towards the commotion, and the music stopped abruptly.

Dove pulled her shoes back on and jogged towards them, heart rate accelerating again, yanking her phone out, swinging her gaze out to the waves where the man had gesticulated. She reached the group as two of them plunged into the water, half running in the waist-high waves, bending to haul at an object bobbing towards the shore.

A woman left on the beach was talking urgently into her phone, voice high with emotion. "Yes, it's a body, we all saw it, and they're bringing it in now."

Dove ran to help the men with their burden, pushing down the dread growing inside her. The street lights from the promenade cast grotesque shadows across the pebbles. Someone had switched on a torch and the thin beam of icy white lit random details of the rescue attempt.

Dove ran into the water, splashing out in strong, steady strides, leaning down to take her share of the weight.

She grabbed a slippery arm, staggering a little. Shifting the weight, muscles tensing, as she almost lost her footing in the shifting shingle and lapping water. Her heart was banging against her ribs so hard that it hurt to breathe. Her hands were clumsy, grappling with the wet body she was trying to support.

The man opposite her was trying to see if the person was still breathing. He reached over and swiped the curtain of dark hair from the mouth, exposing the face to air as they reached dry land.

Her sister's head flopped back, drooping and limp.

"*Gaia!*"

CHAPTER TWENTY-THREE

I didn't start the games because that wasn't what they wanted. They wanted sex in a glass box on the beach. They liked the possibility strangers might be having a midnight stroll and see four middle-aged idiots getting it on.

It's an unlikely source of income, and not without risks, but Caz doesn't know how close we are to losing the whole place. The legal fees and planning permission cost far more than we had saved, and the building cost spiralled.

I'm not losing the only good thing I've ever done, I'm not losing my family, not after losing Mickey. Just to be careful, I've stuck some peel-off tinted sheets on the three exposed sides of Room Six.

They don't know what I've done. While their aim is to be seen, mine is to keep them as inconspicuous as possible. They're playing a whole different game to me. All I want really is to save my business and get on with my life. I've got a baby now, and so my perspective has shifted to adult matters and adult decisions. To the person I have grown into.

One conversation was all it took to send me tumbling back down again. The flash of recognition, heads close together, the scent of his expensive cologne mingling with the wool of his designer suit, expressions bitter and words slicing the balmy night air like knives.

"I know who you are and I know what you did."

Years of silence, a precarious peace ruined in an instant. It wasn't my fault, it really wasn't. But the threat popped out unexpectedly, and settled deep in my heart.

I found myself sitting on the floor, hugging my knees, shaking as I watched the monitors. After a while, I couldn't cope at all and began to pace. All I could see was my sister, laughing, her red-gold hair flying out, then flopping across her face as she did cartwheels on the waste ground behind our house. I saw myself pushing her on the rusty swing when she was tiny, higher and higher, her little hands gripping the chains, legs dangling, the same red-gold hair, but it was girly then. Baby curls, Mum called it. My baby sister.

Should you ever go back? And if you do, can you ever return to the person you are now? I rocked back and forth on the floor of my flash and expensive office, shaking like I had a fever, while he laughed and did a different kind of gymnastics in Room Six.

CHAPTER TWENTY-FOUR

"You know her?" one of the men asked shortly, his breathing laboured after the exertion of the rescue, the urgency of the moment, as they dragged the body to the beach and deposited it carefully on to the pebbles.

"She's my sister," Dove said shortly, as she carefully and quickly examined Gaia, checking for breathing with shaking hands, finding the body cold and still with no sign of life. "Get back on the phone to the ambulance with an update and tell them she's not breathing." She could hear her shrillness, her fear, and the terror rising up from her stomach made her want to scream, or vomit, or both.

The woman nodded and quickly picked up her phone again, and one of the men positioned himself at Gaia's head. "I know CPR, I can help."

"Great, you hold her head steady, open her airway while I start chest compressions." Dove was still working automatically, sure and steady, but inside she was breaking apart.

The woman was back, relaying questions from the 999 call-handler, and the coastguards were already driving down the beach, the flashing lights of their vehicle banishing the evening shadows.

Just as they dumped their kit, Gaia gave a cough and began to retch. Swift hands turned her on to her side, and Dove quickly stroked her hair away from her face as she vomited on to the stony beach.

Gaia had a slash across the side of her head, a sizable bruised lump stretching towards her forehead and more bruising on her shoulder. But she was okay. Tears leaked down Dove's cheeks. She hastily brushed them away as Gaia's eyes focused and she caught sight of her sister.

"Hey," she croaked. She lifted an arm, impeding the efforts of the coastguards, who were trying to fit an oxygen mask.

"Gaia, it's okay, let them help. Bloody hell." Dove let out a long breath, light-headed with relief. "I thought you'd had it then." Tears were streaming down her cheeks but she didn't care. She just sat back on her heels and watched her sister breathing.

More lights lit up the beach, and quick voices exchanged information, before the ambulance crew and police made their way down to the sea's edge where Gaia lay.

"All ready for your brother-in-law to save the day, Gaia?" Quinn dumped his kitbag and knelt beside his fiancée and her sister, as his crewmate brought up the rear with another heavy bag slung over his shoulder.

"*Quinn*?" Dove whispered through her tears. She couldn't comprehend the fact that he was here. But of course, contrary to public perception, there weren't that many ambulance crews working in the area. The chances were high he would be called out to a job in his home town — the ambulance make-ready centre was barely three miles away, and she thanked God that tonight it was this particular incident.

Gaia moved the oxygen mask again, fingers scrabbling with the plastic tubing. "I'm fine. Give me a glass of whisky and I'll be fine. You can bugger off now, Quinn." But her voice was strained, husky, and her face still deathly pale in the glare of the lights.

She attempted a laugh, but the effort was apparently too much, and she sank back on to the pebbles, breathing deeply into the mask.

"You all right, babe?" Quinn said to Dove, resting a quick, gentle hand on her shoulder, concern in his eyes, professionalism in his movements, despite his humour.

Quinn and his crewmate, Dave, kept up a gentle stream of banter, even as they examined the patient, inserted a needle into her arm, and took various vital observations.

Dove felt a rush of reassurance and relief at his steady presence and had to look away as tears threatened again. She was happy to be jostled away as the coastguard first responder was now updating the medical team and the police. In the organised chaos around her sister's body, Dove was at last able to hide her emotion in the shadows.

She moved further away to let the various teams do their jobs, yet never letting her sister out of her sight. She felt like laughing when it became obvious that Gaia was going to be okay, and was even, miraculously, returning to her usual prickly, stubborn self. The patient was talking more easily now, answering questions, trying to sit up.

Eventually, clearly satisfied Gaia was stable enough to move, they strapped her to a stretcher, wrapped in foil and blankets. Quinn picked up his bag and jogged over to Dove as the stretcher party went ahead. "She should be okay but, of course, you know . . ."

"Yeah . . . secondary drowning and all that. Jeez, Quinn, I never thought I'd be doing CPR on my own sister." Dove walked with him as they headed up the beach.

"Knowing you three, I'm surprised you haven't had to do it before." Quinn winked at her. "Seriously, babe, you did a good job, and thank God that man spotted her when he did."

"Did she say anything about what happened?" Now that she was more confident Gaia was going to be okay, her mind was turning back to why she was in the sea in the first place.

"Not really. Sounds like a robbery that went wrong, though. She said she went to get another bag of change for the tills and someone hit her on the back of the head while she was kneeling down at the open safe."

"At her *club*?" Dove was trying to take this in, thinking of the message she had left for Gaia about two hours ago. The club should be busy with customers and staff, and Gaia had an excellent security system. Dove tried to remember the layout of the office where the safe was installed. There was a fire door leading to the alleyway behind the building, she recalled, but that was alarmed.

"Yes, at California Dreams," Quinn confirmed.

"So why the fuck was she floating in the sea down here?"

"Babe, I don't know any more than you do. Are you coming in the truck with us?"

"Yes, of course. Oh shit, and I must ring Ren as soon as we get to hospital," Dove said, checking she had her phone securely in her pocket. Her hands were still shaking, and she fumbled with the device until Quinn closed a warm strong hand around hers.

Together they climbed into the ambulance and travelled to the hospital, Quinn in the back, monitoring the patient, and his colleague driving on blue lights.

Gaia seemed a bit hazy, and kept trying to pull her oxygen mask off. Quinn spoke firmly. "Mate, I know you feel like shit and you want to tell us exactly what happened, but can you just keep this on for a bit?"

Furious amber-brown eyes met Dove's concerned gaze and she gave a shaky laugh. "Don't look at me for help, you know what he's like. We'll get this sorted out, and don't worry, police have gone straight to the club to check everything out, and I'll ring Ren when we get to the hospital. Okay?"

A tiny jerk of a nod and Gaia turned her head back on to the stretcher, closing her eyes, apparently resigned to her fate.

* * *

Gaia turned out to be the last shout on Quinn's shift, so while he and his crewmate headed off to base to return their

131

vehicle, Dove stayed at the hospital. As usual, A&E was full to bursting, but Gaia was taken straight into Resus for monitoring. Two uniformed police officers went into the bay where Gaia was lying, and spent half an hour in muttered conversation.

When they came out, Dove introduced herself and received an update. Her sister was indeed making a rapid recovery, and had repeated her statement to Dove's uniformed colleagues — that she had been getting money for the tills out of the safe when she was hit. She had neither heard the attacker approach, nor seen them, but was confident her CCTV would have captured everything.

Dove sat on a hard plastic seat until Ren arrived. The sisters hugged and she blessed ever-practical Ren, who had brought a flask of coffee for Dove and a small bag of clothes and toiletries for Gaia.

"I can't believe it," Ren said, as they sat side-by-side, half watching the ebb and flow of the walking wounded.

"It was one of the worst moments of my life," Dove admitted, gulping scalding coffee, burning her lips.

"But why was she in the sea? I mean, if she was attacked at the club that means someone must have driven her down to the beach while she was unconscious," Ren said, her brow furrowed with worry.

It wasn't long before a harassed doctor informed them they could see Gaia, but she was sleeping. As far as he could tell, there was a good chance she would suffer no long-lasting injuries, but they would have to wait for further test results.

Dove studied her sister, so peaceful and young-looking, neatly tucked into the hospital bed. Some of her hair had been shaved to allow access to her wound, which was now neatly stapled. The bruising extended down her forehead and one cheek, and Dove caught her breath, tears threatening again.

"I'll stay for a bit," Ren said. "Didn't you say Quinn was coming by to give you a lift home? He must be exhausted, so you get off."

Dove hesitated, reaching a hand down to hold Gaia's, feeling the reassuring warmth, the steady pulse. "If you're sure. And for God's sake ring me if there is any change, won't you?"

"Of course."

They kissed, and Dove bent down and dropped her lips briefly on Gaia's forehead, her long hair brushing her sister's face, but Gaia never moved, just carried on breathing slowly and evenly.

* * *

Dove was silent on the drive home from the hospital, her tired brain turning over this new and unexpected incident. "I guess we need to wait for the CCTV," she said finally, fidgeting with her phone. "But it seems like someone knew her routine, when she would go and get more bags of money for the tills . . . She doesn't remember anything after the blow to her head."

"She'll be okay, babe. She's tougher than anyone I know and I almost feel sorry for whoever did it by the time she finds out who they are . . ." Quinn pulled up outside their house. "Her lungs were clear, and she'll have to stay in for observation, but she's very fit and healthy, so chances are they'll send her home after forty-eight hours."

"I hope so." Dove got out and slammed her door, the sound deafening in the darkness. "You know what I was just thinking, as well?"

"Who the hell jumped her at the club and how you can find and possibly hurt them?" Quinn suggested, leading the way up the garden path.

"That too," Dove admitted. "But actually I was thinking there have been quite a few people getting bashed on the back of the head and robbed recently." Her own injury throbbed in painful memory. "What if our Claw Beach perps have changed MO?"

"Perhaps they thought Gaia was dead and panicked, try-ing to dispose of her body? It's very different to what you said

133

before, about luring men out to rob them. This was inside her club and she's a woman," Quinn pointed out, pulling off his green uniform shirt with a sigh of relief, and padding barefoot and bare-chested to the fridge. "The only connection, really, is the blow to the head, isn't it? God, I'm starving — if only I could just sit inside the freezer cabinet for a bit to cool off . . ."

"Please don't, you'll make all the ice cream melt." Dove reached past him to the high cupboard for wine glasses, before grabbing the loaf of bread from the counter. "I'll make you a toastie" She began peeling off her own damp clothing, her T-shirt stiff with drying seawater, as she perused the menu.

Layla was waiting for them sit down, her elegant grey body bolt upright in the middle of the living room, her tail switching crossly, green-gold eyes wide.

"I suppose you fed her?" Quinn queried, catching the feline disapproval as they finally collapsed on the sofa.

"Of course." After her first mouthful of white wine, Dove lay down, swinging her bare legs across Quinn's lap, closing her eyes. "Oh shit, my brain is literally fried right now. Poor Gaia." One hand still clutched her mobile phone, and she brought it up to her face, checking for the hundredth time since they had left the hospital for missed calls.

"I think my theory about getting rid of the body is bang on," Quinn told her. "Hey, we should switch uniforms for a bit. You did a good job with Gaia on the beach."

"Green so isn't my colour," she told him sleepily.

* * *

Dove almost overslept the next morning, having woken with a jump from a nightmare at 3.30 a.m., so convinced she had missed a call from the hospital about her sister that she crept downstairs and placed a call, only to be told by the sleepy-sounding nurse on duty that Gaia was fine and reading a magazine.

By the time she had gone back to sleep it had been half past four and she now felt bad-tempered and gritty-eyed. Quinn, who slept at any time and generally anywhere like a cat, was snoring as she now padded wearily out of the bedroom.

Her phone buzzed with a text as she hit the shower and she reached out a wet hand to check the message. It was from Ren:

Gaia fine & v pissed off she has to stay in until they finish running some more tests, but don't worry she's ok. Will stay with her as Eden opening the shop x

She felt herself relax a little, the memory of Gaia's limp body and lolling head fading slightly. Despite Quinn's lazy humour and his gentle banter last night, she knew he had also been shocked. He was very fond of his soon-to-be sisters-in-law, and having no other family, had assimilated neatly into her slightly odd set-up. But humour was Quinn's way of dealing with things, was in fact one of the reasons he could do such a demanding job, she thought, drying herself and walking naked down to the kitchen for much-needed coffee. She checked the time and hastily accelerated her routine.

Packing her bag, she discovered the note from last night, wedged between her iPad and notepad. For a second she studied it again, before stuffing it back in. It would wait.

* * *

Usually one of the first to check in at the office, today Dove rushed into the briefing room with minutes to spare and sat down next to Steve. He raised his eyebrows at her but she made an *I'm fine* gesture, and turned her attention towards the whiteboard.

DI Blackman kicked off, immaculate in a grey suit and pale blue tie, and apparently full of energy. "Right, we are getting somewhere with our timelines now." He indicated the board. "Dionne Radley left work at 11 p.m. and walked alone to the public toilets opposite Kenny's Irish Bar. She changed and left her bag there, and we assume she was going to collect it later on. She left her main phone in her bag, probably accidentally."

DI Lincoln, who was pinching his forehead between finger and thumb, as though to draw some ideas out, continued. "Dressed to party, she then met Ellis Bravery at the roadside and they took a taxi to the Beach Escape Rooms, arriving at just after midnight. Pete?"

DS Wyndham nodded. "Maya and I spoke to Oscar Wilding's neighbour last night. She rang back just after we left the brief, had only just picked up our message so we went straight round." He paused, glanced down at his notes. "She confirms she saw a woman matching Aileen Jackson's description arrive by taxi at his house at around half eleven. The woman, probably Aileen, went in, and around fifteen minutes later they both came out and started walking towards the town centre."

"We pulled CCTV and they are caught on the seafront cam on the west end of the pier at just past midnight. Looks like Aileen was very sure her husband was at work, and quite happy to be seen out on a nice romantic stroll with another bloke," Maya commented.

"But he wasn't at work, because his manager confirmed he never showed up, and he sure as hell wasn't at home because otherwise his wife wouldn't have been hitting the town," Josh said. "Perhaps he set her up and followed them to the pier?"

"Get on to it. Dig deeper into Billy Jackson's background as well as his wife's," DI Blackman said grimly. "Moving on, we need Jamie Delaney in for an interview to review his statement. Steve?"

"I rang this morning and the baby is fine. They are all back home, so Dove and I will get it done ASAP. We'll go and pick him up because they don't have a car." Steve looked down at his iPad. "Jamie and Caz said in their statements initially that Jamie was working all evening, locked up and went home at half past eleven. She was at home with the baby all evening."

"Convenient, considering our illicit foursome began arriving half an hour later," DI Blackman mused. "No prints from the supposed break-in, and no sign our victims were carrying bolt cutters. From their previous text messages it seemed like this was a planned event, suggested by Ellis, and yet nobody even mentioned an illegal entry of the premises. The phones, as far as they knew, were safe, so why would they leave that part out?"

CHAPTER TWENTY-FIVE

Dove's phone rang as the briefing finished. It was DI Rankin, responding to her message from last night.

"I've got the note, and I'll drop it off downstairs in about fifteen minutes if that's okay?" Dove paused. "My sister was attacked at her club last night. I realise the circumstances are different but I wondered if all of this could be connected to our Claw Beach perps?"

"Right, California Dreams. Okay, I'll look into any connections. You must be known there . . . Any suspects? Someone who might be doing a bit of dealing on the side maybe . . ."

"None. Gaia runs a tight ship, and a clean one, but I'll keep thinking," Dove told him.

"Call me any time. Sorry to hear about your sister." He rang off.

Dove rummaged for a packet of sweets, opened it and tipped the lot into her mouth, feeling the sugar hit her bloodstream.

Steve was watching her curiously. "What's happening now?"

She told him, and he gave a low whistle. "It's all going on with you at the moment, isn't it? How's Gaia doing?"

"She should be fine, they are just waiting for a few more test results," Dove said gratefully. Worry for her sister sat heavily at the back of her mind, despite the intensity of their case. "Now back to our escape-room victims and Mr Jamie Delaney." But she couldn't stop herself quickly checking she had lots of battery life in her phone, and that there were no new messages from the hospital or Ren. Satisfied, with an effort, she shoved everything else to the back of her mind and focused on their case.

With the Jamie Delaney interview imminent, it was important to spend a little time checking through the statements, looking for red flags and tripwires, basically anything that didn't seem right, or contradicted the actual events as they currently knew them.

Dove was checking the mobile phone records, ticking off numbers on the printout with her pen. "Jamie made a call, look, at 12.20, to Caz."

"He was walking home by then?" Steve suggested. "They live on Ship Street, don't they, so that's maybe a half-mile walk."

Dove pulled up the maps and studied them, before she swung her chair round. "Which means he should have been nearly home, but according to the triangulation he was on the pier. With the cell sites, that means he was still very much in the vicinity when the victims arrived."

"Any street cam in that area?" Steve took his glasses off, gave them a rub on his shirt and perched them back on his nose.

She scrolled through. "There's one on the corner of Ship Street and Coast Road . . . Hang on." She rewound the footage and studied the blurred figures, the light traffic. There was a pedestrian crossing to the east of the camera.

Steve was looking over her shoulder. He poked a finger at the screen. "They live at 110, which is two houses up from the corner. What's going on there?"

There was still no sign of Jamie but a light-haired woman carrying a baby was caught walking swiftly towards the crossing at, Dove squinted at the clock in the corner, 12.30 a.m.

The woman was caught again on the next street cam, which faced down the promenade to the beach. The security cameras on the pier had been damaged so this was the last sighting but Dove was sure it was Caz. She sat back in her chair. "So Jamie called his girlfriend and whatever they discussed was so urgent she had to take the baby down to the escape rooms?"

"I can't wait to ask him what he said to her," Steve said grimly. "Let's get moving."

Outside it was hot but muggy. Purple-bruised clouds were massing in the sky and white-tipped waves out at sea promised a hell of a storm later. The wind had got up too, but was more like a dragon's breath than any relief from the heat. The beach was a mass of squirming kids, colourful striped umbrellas and yelling parents. Lifeguards in their red Portakabin huts scanned the tourists with binoculars, and Dove was instantly taken back to last night and Gaia.

Keen to discover any updates, and as her sister's phone had not been recovered, Dove rang Colin at the club as they sat in the inevitable traffic jam on the coast road.

Colin was Gaia's manager and sidekick, a capable, gentle man with heavily gelled blonde hair and a penchant for leather bracelets. He had been shocked by the attack on his employer, but could only tell Dove the police had been round and checked out the crime scene.

"I wasn't working last night because it was my night off, or I might have been able to help her," Colin said, his voice strained with emotion. He was devoted to Gaia and the club, and Dove knew the staff adored him.

"Did you see the CCTV?" Dove asked quickly.

"Yeah. Bloke with a hood pulled down over his face. Big bloke smashed Gaia over the head with a baseball bat. Bastard!"

"Just the one attacker?"

"Just him, and after he hit her, he took the money out the safe and ripped her jewellery off. There was a few minutes' time-lapse there, where he went out of the room, perhaps checking nobody had heard him? Anyway, he was back quickly enough and he dragged her body out of the fire exit. Fuck me, Dove, I'm so glad she's going to be all right." Emotion spilled over and he gave a ragged sigh. "I'm going out on my board later, this kind of stress makes me head for the waves." Colin was also an avid surfer.

"Me too, to both of those things. Can you keep me updated? Oh, and anything you need, just let me know, and I'll try and sort things until Gaia gets back," Dove told him gratefully. Worry for her sister had settled into a tight little ball deep in her gut, and she had to work hard to get rid of constant replays of Gaia hanging lifeless as she was dragged from the waves.

"No problem. Uri's coming in today as well," he said, with a slight edge to his tone.

Uri Marquess was one of Gaia's financial backers, and Dove was fairly sure he was one of her sister's ex-boyfriends. He was a shady character, who operated mostly just the right side of the law, dipping into the illegal side occasionally but covering it well, with a fair amount of smooth charm. Like Colin, Uri was devoted to Gaia. If he found out who had hurt her sister before the police did, Dove was fairly sure the person would never be found. She had worked with people like Uri in her previous job. If you were in with them, you were family. If not, you were fair game.

Jamie Delaney was cleaning the windows of his office when Dove and Steve walked up the pier. Seagulls floated above on lazy wings, squawking and arguing amongst themselves, and the sea was dotted with paddleboarders, kayaks and inflatable rubber rings. The odd jet-ski flashed past, and far out in the English Channel larger ships and dredgers could be seen against the stormy skyline. The forensics teams had finished, but the pier remained shut to the public. Crime-scene tape and traffic cones stretched along the bollards between the wooden boards and the pavement.

"You said there was something you wanted to discuss down the police station?" Jamie, hazel eyes bloodshot and shadowed from lack of sleep, seemed defensive. He thumped his bucket of soapy water down, sloshing some over the side, and folded his arms as he faced them. "I thought Caz and I already made our statements. We also got told we could reopen on Friday. You lot have all finished, so we could get some customers in now. Some of us have to make a living."

"We have uncovered some new evidence in the course of our enquiry," Steve told him evenly. "Therefore, as I mentioned on the phone, we need you to come down to the station for interview."

"I told you I could've got the bus later on," Jamie said, emptying the soapy water fairly close to the police officers' feet. "My solicitor can't make it for another half hour."

"So we've come to give you a lift," Dove said cheerfully. "We were glad to hear your baby is okay now."

His expression lightened a fraction. "It was a pretty stressful night. Caz is at home with her now, probably trying to squeeze a nap in."

"I've got one of my own," Steve offered, with a genuine smile. "No sleep since she was born, or it certainly feels like it."

"Tell me about it. I'll just get my keys," Jamie said. "You want to come inside and check I'm not leaving by the back door?" But the edge was gone and his tone was easier, more jokey and good-natured. Amazing what a bit of dad bonding could do, Dove thought.

"Sure, I'd kind of like a quick peek at the control centre." Steve, still apparently in 'good cop' mode, followed their suspect towards the office, while Dove watched.

The two men vanished through the doors, but Dove hesitated again, taking in the sleek glass escape rooms, glittering below the massing storm clouds. Various controls and panels dotted the sides. Something about their uniform, almost alien appearance made her shiver. Being locked in anywhere had never seemed like a great option to her. Blue-and-white tape was fluttering in the sea breeze, a stray piece of newspaper blowing around the otherwise immaculate boarding. She followed the men inside.

The main office was large and airy, fans working hard to combat the heat outside. Jamie was showing Steve the main control panel, totally at ease now, explaining how each game worked, the different levels you could play at, and other technical details.

Dove studied these for a couple of minutes. At first glance, it looked like a giant, complicated mass of cogs and switches. But closer inspection showed the main panel divided into six smaller ones, with tiny printed labels like *Adventure in Space* and *Pathway to Heaven*. The most sinister was a black switch labelled 'Level Three', which said *Hell Speed or Die Trying*.

To the right, one for each escape room, there was a bright red emergency shut-off valve, and a button marked *STOP*. Jamie pointed these out now. "Like I said before, we had to get the engineers in a couple of weeks ago because we had issues with the outflow pipe and valve on Room Six." He shrugged. "It got fixed, though."

"Is there an emergency shut-off outside as well?" Dove asked.

"Sure, just the other side of this wall. The electrics all feed through and there's a weatherproof panel," Jamie told her.

"The office wasn't affected by the break-in?" Steve asked casually, still staring at the gaming panels.

"No. You can only access the gaming mechanism from in here. I guess they just wanted to get in, have some fun and get out." He shook his head in apparent genuine sorrow. "Poor buggers. But you said you got some new evidence?"

Jamie's wide hazel eyes were framed by very pale lashes which, combined with the bleach-blonde hair, gave him a striking appearance. His body language and tone said he knew it, Dove thought. But at least he seemed coopera-tive. Her mind wandered back to the emergency shut-off. From Jess's notes she recalled the panel had been damaged. Someone had made sure the victims could not be saved.

Steve nodded. "We'll go through it all at the station. Thanks for showing us around. It's a neat place, isn't it?"

Jamie smiled. "Well, we had a job convincing the planners, but yeah, we love it." He looked towards Dove. "Do you surf?"

She was studying a small collection of paddleboards and other sports equipment, which were propped in the corner of the room. There was a rack of wetsuits, all black and mostly entry-level quality. Dove took a guess: "It's my thing. Perfect to de-stress after a tough job. My fiancé says I'm only really happy when I'm out at sea. Is that your wetsuit? A Rip Curl Flashbomb. Nice one."

Jamie wandered over, seemingly completely relaxed now, and ran a hand across the suit hanging on a metal dryer, stretching it out so they could see the material. "It is. No zips! I keep mine down here so I can escape off the end of the pier when I'm not working. Sometimes we have friends round and we kit them out too. Caz hasn't been out in a while, with being pregnant and then the new baby and everything, so her stuff is all at home."

By the time they got Jamie to the station and his solicitor had joined them, Dove felt essential groundwork had been laid. When they sat down in the interview room, Jamie seemed at ease, still trying to talk about surfing with her and asking about the MCT job description. She wondered at his mood switch down at the pier. Was it because she and Steve had made him feel comfortable, or was he super smart and playing along?

Now the recording had started, he appeared a little nervous, and apologised. "I feel like you're arresting me or something," he said, still smiling but looking quickly at his solicitor as if asking for the man's reassurance.

The solicitor was swift to offer what was required, and jumped straight in. "This is routine questioning, Jamie, as I told you, nothing to worry about."

Steve went carefully over Jamie's statement, before he started to trip him up over a couple of blatant lies. "You said you called your girlfriend, Caz, to tell her you were on your way home before you locked up at eleven?"

"Yes." Jamie's voice was steady, and his hands neatly clasped in front of him.

The sharp, bony face still sported a pleasant expression, Dove thought, but how much of his character was he showing? If he had committed the murder, he was pretty cool about it. It was like watching an actor reading unfamiliar lines. Something felt way out of kilter.

Steve pushed the phone records over to him and highlighted the time issue, before moving swiftly on to the street cam. "There is no sign of you making your way home, but ten minutes after that call, we see a woman who we believe to be Caz Liffey leave your house carrying what appears to be your baby. She features again here." Steve placed the second photograph in front of Jamie and his solicitor. "But she never makes it past the pier to the next street cam on Coast Road, so she must, by process of elimination, have gone on to the pier."

Jamie still seemed calm as he looked at the evidence in front of him. "I walked down the wooden steps to the beach after I locked up, and I think I called Caz there." Cool eyes met Dove's. "She said the baby wasn't sleeping. She thought maybe it was colic or something, so I told her to bring her down and we'd walk along the beach for a bit. Caz came down to the pier and hit the beach the same route I used."

"Wouldn't it have been easier for her to walk straight across the promenade and down on to the beach via the sloping walkways, rather than go down the steep flight of steps near the pier?" Dove queried.

"I suppose it would have." He frowned as though thinking hard. "But she's been really exhausted and emotional since the birth. The midwife said she was suffering from postnatal depression as well and she's been prescribed some medication for it. I guess, that night, she just wasn't thinking straight."

CHAPTER TWENTY-SIX

Jamie took a sip of water and smiled at Steve and Dove, repeating his initial question as if to show them he hadn't been caught out at all. "Now, where's this new evidence you said you had?"

"Moving on, then," Steve said equably. "I assume you know you have a historical connection with one of the victims, Ellis Bravery?"

Jamie's jaw clenched now and he looked at his solicitor, who peered over his half-moon glasses. "My client is aware Ellis Bravery used to be a neighbour of his parents, yes. It is a distressing subject for him, so unless these questions are entirely relevant . . ."

"Which they are," Dove assured him. "Mr Bravery was also questioned in relation to the attack on your sister, Mickey Delaney, wasn't he?"

Jamie's shoulders sagged now, and he bit his lip. "I . . . I was shocked when I heard, because you know . . . well, you must know what happened to Mickey and how she is now."

"This isn't relevant to the current line of questioning," the solicitor said, as Jamie slumped forward, chin dropping into his cupped hand. "Do you want to take a break, Jamie?"

Jamie shook his head. "No, I'm good. It's just when anyone mentions Mickey . . . It isn't something you get over, what happened."

"Jamie, can I ask you again, what happened on the night of July twenty-fifth?" Steve said quietly.

Jamie folded his arms, expression wary and lips pursed. Dove could almost hear his brain ticking over now. His shoulders were tense. Was it the mention of his sister, or of Ellis Bravery, that had caused the sudden change?

His solicitor sat quietly, pen poised, but his eyes darted from his client to the police officers.

"Jamie?" Steve repeated the question quietly, and Dove could sense the tension in the room ratcheting up a notch.

"No comment. I don't have anything to add to my original statement," Jamie said firmly, sitting back and wrapping his arms tightly around his chest.

The solicitor cleared his throat and thoughtfully scratched a spot on his chin. "I may need a few moments alone with my client."

"Of course. We appreciate your client's cooperation," Dove said smoothly. "But you must see we have to follow up on all our leads." She tapped the photographs on the table in front of them. "We are just trying to establish a timeline and from these photographs Jamie clearly wasn't where he said he was in his initial statement."

While Jamie conferred with his solicitor, Steve and Dove headed for the coffee machine.

"What do you think?" Steve asked, rummaging in his pockets for loose change. He keyed in his selection and dropped a few coins in the slot, then thumped the buttons on the snack machine. It only ever responded to treatment that stopped just short of violence. A packet of salted peanuts and a Dairy Milk chocolate bar tumbled down into the drawer with a clang.

"I think he's lying about the whole thing, and he's just wondering how to play it."

"He's been pretty cool until now. If he is responsible for the murders, Caz might be in on it too," Dove said. "*Her* statement says she never left home that night, and here she is walking around at past midnight with the baby."

"If she doesn't actually know, perhaps she suspects what he did and is terrified we'll find out," Steve mused, checking his watch. "We'd better get back."

Dove scrolled quickly through her messages as they walked down the stairs. She had a voicemail from her niece, Delta, which she decided to leave until after the interview. The girl would have texted if it was urgent.

* * *

Back in the interview room, it was evident Jamie had taken control of himself. He was slightly paler than he had been, but sitting back at the table with his fingers clasped in front of him, he said, "I would like to change my statement."

"Great. Tell us what really happened that night." Steve tapped a pen on the table, his gaze never leaving Jamie's.

"It's tough, paying back the business loans. The fight with the planners took a lot of our savings, and although we are fully booked most days, it's still hard. I've got a credit card that needs paying off and . . ." He glanced at Dove and Steve, hands spread. "Caz doesn't know we are in quite so much debt. I wanted to keep it hidden, what with the baby and everything. I didn't want her to worry . . ."

"Go on. You need extra cash," Dove said.

"Last month this bloke stopped by, said he was on this Fantasy Play site and . . . I looked and it seemed like a thing for swingers but nothing illegal. The man offered cash if I would let him and his friends use one of the rooms occasionally, like once every couple of months." Jamie sighed. "It seemed like a cash-in-hand answer to our money problems."

"Who was this man?"

"Oscar Wilding. Red hair, softly spoken. Tall, skinny bloke. Not what I would expect for, well, this kind of thing. He looked more like some kind of retired schoolteacher.

Crazy name too, right?" Jamie frowned. "Anyway, he seemed a bit odd but nice enough, so I said yes. He came with two men and a woman last month after midnight. I let them in and left them for an hour to do whatever."

"Do you have any contact details for Oscar or any of the people he used the room with?" Steve asked.

"No. He just turns up sometimes, books in and gives me the cash before they . . . um . . . He always said it was before they 'play', and I think he could tell it freaked me out a bit. He liked that. The whole thing makes me feel a bit sick, but if they want to pay for it, you know . . ." His voice trailed off, and he glanced at his solicitor again.

"The glass on the beach side of Room Six is tinted," Dove said, remembering from Jess's notes that this was the only room where the glass was.

"I put those stick-on sheets up last month." Jamie looked at her. "The Fantasy Play guy paid £1,500 for an hour. He kept asking about the view from the beach and I thought he was worried about being seen, but turns out that was what he wanted." Jamie rolled his eyes in evident distaste. "That was the last thing I wanted, of course, so I added the stick-on sheets. Oscar never mentioned it, so I guess he didn't notice."

"Okay, so moving on, you have this cash-in-hand business on the side. What happened on the twenty-fifth?" Steve said.

Jamie shrugged. "Oscar showed up as planned, and he had Ellis Bravery and the two women with him. Of course it was a shock to see Bravery . . . I can't even begin to describe how I felt, but I would never have killed him." He relaxed a little, shoulders sagging. "It brought it all back, and all I could think of was Mickey lying in hospital."

"Did you speak to Ellis?" Steve asked.

"Yes, I had to, but only to greet him as I left to go back into the office. He . . ." Jamie paused, as though considering his choice of words. "He didn't seem to recognise me, or maybe he did but he hid it well. I used to be this lanky ginger kid and, well, I guess I look different now."

Again the little note of something, Dove thought. Arrogance? Self-assurance?

Jamie smiled at both officers, genuine pain in his face, palms upturned. "I'm sure you can imagine how I felt, seeing him."

"And you are sure there wasn't any kind of conversation between the two of you? It must have been tough knowing he was paying to use your business for sex," Dove suggested, glancing down at her notes. He did look very different to how he'd been described — muscular, filled out, the hair and eyebrows dyed, arms filled with leather bracelets, studs in his ears and nose. An actor filling a role perhaps. But lots of people changed their appearance, especially during those formative years. Would Jamie really have let the man he believed attacked his sister walk past without even a comment?

Jamie ignored this, and continued, "It's not illegal to rent your business out after hours."

"I'm sure you declared all of your extra income." Dove nodded at him, smiling encouragingly.

Jamie fidgeted. "Probably. I might not have filled in all the paperwork yet."

"Paperwork and illegal earnings are most definitely the least of your worries at the moment. So you let them in, took the money, went back into the office to babysit them for an hour. You called your girlfriend while you were there," Steve stated, looking at the photographs and documents in front of them.

"So? Of course I called her!" A flash of anger or fear, and Jamie pushed his chair back, half standing, shouting at them. "The man I believe nearly killed my sister was having sex less than fifty yards from me."

"Sit down please, Jamie," the solicitor said.

"You said Ellis didn't seem to recognise you. That must have hurt," Dove added, keen to push on, now they had accessed some kind of emotion.

Jamie slumped back down, hands busy now, fiddling with the studs in his ears, tapping his knee. "Okay, you know

I called Caz and told her Ellis Bravery was here. She knew how stressed out I would be, so she picked up Lila and came straight down. We stayed in the office until one and then I went and let them out. Caz and I locked up and went home. We walked along the beach to opposite Miles Road. Lila was crying, and we were so freaked by bloody Ellis Bravery. Then we went home via the cut-through straight into our street," Jamie explained.

Neat, thought Dove. He had dodged the next question about cameras. They had combed all the footage in the area, and there were no cameras covering the route he had described.

* * *

"So what time did you eventually get home?" Dove continued.

"I don't know, maybe around quarter to two?" Jamie drained his water, playing with the empty plastic cup with slightly shaking fingers.

"So what do *you* think happened to your Fantasy Play customers?" Steve queried.

"I can only assume from the evidence they came back, broke in, and went back into Room Six for another round," Jamie said blandly.

"Your personal bank records show cash deposits of fifteen hundred pounds for March, April, June and July. Can you confirm these are all from your Fantasy Play clients?"

"Yes."

"And you never had any trouble with them before? Nobody tried to get back in? Oscar paid up when they arrived?" Steve asked.

"No trouble," Jamie admitted. "But this time they were all hammered. One of the women, the one in the black lace dress with the long brown hair, she dropped an empty bottle of vodka into the bin over there. I bet your investigation team have got that somewhere, as they seem to have bagged up every cigarette end and piece of fluff in the place."

"Which seems rather unlikely," Dove told him. Dionne had managed to get drunk very quickly, considering she had come straight from work, and evidence on the timeline showed she'd met Ellis just after she changed. And the thought of Jamie confronting the man who was basically his worst nightmare and literally saying nothing but 'Good evening' still wasn't ringing true either. "So they had their fun, paid you, walked out and then somehow got hold of a pair of bolt cutters, which enabled them to return to Room Six. For what purpose?"

Jamie blinked, his cool hazel eyes now fixed on Dove's face. Nervous energy all used up now, he was back to sitting straight with his hands clasped on the table in front of him. "I have no idea."

* * *

When Steve and Dove reported back upstairs, DI Blackman agreed Jamie Delaney should be held in custody for thirty-six hours pending further questioning. "He lied. She lied. And he has the motive and the means." The DI ran a hand over his shaven head thoughtfully. "We need to talk to Caz next. Let's go through the forensics again first."

Dove headed outside to grab some food, but Steve insisted he would rather eat chocolate at his computer. His short-lived attempt at a healthy lifestyle had ground to a halt as summer arrived.

Dove went outside to join the queue for the food van, stretching her aching arms and back in the cloudy sunshine. The thunder clouds were still stacking up over the sea, and the heat was sticky and uncomfortable. Her head was aching, but she couldn't tell if it was from her recent injury or just a response to the imminent break in the weather.

"What do you want, love?" The man behind the counter of the food van was scarlet in the face, sweat beading his bald head.

She ordered a Coke and a bacon sandwich, stacking her glass with ice from the rapidly melting bucket on the counter.

"Not going for a fruit salad today?" Lindsey appeared behind her and reached for a pre-made prawn and pasta box.

Dove grinned. "Enjoy your healthy food and I'll enjoy mine. Do you still want a coffee later? Four sugars, isn't it?"

"Whatever, Milson." Lindsey stuck a middle finger up at Dove and paid. They carried their food back to the office together.

"You got anything worth talking about?" Dove asked.

"I have, actually. Oscar Wilding was having an affair with Aileen Jackson. He does a few odd jobs for the blessedly nosy neighbour, Caroline, who lives across the road. She doesn't seem to have a life, but is devoted to her cat." Lindsey smiled as they negotiated the door with their cups and packages. "She's a sweet lady who knows the whole street intimately. She recalled Mr Wilding chatting to Aileen when she put the bins out, about six months ago. Said he came back fairly often after that, always at night, and I need to check, but I'm guessing when the husband was working the night shift. The neighbour said it was love and they were planning to run away together, but that may be her embellishing a little."

"I don't suppose the neighbour saw them on the twenty-fifth?" Dove suggested, considering Aileen's apparent return to a more exciting lifestyle.

"She did indeed. She claims Mr Wilding arrived in a taxi, picked up Aileen, and they both left at twenty to eleven, which ties in with the taxi driver's statement about picking up the couple and dropping them on the seafront at five to twelve," Lindsey said. "Boom! What have you got?"

Dove told her, and added, "So now we have to speak to Caz Liffey and find out her version of events, because they both lied on their initial statements, didn't they?"

"Seems kind of sick if they were in it together, sat in the office with the baby while our victims died," Lindsey observed, as they entered the office. "I'd be interested to see more of the Mickey Delaney case and find out if Bravery should have been in the frame for her attack after all. Didn't the DCI say his alibi was based on some motorway-cam footage? Worth looking into." She took a gulp of her drink as they headed up the stairs. Anyway, I'll catch you later."

"Sure. Thanks, Lindsey."

"Oh," Lindsey paused at the door and turned back, "cameras at the escape rooms feed back into the office, so whoever's working can keep an eye on the players. Could it have been some kind of retribution? Sitting down and watching Bravery and the others drown?"

CHAPTER TWENTY-SEVEN

Jenna's asking me a question, but today I don't feel like answering. I concentrate on the rise and fall of my chest, on my lungs working, on my heart beating, but it's all too loud, too strong, like I'm underwater.

Jenna is talking again, but her voice is soothing now. She is my best friend and sometimes she makes me mad, but I trust her. I can hear another female voice too, and this one is sharper. A hand on my arm takes me back to the car journeys. I don't trust Caz.

Caz pretends to like me because she fancies my brother. She's all whispers and insincere little touches on my arm or hand as we sit on the back seat.

Jenna is saying something about training now, and Caz is correcting her . . . I drift along with them. Sometimes I reply but they ignore me.

I made the squad, so now I get another six hours' training a week. Mum got over her stress about driving me to practice, but it means we have to lift-share with Caz, which sucks. She hates me because she's two years older and only just made the squad, but she pretends to like me.

I've been pushing and pushing my body, just to show Coach he made the right choice, and I know I've been noticed. It gives me such a buzz to step out on to the mat and do my routine. I don't fear anything when I'm out there, but before and after, the chatter, the envious glances as I come off the mat, make me shake inside.

I don't need everyone to like me, because I'm not here to make friends. I'm here to go to the Olympics. Even Jenna says I'm just lucky. Lucky to get picked, lucky not to have an injury, lucky in competitions . . . She doesn't get it. It's not about luck, it's about sheer hard work, and forcing myself to do it.

Jenna and I are the same age, and sooner or later it's going to come down to me or her. I hope we can still be friends but I guess I can survive if not . . . I don't think Jenna wants it as much as me, but her mum wants it more than anyone else. She's a total bitch, Jenna's mum, and she hates me too. In fact, if I think about it, more people hate me than like me in gymnastics.

Caz is saying something about the weekend now, about going out . . . Probably to watch the football, so she can stare at Jamie . . .

On Saturday after the summer regional competition, we went out to the old swings, just me, Caz and Jenna. It was great just sitting on the swings in the sunshine, twisting the chains round and round, then letting go so the wooden seat whizzed round in the opposite direction. Pretending to be a little kid again, like none of it matters.

Jamie was hanging with his mates in the far corner, near the woods. They were kicking a ball around, probably smoking in between games like they usually do. I should tell Mum. Caz was watching Jamie like she usually does, and Jenna started on about how Nathan fancies me so I should go out with him.

I was happy until I saw him watching us. He lives here too, so he has every right to be hanging around, trimming the hedge, mowing the strip of lawn that separates the dirt track from his garden. No one else noticed.

The other girls carried on chatting. Jenna blew bubbles with her pink gum, and Caz talked about her plans to travel the world. She's so in love with my brother, it's embarrassing, because Jamie pretty much ignores her. A lot of girls like him, despite the fact he's ginger and lanky. Funny, people always say he has ginger hair, but mine is usually described as red. Another difference between us.

Funny, because although Jenna and Caz are still talking, I think I can hear my dad's voice, even see his face quite clearly. I can't tell what he's saying, but the other girls have gone quiet, and I'm back on that summer's day.

I carried on winding and unwinding the swing, letting the chat flow over my head, watching the man with the hedge trimmer. If he ever tries anything, I'll be ready . . . I rubbed the bruises on my arm. I bruise really easily, so I always have bruises. Lucky, really . . . There's always an excuse for everything.

I think this might be one of those memories I'll look back on when I'm old and grey and laugh at. I hope so anyway, because just now, for some reason I'm crying. My face is wet but my skin is hot again. As though I'm in the sun and someone has thrown water at me. I'm back in the under-tens at gym club, hardly daring to come out of the changing rooms and face the confident, beautiful girls, the strong, laughing boys. And when I did, just by the door, one of those girls was at the water fountain. She looked up as I went past and deliberately put her hand under the jet, directing the icy water right into my face.

"Caz!" A voice scolded. But there was laughter and my face was burning as I forced myself to carry on walking.

Everything seemed to be impossible back then, when I was just a skinny kid with long tangled red hair scraped into a ponytail and a crappy second-hand green leotard. I have gymnastics to thank for the fact I now look like one of those hard-faced, confident girls I used to admire. But I'm not like them on the inside, no matter how much Coach praises me, no matter I'm in the county squad, the national squad, and an Olympic Pathway contender. And they still hate me.

* * *

The beeping is getting louder, and my heart rate increases, picking up the rhythm. There is music pumping out, coloured lights flashing, and the evening summer heat is almost tropical . . . A woman is shouting, and other voices join in, panicked, but quickly fading as I realise where my memory has led. Dad took me and Jamie to the funfair down in Lymington-on-Sea today. It was so cool because he just dropped us off to meet our mates and then picked us back up at eleven!

Jamie whinged (of course) but took the free lift home because his stupid scooter was broken. The night was alive with the noise and neon colour of the fair, the smell of summer, sweat and burgers. I won four goldfish in a plastic bag on the rifle range, and when we got home, I let them swim free in our pond.

I stayed outside watching the ripples in the dark water, watching the lights go out in neighbouring houses. By the time Dad called for me to hurry up, the only light left on was in an upstairs room in the house next door.

CHAPTER TWENTY-EIGHT

Dove ate her bacon sandwich while she went back over the forensic evidence from the Beach Escape Rooms. Okay, so if Caz and Jamie had been in the office, either one of them could have swum down to block the outflow pipe. Probably Jamie, she supposed, as it was his vendetta.

She chewed a thumbnail thoughtfully, running over the sequence of events. Suppose Jamie had threatened Ellis when he arrived for his sordid night out. Maybe Ellis had laughed in his face and Jamie just snapped? The man he was sure had put his sister in a coma was now getting it on in the escape room without a care in the world.

No wonder the security cameras had been damaged to avoid too much evidence being captured. Did they plan it hastily together, Caz and Jamie, including the feeble idea of the break-in? Or, she stopped with her drink halfway to her mouth, had Jamie already put the workings in place by the time Caz arrived to comfort him? Did they argue, and did she try to stop him from going ahead and murdering four people?

The photographs of the outflow pipe and accompanying notes indicated no evidence had been found on any part of the structure. The seawater would have washed everything away, Dove thought, skimming the documents, and licking a stray splash of brown sauce off the back of her hand. Fingerprints from the control panel and the emergency shut-off valves, both inside the office and outside, had Caz's and Jamie's prints on them.

She peered at a footnote. A partial oil-smeared print had been identified on the outside emergency shut-off valve. The print was still being processed.

Dove had picked up her phone to call Jess and see if she had any further information on the last print, when saw a new voicemail. Delta! She had forgotten to listen to the last one. With a twinge of guilt, she called her niece.

"Hi Delta. What's up?"

"Oh, Dove, I've been trying to call you and I know you're at work but . . . Nothing's wrong, really . . . Actually, could I stay with you for a bit?" Delta was normally cool and laid-back, but now her voice was quick, and her words tumbled over each other.

Dove was surprised by the request. She knew Ren and Delta had fallen out over Delta's current job choice, but she thought Delta was happy with her friend Abi, in a flat-share in the slightly dodgy area of Highcourt in Lymington-on-Sea. "Are you not still living with Abi? Or did you two have a fight or something?"

There was a slight pause. "Dove! We aren't ten . . . It's just . . . the landlord is having the flat decorated and the place stinks of paint. You know how I get migraines . . ."

This last was true. Delta had had to cope with a lot during her teenage years, seen and experienced things nobody her age should have done. The doctors thought the migraines might be as a result of some kind of PTSD, although the girl had never displayed any other symptoms, constantly assuring everyone she was fine.

"You could stay with your mum? She'd like that," Dove suggested.

"She wouldn't. She'd go on and on about how I need to get a better job and stop bumming around as a pole dancer." Delta's usual sarcastic tone had returned.

This was probably true, Dove supposed. "You're always welcome at ours, but the couch isn't the most comfortable, and with both of us working shifts . . . Although Quinn is supposed to be on a few days off now, he might go in for extra shifts because of his training."

"It's fine, I won't then!" Delta snapped.

Dove realised her ham-handed efforts to persuade Delta to move back in with Ren were not working. "Don't be silly, we'd love to have you. I just wanted you to know it's probably just as uncomfortable as Abi's flat at the moment. When do you want to come?"

There was another pause, longer this time, as if Delta was considering the offer. "If you're sure, could I come tonight?"

"I . . . Yes, you can." Dove glanced at the computer screen and back at her watch. "Look, why don't I pick you up from work, and we can go to Ren's together and then back to mine. You were still planning on coming over to hers later, I take it?"

"Sure. Yeah, thanks, Dove, that would be great. It's only for a couple of days while the . . . while the painter finishes."

"Is everything else okay?" Dove queried. She couldn't help feeling the landlord of this particular block of flats was very unlikely to be redecorating. She had been out to the flats a few times in the course of investigations and the whole place stunk of rats and piss.

"Fine. Dove, have you heard anything else about Gaia yet?"

"No, but she should be out tomorrow. All the tests have come back normal and she's gagging to get back home." Dove wondered if it was Gaia's accident that was upsetting her normally level-headed niece.

"Everyone's talking about what happened at the club," Delta said quietly.

"I'm sure. But I know Colin and Uri will be keeping an eye on things until Gaia gets back to work." Dove paused. "Delta, do *you* know anything about the robbery?"

"No." It was a little quick and a little sharp. "Of course I don't, but people are saying it must have been an inside job, so there are lots of accusations flying around, especially from the new girls."

"Just try and encourage everyone to cooperate with the police," Dove suggested. She didn't think Delta would be holding out on some vital piece of information, because she had been brought up around Dove's work and knew better than that, but still, the girl was definitely on edge.

Delta sighed. "Most of them don't like the police at all."

"Well, ignore the haters and concentrate on the employees who owe their livelihoods to your aunt," Dove told her. "Delta, I've got to go, but I'll pick you up later unless I get stuck here on something."

CHAPTER TWENTY-NINE

He was watching me when I arrived home today, the man next door, but I went out into the back garden anyway and worked at my walkovers, my back flips, my jumps until I couldn't move any more. My homework books waited in a pile on the grass, but I couldn't be bothered to open them.

So I flopped down by the pond. It was so gross. Filled with rubbish, cigarette ends and oil. My fish were floating on their sides, poisoned by the shit in the water.

And then I looked up and saw he'd started trimming his hedge with hand clippers, precisely snipping away feathery leaves. He stared with that intense, slightly calculating look. He didn't even flinch when I stared back at him. I've never ever challenged him before. Instead of turning away, he smiled and nodded at me, as though he had been waiting for me to acknowledge our connection.

It freaked me out. I grabbed my books and ran inside, into the kitchen. I grabbed a sports drink from the fridge and banging the door closed. All the magnets from our holiday to Spain and certificates from school fell to the floor.

The kitchen was empty, but I could hear Mum upstairs, telling Jamie off for leaving his clothes all over the floor of his bedroom again.

Mum's voice is bringing me back to normal. The feel of the cool black lino tiles on the kitchen floor under my bare toes, the squashy cream leather sofa next to the shelf of cookery books. It's all just like anyone else's house. I can hear the murmur of the TV, the beeping of the timer on the cooker, but I'm drifting again . . .

I'm safe now.

It will be okay.

CHAPTER THIRTY

Jess had no further information on the partial print on the shut-off valve, but suggested it might be a match to one of the plumbers who had completed maintenance on the system the week before. "As far as they can tell, the system was working perfectly, but with the bung in place and the emergency shut-off disabled, there was nothing to stop the water from filling the room."

"And we didn't get anything from the hatch to the actual room?" Dove queried hopefully.

"Sorry, love. Lots of prints on the shiny glass and chrome including all of our victims, the two owners, and numerous unidentified yet." She paused. "There was one other thing. The lock on the roof hatch in Escape Room Six is a simple bolt-and-padlock affair. The padlock was cut using the same bolt cutters as the main entrance gate."

Dove digested this for a moment. "There's still the issue of why didn't they just open the hatch and get out when they saw the water rising so fast?"

"There was plenty of alcohol in their systems — perhaps they just got confused and simply couldn't find the way out," Jess suggested. "It was dark. They were pissed. They may not have realised how serious it was until it was too late."

"You think?"

"Not really," Jess admitted. "But I'm just throwing it out there."

"Two more things," Dove added. "Did you get a vodka bottle from the bin?"

There was a pause. "Yes, with DNA and prints matching Dionne Radley and Ellis Bravery. Cigarette butts showing DNA matching all four victims, and a used tissue matching Oscar Wilding's. You saw the report from inside the room? Condoms, phones, etcetera.?"

"Yes, thanks."

"The water samples showed blood matches to Dionne and Oscar, plus there were traces of vodka in there."

"They took supplies in with them?" Dove supposed that made sense in terms of busting the blood-alcohol levels. "No trace of any other empty bottles or cans on scene though?"

"No."

"Great, thanks, Jess." Dove ended the call, and opened another packet of sweets as she went back to her computer. They were missing something. She could feel it. The focus kept shifting from victim to victim, but surely Ellis Bravery was the key. He was the link to Caz and Jamie, to Jamie's past . . .

"Wetsuit!" Dove said suddenly, looking up from the masses of photographic evidence. "Jamie keeps his wetsuit at the office, and it was hanging on the dryer when we went to bring him in. There was a box of other stuff too — gloves, masks, fins . . ."

"So?" Steve glanced over from his own computer.

"So what if he wore the suit and the gloves to swim down and put the bung in place? It would be sensible to avoid any skin contact in case we could trace DNA or prints on the bung or pipe . . . I mean, it's unlikely because of all the seawater washing around, but if he was being careful . . ." Dove suggested. "So much evidence was bagged and tagged from the whole place, but there isn't anything to say the wetsuits were checked."

"True. It's hot weather, so unless he thought ahead, as you say, why would you put one on when it's sweltering outside? But I'm not sure how you'd prove which suit had been worn recently. He could have worn it any time in the last few weeks," Steve pointed out.

The DI called them into his office. "Caz Liffey is downstairs wanting to change her statement. She must have freaked out hearing Jamie would be staying with us for a little while. I want you two to interview her, and Maya and I will then talk to Jamie again, depending on what she says."

"Yes, boss," Dove said. Her heart was thumping hard. It was that same thrill of excitement she got every time the chase began, and the suspect was twisting around trying to escape. Would Caz admit to the murders or did she really not know exactly what had happened the night of the twenty-fifth?

Caz, small and muscular, with her long, yellowish hair piled on top of her head in a plastic clip, was huddled on a chair in the interview room, looking as if she was about to burst into tears. She kept blinking and gnawing at her bottom lip, and she had a smear of something that looked like toothpaste on her chin.

Her solicitor sat next to her, files open and pen ready. "My client would like to revise her statement regarding the night of July twenty-fifth. She has been under extreme stress, suffering from postnatal depression and insomnia. In addition, last night her baby girl had to be admitted to hospital, which has placed additional strain on my client's mental health."

"Would you like to tell us what happened, then?" Steve suggested, smiling at her. "We're so glad your baby is okay now. It must have been terrifying."

Caz pulled a strand of her hair around and put it in her mouth, chewing the split ends. Her shoulders were hunched forward and her eyes shadowed with purple bags. Eventually she pushed her hair away and answered, eyes darting wildly from one person to the next. "Yes! It was awful when she was just fitting and I thought she'd stopped breathing . . ."

"Would you like another glass of water, or a hot drink?" Dove asked gently, noticing Caz had already drained her plastic cup.

The other woman glanced down at the cup, vaguely, as though she had only just noticed it. "No . . . Thank you. I want to tell you something first. Jamie told me he'd seen Ellis Bravery in the street in Abberley about a month ago, and I was shocked. I never thought he'd show up in the same town as us. Turns out he'd been living here all along. Ironic." Caz abandoned her hair, and pulled her sleeves down over her hands now, long cuffs covering her small, stubby fingers.

"I imagine it's been emotional for you both," Steve commented.

"Yes! We went to visit Jamie's parents the next day, and although I told Jamie not to tell them, I think he did, because they were kind of not with it all morning." She dipped her gaze, picking at her cuffs now, with restless stubby fingers. "Mickey was my friend and we were in the gymnastics squad together. It is almost impossible to believe she's been lying in a bed for almost five years." Tears slid down her cheeks, and she sniffed.

"So what happened that night, Caz? Did you kill Ellis Bravery, Dionne Radley, Aileen Jackson and Oscar Wilding?" Dove asked.

For a moment Caz sat open-mouthed at such a direct approach, and glanced at her solicitor before answering. "Of course not! We would never do that. But when Jamie called to say Ellis was actually in the escape room, I panicked." She paused and shifted on her seat as though it was uncomfortable. "When Jamie said we had another booking from the Fantasy Play man, I was pleased. We needed the cash to pay back our loan, and he paid well. But then he called me and at first he could hardly speak . . ."

"Go on."

"He told me one of the men was Ellis Bravery."

"And just to recap for the recording, Ellis Bravery is the man he believes is responsible for Mickey's attack?"

"Yes." She blinked hard, eyes wet, voice trembling. "The police really screwed up on Mickey's investigation. Everyone knows it was Ellis and here he was walking around free, coming into our business to have sex. At least these women were legal, I suppose, but I guess he moved on from underage girls."

"So you picked up the baby and went over to the pier," Steve prompted.

"I suppose. I hardly remember what happened after he called, only that I needed to help him," Caz said. "I panicked. All I was thinking was that I needed Lila safe and Jamie safe, and then nothing else would matter." She was crying properly now.

"Caz, do you need a moment?" the solicitor asked.

She shook her head, dragged a tissue from her pocket and blew her nose loudly. "Sorry . . . I'm sorry, it's just everything is such a mess . . . I don't know if I went to the pier . . ."

Steve placed the street-cam pictures on the table between them. "Yes, you did, because this is you walking towards the pier at 12.20 a.m."

Caz stared at the images, blinking hard.

"What happened when you arrived?" Dove asked softly. "You said you were worried about Jamie. How did he seem?"

Caz took a long, ragged breath and pressed her fingertips to her forehead. "He was crying. When I got in and put Lila down in her basket, Jamie freaked out completely, started throwing pens around. Oh, not at us, just at the windows and he kicked the bin over . . ."

"Caz, did Jamie speak to Ellis when he arrived with the other Fantasy Play clients? Did they maybe have a quick conversation?" Dove asked.

"No! Oh no, Jamie said he was so shocked and Ellis didn't seem to recognise him, so he just let them all in and came to the office to ring me."

"Did you see the four people in Escape Room Six as you arrived?" Dove asked.

169

Caz shook her head. "No. It was dark, and there wasn't much of a moon that night. The lights were off except in the office and Escape Room Six is below the level of the pier." She seemed to have calmed down a little and recited the rest of her new statement without much emotion. "We decided it would be best if I stayed until the Fantasy Play people had gone, and I would show them out so Jamie didn't have to face them," she said carefully. "There are cameras in the office, and I recognised Ellis Bravery, the filthy old perv, on the screen."

"Did you know him well when you were younger?" Steve asked.

She shrugged. "I just knew him as one of the neighbours. My stepmum used to sell him duty-free cigarettes she got from a friend, so he came round sometimes." Caz sighed. "But it was always Mickey who would spot him perving behind the hedge . . . She was almost scared of him, but the rest of us hardly noticed him. Like everyone said, in the end there was nobody else who could've tried to kill her. I don't know who found out that Ellis had been involved in a child-porn investigation, but mud sticks, doesn't it?"

"Your stepmum was still happy to invite him to her home and sell him cigarettes, though?" Steve said.

Caz shrugged. "We needed the extra cash. She didn't care what you'd done as long as it wasn't directed at her, and she never paid much attention to gossip. She was in the minority."

"Going back to the night of the twenty-fifth," Dove said. "What happened after the hour was up?"

"I went to show them out. Jamie was just sitting on the floor in the office cuddling Lila. He didn't move or react at all when I said the time was up," Caz said. "The hatch was already open and they staggered a bit when they came out, pissed as farts, thanked me and I let them out and locked the gate behind them. All I was thinking about was getting back to Jamie and Lila and us all being safe."

"You showed the Fantasy Play clients to the main gate and locked it behind them? These four people?" She pushed her iPad across to Caz who studied the faces and nodded briskly.

"Right out the front gate. I just said good night and locked up. They'd already paid Jamie, and as I said, they were drunk, so we were hardly going to stand around having a chat, were we?"

"Did you see which way they walked, or if they got a taxi?" Steve made a note on his paperwork.

"No, sorry. What with everything that had happened, I was so desperate to get Jamie and the baby home, and it was such a shock to see Ellis after all these years," Caz said. "After I locked up, I went back to the office, turned all the lights off, locked up there, and we walked home down the beach way . . . It was warm, Lila was crying a bit, and Jamie was still completely silent, like he was stunned or in a trance. We went home, fed Lila, and went to bed. Next thing we knew we got a call saying there were four dead bodies in our escape room."

* * *

DCI Franklin called a quick briefing in the incident room at 2.30. "I'm aware we're not all present, but I think we are making significant progress on this case, and I wanted to clarify a couple of things. Mainly so we can stop chasing a few of these leads." He indicated the whiteboard, which had so many individual strands that it looked like a ball of wool gone rogue from someone's knitting. "Jon?"

DI Blackman took the nod from his superior and proceeded. "Aileen Jackson seems to have been planning to run away with Oscar Wilding. She probably had another phone to communicate with him, which we are currently trying to locate." He paused and glanced down at his notes. "Her husband Billy, as well as working at Tesco's, sometimes does a bit of cash-in-hand for a friend who runs a business providing plumbing and heating engineers. Josh?"

DC Conrad was swiping through documents on his iPad. "He was with his mate, Keith Arkle, when the business was called in to the Beach Escape Rooms to fix a faulty out-flow pipe, and an electrical fault. We spoke to Keith and a couple of his other employees, and they confirmed it was the first time they had been called to that particular venue, but they fixed the problem within the hour. I've got the details. It was just a short circuit in the wiring behind the panel. The partial print the lab lifted from the outside panel is a match to Keith Arkle."

"So if Billy had found out about his wife and Oscar, and maybe followed her that night, he had working knowledge of the mechanisms used for the murder," DC Pete Wyndham commented. "Hang on, isn't the valve a manual shut-off?" He was looking at the photographs now up on the big screen on the wall.

Josh pointed a little to the left of the control panel. "If the electrics fail, the system for the affected room is supposed to shut down automatically, and if that fails to activate, yes, you twist that wheel and lock it by hand."

Pete frowned, nodding along. "So essentially, what you are saying is, nobody twisted the wheel?"

"Pretty much," Josh agreed. "The only way out was the entrance/exit hatch. It should have still been possible for them to escape, or at least float on top of the water, if their normal reactions hadn't been impaired by the substances they had imbibed. Dionne's husband claims she never learned to swim, so that would put her at an immediate disadvantage."

"But if somebody slid the bolts on that, they had no chance of survival, poor buggers," DI Blackman put in, picking up his coffee mug and taking a thoughtful sip.

"We also have Tomas Radley, Dionne's husband, who claims their marital problems were common knowledge and they were going to file for divorce, yet Dionne is creeping around changing clothes in a public toilet and pretending she's at work when she could have just told him she was off on a jolly," Steve pointed out. "He already knew she was having affairs, so why the secrecy?"

"Unless the secrecy from Dionne was all for Ellis?" Dove suggested. "He's got the most to lose, hasn't he? High-flying entrepreneur, with trophy girlfriend who sleeps soundly, and hears what she wants to hear as long as he keeps the money coming in. Not to mention he's left his brush with child pornography behind him and buried his involvement with the Mickey Delaney case so successfully, he didn't even recognise Jamie."

"Maybe he *did* recognise Jamie?" DI Blackman commented. "We only have Jamie's word that he didn't. But he was having a party night with his friends, so he wouldn't have wanted to rock the boat. Was he intending to speak to him afterwards? Jamie already admitted he was totally thrown, and quite understandably so."

"I just can't see them both letting the moment pass," Dove said. "Maybe Jamie started an argument, maybe accused Ellis in front of his friends, in front of Dionne, who he appears to have been seeing for a while according to Tracey at Camillo's. Perhaps Ellis, now, as you say, the high-flying businessman instead of the out-of-work neighbour, threatened Jamie to keep his mouth shut . . . Maybe threatened to bring down his business?" Dove struggled to run with her strand of thought, but Steve was nodding.

"Ellis has a lot of property interests, and he sits on the town council. He's turned into Mr Respectable." Steve was flicking through his notes.

"Jamie and Caz were both there at the same time as our victims, they both admitted lying in their original statements, and they had motive and means," Lindsey said. "I can't see we should be looking anywhere else now."

"Caz has gone home, but DC Amin and I are having another chat with Jamie now. *If* he did it, for this to go through, the CPS are going to want hard evidence and at the moment it's all circumstantial," DI Blackman said, and DI Lincoln nodded in agreement. "Josh and Lindsey, find out exactly where Billy Jackson was during those four missing hours on the night of the twenty-fifth, so we can eliminate him from our enquiries."

"Caz said she and Jamie went to visit his parents in Salthaven the day after he claims to have seen Ellis in the street. She says they agreed *not* to tell his parents, but thinks Jamie *did* tell them. So Russ and Claire Delaney were also aware Ellis was still in the area," Dove added.

The DI nodded. "Might be worth talking to them, just to verify where they were on the twenty-fifth. It must be a big shock, to discover the person who you believe tried to murder your teenage daughter, by throwing her into a quarry, is back in town. I wonder why he moved back in the first place?"

CHAPTER THIRTY-ONE

"I want to take another look at the Beach Escape Rooms," Dove told Steve, as the team filed out towards the coffee machine, splitting into various partnerships for the afternoon.

He shrugged. "Can't do any harm, and I agree with Lindsey, we need to nail Caz and Jamie somehow. None of the others are really in the running, unless it was Billy Jackson, and if he was responsible, we can't prosecute a dead man."

They parked on the side of the road next to the seafront, and headed towards the pier. Despite the weather becoming heavy and stormy, with spots of rain splashing on the dusty pavements, and the waves cresting white-tipped and ominous out to sea, the town was still busy with tourists.

As they passed the amusement arcade, Dove gave a fiver to a man pulling a shopping trolley full of his possessions. He was dressed in a brown towelling robe, and his tangled dreadlocks fell to his waist. He walked slowly, with dignity, and thanked her for the money.

"Dove! You keeping all right, my darling?" His voice was low and musical, and Dove knew that stashed amongst the other bags in his trolley was a battered trumpet in a blue velvet case.

"Fine, thanks, Ron. You okay?" She smiled at him.

He nodded slowly, taking in Steve. "He's looking a bit worried. What have you two been up to under the pier? Thought you were with that nice medical bloke." He cackled, and Dove laughed.

"What do you think? Honestly, Ron, your mind is stuck in the gutter, mate."

"Got myself a phone a while back," he announced proudly, still looking warily at Steve.

"I know, mate, you told me. That's good. Take care of it," Dove told him. She had met Ron when he was being beaten up by a group of teenagers on a stag weekend. Luckily she had been with Quinn, and the two of them were able to scare off the kids and help the old man to recover. She'd kept an eye out for old Ron ever since.

"You going to be coming back this way?" the old man said.

"In about an hour, maybe less."

"Could do with some fish and chips to tide me over till the bars open." Ron grinned, showing rotten and gappy teeth. He was well known along the seafront, and a few of the bars let him busk outside on summer evenings, giving him the odd free drink and letting him earn a few pennies. He lived with a few other rough sleepers in the derelict leisure-centre car park in a makeshift tent, but when it got crowded in the summer months, he often moved under the pier for the long hot nights.

"I'll get you some lunch," Dove told him.

"Ta, Dove, my Lovey-Dovey . . . It's gonna rain tonight, isn't it? Big storm coming up from the Channel . . ." He nodded, hair flying, and wandered on, shopping trolley creaking and rattling over the pavement, unexpectedly humming a Justin Bieber hit to himself.

Dove smiled. "We need to come back this way and keep an eye out for him. He only ever asks for me to buy him lunch if he's got some information."

"Lovey-Dovey? And how did he get a phone?" Steve asked innocently, his mouth curving into a knowing smirk.

"I know it's cringey, but he likes calling me that. As for the phone, no idea. Everyone's got a phone these days," Dove said airily. Her days of source handling might be over, but that didn't mean she would ever pass up a good contact if she could help it, and Ron, if he wasn't paralytic, was an excellent contact.

He reminded her of the homeless people her dad had worked with under the pier in Santa Monica in Los Angeles. The actors and musicians, the lost people and the drifters, all of whom had been flushed off the streets on to the beach. With a few charity partners, her parents had helped set up a drop-in centre for those needing healthcare and looking for accommodation or jobs. The centre was still running, but her parents were currently living back in their rural commune.

It had been a good childhood, but it had shaped her and her sisters in a different way to a lot of their friends. It wasn't just their unusual names, although that had been a factor, especially when the family moved to the UK.

She had lost count of the amount of times someone had taken the piss because she was called Dove. As a kid she'd become ashamed of it, but now she understood its origins she was proud, and felt the haters could do their thing somewhere else.

Dove and Steve signed in and were admitted under the crime-scene tape. There was nobody on the site.

The office smelled stale and musty, and Dove looked around with fresh eyes, picturing the night of the murders, noting the white dust and odd plastic bag from the forensics teams. The wetsuits were hanging on the rack, and she slipped on her gloves and picked up Jamie's, with its distinctive logo.

Steve walked over. "Anything?"

She turned it over, examining the fabric, before carefully putting it down and picking up the next suit along. After fifteen minutes, she regretfully put them down. "Nothing. You're right, of course, there's no telling when his suit was last used, and even if he was in the sea with it that night, with

177

the residual heat in this room it would be bone dry by the morning when we pitched up."

Disappointed, they went back out on to the road, and Dove popped into Marine Fish 'n' Chips to buy food for Ron before they walked swiftly down the steps to the beach.

"You think he'll be under the pier?" Steve queried, peering under the damp, sour-smelling structure.

"Only for the day, with a storm coming," Dove explained. "You stay here, and I'll find him. He's a bit unsure of you. No offence."

"None taken." Steve leaned back against the seawall and sipped his takeaway coffee. Above him the stormy sky turned a dark inky blue, and the seagulls circled on huge white wings, their screeching calls half lost in the wind.

There were five or six people huddled under the pier, just above the high-tide level, and Ron called out a greeting before shambling over to her. "Ta, Lovey-Dovey, just what I need."

She handed him the warm parcel of fish and chips, and he began to tear at the fish with his hands, stuffing chunks into his mouth, licking his dirty fingers with relish. When he was half done, he began to talk. "Let's take a little wander down to the sea."

She strolled next to him as he wolfed his chips, keeping a cautious eye on the remaining inhabitants under the pier. The rain was heavier now, refreshing and streaming down her face, soaking her shirt. It had magically cleared the beach too, so Ron and Dove were able to walk down to the low tideline without interference. The wooden struts of the pier looked almost black against the ominous skyline and sheets of rain. Seaweed hung in lurid green tendrils, and further out, the waves crashed and foamed.

"I've got something for you," Ron told her, giving quick looks left and right. "It's on the phone. Here." He shoved the device into her hand and she swiped to unlock it. "Check in the videos."

Dove wiped her face on her shirt sleeve and pushed her wet hair back from her forehead. She peered at his collection and hit play on what seemed to be the newest one. It was shot during the night, and showed a figure swimming in the sea, swimming strongly towards the wooden steps at the end of the pier, hauling themselves up, hand over hand, before vanishing over the edge.

"That was after." Ron, breathing heavily, leaned over and stabbed a finger at the screen. "I didn't get any video of the first bit but I took a couple of photos."

The camera on the cheap phone wasn't designed for night shoots and, like the video, the footage was blurred and grainy, but it was possible to make out a figure swimming under the struts of the pier towards Escape Room Six.

"This person swam out, did something underwater and then came back. It was the night them people got murdered, so I thought you should know," Ron told her importantly.

"Why didn't you tell me earlier?" Dove asked cautiously. The footage was gold dust for showing what had happened, but pretty crap in identifying who the swimmer was. A pale blur of a face was the only image captured.

He shrugged and coughed, a hacking deathbed rasp. "The coppers came asking the morning after but I don't talk to nobody but you, Lovey-Dovey, and you wasn't there."

"I was up on the pier," she told him. "You've got my number." In fact, hers was the only number in his phone, which caught at her heart a little when she noticed. She pressed a couple of buttons and quickly sent herself the photos and video.

He turned away, humming, and she understood. To Ron, sometimes days could pass in an alcoholic stupor, and he would have no idea of time or place. He thought he had found her as soon as he could. Despite having her number, he had never once called her, always preferring to find her on the beach near her house, or he would be wheeling his shopping trolley up the coast road as she arrived home from work.

"Thanks, Ron." She slipped him some notes. "Get some more food when you need it, not the bloody drinks, okay?"

He laughed. "Ta, Lovey-Dovey." He pocketed the phone and shambled back under the pier again, heading back towards his shopping trolley, barking swear words at the four men who were hunched on a filthy duvet sharing what looked like a two-litre bottle of White Lightning, despite the fact they had stayed a respectful distance from his possessions.

* * *

As Dove had already noted, the footage, even cleaned up, was poor, and DC Josh Conrad, who had a tech background before his transfer, had done his best.

"You can see the swimmer is wearing a wetsuit, but it isn't Jamie's one with the distinctive logo," Josh said. "I can't zoom in any more without losing the image completely. It's a cheap phone, and these things never take good pictures at night. If you didn't get a bit from the street lights on the promenade, you wouldn't be able to see anything at all."

Dove was biting her thumbnail, still staring at the images. She remembered Caz saying she hadn't been able to see the victims in Room Six because it was dark, and it was true, but Caz and Jamie clearly hadn't factored in someone hiding under the pier, or the street lights west of the pier casting a dim light as far as the high tidemark. "It could be either of them, or neither of them, couldn't it? The other wetsuits in the office were all black with the odd small logo on the chest."

DI Blackman was not impressed by Dove's phone footage. "You say they came from a homeless man on the beach?" He studied her, cool grey eyes assessing. "Do you know him?"

Dove explained about the beating. "Quinn and I have both seen him on and off ever since. He'll never make a statement, and he has chronic alcoholism, so he's not a reliable witness either. When we went to pick Jamie up for his interview, I admired his wetsuit and he said that Caz keeps hers at home. I know we can't identify her from the footage, but we can mention it during an interview, can't we?"

He nodded. "It's worth a shot. Jamie isn't budging from his story, which does tie in very accurately with his girlfriend's. Though if we can't get anything concrete, we'll have to let him go again."

"We could at least see if the wetsuit thing rattles them both enough to make any cracks show?" Dove suggested, aware this was grasping at straws.

"We haven't got much else." The DI leaned back in his chair, frowning. "We'll get a warrant to search Jamie's and Caz's place. And Dove? I want some more background on both of them. Let's find out if either of them have crossed paths with Bravery since Mickey's attack. The DCI is on board with this, by the way. Go and see Jamie's parents. Something must have triggered Jamie, if he is our perpetrator. He certainly seems adamant Bravery was responsible for his sister's attack, despite the fact he was cleared. Does he know something else about Bravery that he isn't sharing? Has he found out something recently that has made him so sure? Find out."

"Yes, boss."

Caz and Jamie lived a short walk from the pier, in a tall, narrow house near the end of Ship Street. Caz answered the door with the baby in her arms. Her hair was tangled and caught up in a messy knot, and she was wearing a short pink dress. Her bare feet were dirty, and the baby girl was crying.

DI Lincoln was heading up the search, and he explained the procedure to the fuming mother, before Dove and Steve ushered her into the tiny living room.

"What the fuck do you think you're doing?" Caz screeched at them. "I've had zero sleep. Lila won't stop crying. Bloody Jamie's stuck at the police station and now you're treating me like I'm some bloody serial killer!"

CHAPTER THIRTY-TWO

Caz was rocking the baby, trying to pop the dummy back in the little girl's mouth, but the screaming continued until Steve offered to hold her. "Shall I try? I'm not saying it will work, but when my first one had wind, sometimes she liked to be held like this . . ."

Caz hesitated a second, before carefully relinquishing her baby. Steve cradled the child, before turning her towards his chest, putting her up on his shoulder, and gently patting her back. He walked a little way across the room, still patting, while Caz watched closely, teary-eyed and exhausted.

After a while, the crying stopped and the baby let out a burp that made them all smile, and promptly went straight to sleep. Steve handed her back, and Caz sighed heavily. "I should hire you as a nanny. Why wouldn't she do that for me?"

"It's easier when they aren't your own, and you've had a good night's sleep," Steve pointed out.

Once the sleeping baby was settled into a padded basket, Dove offered to make tea. Caz, clearly torn and on the edge, first scowled at her, then nodded sharply, and slumped on the sofa, one eye always on her tiny daughter.

Lila had certainly provided an excellent distraction from the white-suited, white-booted figures who moved calmly and methodically from room to room.

Dove found the milk and shoved some mugs on to a tray ready to take into the other room. She glanced out of the window. The rain was still hurtling down from a grey sky. The tiny courtyard back garden contained a rusty child's swing, some neatly stacked bike tyres and two mountain bikes. A rather parched-looking red rose jostled for space with ivy on the back wall. The gate, she assumed, led straight out into the alleyway.

In a corner, rapidly dissolving into a mess of charred puddles, was the remains of a bonfire.

"Caz, Jamie mentioned you keep your wetsuit at home. Can you let me know where it is?" Dove asked, after they had all taken a sip. It was like a weird tea party where nobody was sure what to say. Or maybe Caz was just so shattered she didn't care anymore.

"I . . . I don't know. I haven't used it for ages." Caz waved a hand. "Maybe upstairs in the spare room with all the boxes. We had to make way for Lila's crib and her changing table. I expect it got packed up. I might have even given it away by accident." She rubbed her eyes. Steve had closed the living-room door, but the activity could still be heard. Heavy footsteps on the stairs, quiet instructions from DI Lincoln.

Dove got up and stood at the window. The monsoon-like torrent of rain was easing off, clouds moving away inland, leaving everything wet and sparkling in the weak sunlight. She turned back to Caz, "You lived next to Jamie when you were kids?"

Caz looked wary, but she nodded. "On the same road as him and Mickey, yes."

"Were you friends with Mickey?"

"Yes, of course. I told you. We used to belong to the same gymnastics club, although I'm two years older than her so we didn't really train together much. She was lovely, and it broke their family apart when she was attacked." Caz sat huddled, hands wrapped around her mug. "I think we all lost faith in the police after that. Nobody else would have attacked Mickey, and now . . . Now we just wait and see what's going to happen. The doctors aren't hopeful, you know, but Jamie and his parents think she'll just wake up one day."

Caz looked at the framed photographs on the wall. They all showed Caz and Jamie on their travels, smiling, tanned, happy. "You know, the gymnastics coach was always very touchy-feely, and he was interviewed, but he would never have killed Mickey because she was winning. His team was everything to him. I heard he died in a car accident. Shame, he was a nice enough bloke."

"Jenna Essex was interviewed too, on Mickey's case, wasn't she?"

"Ridiculous." Caz snorted with slightly hysterical laughter and fumbled for a tissue. "Jenna's a ditzy girl. She couldn't hurt anyone. She always was a gossip, but she'd never hurt Mickey. Too much kudos in being Mickey's supposed best friend. Jenna's mum is a right fucking bitch. She used to make a scene if her precious girl wasn't on the podium at every competition."

There was a touch of ice in Caz's voice when she talked about Jenna, and a whole lot of venom when she spoke about her mum. Interesting. Dove wondered about their relationship. "Do you still keep in touch with Jenna?"

"No," said Caz shortly. "I imagine she's still teaching at her mum's dance academy out Lymington way. She was really cut up after it happened, kept visiting Mickey in hospital, convinced she'd wake up."

"It must have been awful," Steve said sympathetically.

"Yes, it was. It is." Caz looked up with red-rimmed eyes. "After Mickey's attack, it was me who persuaded Jamie to get away, to travel for a bit. It got to him so much. He's seven years older than Mickey and he was always the protective big brother. He blames himself for not being there when she was hurt, for not being able to make her better . . ." She trailed off, lost in her memories.

"You were saying about going travelling?" Steve prompted gently.

"I was going myself, but couldn't afford it yet, and I was only sixteen. He came back every six months to see Mickey, you know, from wherever he was. Once I'd saved up enough, I did my diving-instructor course, and got a job in a holiday resort in Thailand." She smiled at the memory, glancing out as the sun broke through the clouds, creating a halo effect over the road, which steamed after the sudden change in the weather. "This hot stormy weather and sudden rain reminds me of travelling."

"And you stayed in touch with Jamie?"

"On and off, but we met again in Koh Samui and later at a backpacker's hostel outside Cancun in Mexico. I had some time off, and we were emailing, and realised we were going to be in the same place at the same time. He'd just done his instructor course, so we travelled together after that, ending up with six months in the Maldives, working for a tour operator. It was heaven."

"And you came back to Abberley?" Dove queried.

"We both still felt the UK was our home and we wanted kids. Jamie wanted to be near his parents when Mickey . . . well, if anything happened to Mickey. Five years is a long time to be in a coma. Something will happen soon, good or bad, and decisions will have to be made. Jamie knows I'll support him," Caz explained.

"Caz, are you sure Jamie never mentioned Ellis Bravery speaking to him, either the night of the twenty-fifth, or earlier in the month when he saw him in the street?" Dove was slipping the top back on her pen, pocketing her notebook and iPad, keeping it casual.

For a long moment Caz was silent, then she turned back to Dove, shutters down, her face stony again. "Nothing. He said nothing to Jamie apart from greeting him. I told you, Ellis never recognised him."

* * *

185

After the search was complete, the team exited the house. DI Lincoln caught Dove and Steve before they got in the car. "Can you two go and have a word with the woman opposite? Number 213. Miss Serena Cardew. She asked one of the SOCOs what was going on and then said she had some information for us."

Steve nodded. "Can do, boss. Nosy neighbours are often the best type to have."

DI Lincoln agreed. "We've got a few bits and pieces, but nothing that jumps out from the search apart from the recent bonfire in the backyard."

Dove, hearing the change in his gravelly voice, from monotone to something approaching bloodhound alertness, felt her own pulse begin to race. "What is it?"

"All bagged and tagged, but it looks like someone tried to burn a wetsuit."

CHAPTER THIRTY-THREE

It's so hot again. Not desert heat, just sweaty, muggy and making me breathless.

The summer has been so hot. Not like normal The last couple of days, we spent time in the woods, hanging out by the quarry. Jamie made a rope swing that went right out over the drop. I can see him laughing, daring the others to have a go, his hair bright in the sunlight.

As always, down by the quarry, hidden from the grown-ups, there is smoking, drinking, people hooking up and breaking up. Gymnastics training always comes first for me, but I think this summer I've finally figured out I can be both an elite athlete and a teenager.

So I've still been getting up to train at four, making sure I get my homework done, putting in just enough effort to cruise by in the middle of my year group. After school I train again, Coach straightening my body in the gym, adjusting my posture with steady hands. Both of us strive for perfection.

In the evenings, I shower and hang out in the waste ground behind our house, by the swings. There's often a big gang of teenagers from the estate who play football. Salthaven is a small town, so the matches get really fierce. There's a lot at stake.

It's been so hot, I've just been wearing shorts and a bikini top. I'm no match for Jenna in her pink lace hot pants and bra (covered

*with a large hoody until she is out of the house because her mum would
totally kill her).*

*Two weeks after he rejected me, Nathan decided to ask me out.
Thinking he was taking the piss and it was a joke, I said no, but we
hung out as friends and gradually drifted into being boyfriend and girlfriend. I can feel every last touch, taste Nathan's mouth on mine, hear
his voice telling me he wants to leave school and join his dad's decorating
business, telling me I should aim big and hold tight to my dreams.*

*It was such a sweet, innocent kiss, that first one, and so far from the
pressures of my life. The others gave us less hassle when it became obvious
we were together. A few dates at the football field, hanging out and sharing
a can of cheap fizzy wine he'd got his brother to buy at the garage.*

*Then, when he wanted more, I said no, pushed him gently away,
both hands against his chest. He was probably disappointed, but he's
nice and he didn't want to hurt me. We broke up a few days later, just
as the summer holidays were about to start. I guess I should have been
sad, but instead I felt a vague sense of relief, like I'd ticked off another
experience, like I'd joined the gang properly.*

*Jenna started dating him not long after that and she was soon
texting me, telling everyone they'd gone all the way, giving me way too
many details. Made me cringe. But I'd gone by then — travelling for a
four-day competition in Liverpool. I couldn't let any of that get to me. I
had to focus, on my routines, my timing, my vaults. All the things that
matter more than a stupid teenage romance.*

*And anyway, Jenna was left at home because I got the last place
on the squad this time and there's no room for her.*

*I can feel a mosquito bite my arm, a sharp prick of pain, and I
want to rub the sore place. My face is wet again. Is it tears or sweat?
I want to wipe it away, but I can't move . . . I shout for my mum, for
Jenna, to help me, but they don't hear.*

CHAPTER THIRTY-FOUR

The woman who lived opposite Jamie and Caz proved to be a delightful elderly lady, recently confined to a wheelchair after a boating accident. "I get so bored, I spend a lot of time watching the street. I might write a book one day, but then again I have been promised a mobility scooter so I'll be out and about soon." She beamed at them, and offered tea and biscuits.

"No, thanks. You mentioned to one of our colleagues you have some information you want to share?" Dove said.

"I do." She wheeled herself into the spotless living area, and deftly leaned over to pick up a newspaper. "Your other colleagues have already been around knocking on doors asking if anyone saw anything on the night of July twenty-fifth, but I didn't." For a second her face clouded. "Sometimes the pain is bad and I have to medicate, you know, so I slept like a baby that night."

Steve nodded encouragingly.

"Their baby doesn't seem to sleep much, Caz's and Jamie's. I hear her wailing sometimes. Nice couple they are, and we've chatted a couple of times."

Dove waited, as the woman paused to sip from a glass of water, "But I did see a woman, not much more than a girl,

189

arrive on a moped, or a scooter thing, the night before the murders. She was very late, after midnight, but I like to watch films until about one, so I was here in the front room. The curtains were open, and as it's been so hot at night the windows are all on the vent, so I can see right out into the street."

Dove shot a glance across from the sofa to the window. It was true, the houses were directly opposite one another. "Did you recognise the girl?"

"Not at the time, but in yesterday's paper I saw her picture." Serena tapped the newspaper and handed it to Dove.

Linked to the main feature on the murders at the Beach Escape Rooms was a piece on Mickey Delaney. The journalist had re-hashed the cold case, bringing up the fact she would have been in a coma for five years next month, adding one of the murder victims had been a suspect in Mickey's attack.

Dove rolled her eyes. Ellis Bravery had never officially been a suspect, just one of the many people questioned in connection with the incident. But the press liked the stretch the truth . . .

This was something the press had been gorging on ever since the identities were released, despite the fact that community engagement and support from the police appeal had initially been high. Below the inky paragraphs were photos, the largest and most poignant of which was captioned *Mickey and best friend Jenna celebrate a competition win, just weeks before the attack*.

The two girls were beaming for the camera, arms around each other, cheeks touching, holding up their medals. Dove looked up at Serena. "You mean the late-night visitor was this girl? Jenna Essex?"

The woman nodded. "Exactly that. Jenna . . . Essex? was at Caz's house. A very pretty girl and she doesn't look a day older than this photograph, even though I suppose she must be, what, eighteen or nineteen now? She seemed to be in a hurry — upset, I would say, and she was carrying a box, a small plastic box."

"Do you have any cameras outside your house?" Steve asked.

"No, but I'm getting one of those doorbell cameras fitted soon."

Dove assumed the street cam would have picked up Jenna's arrival. But perhaps she was a regular visitor. "Have you seen her before?"

"No, never. Caz seemed to have been expecting her because she was waiting with the door open." Serena paused. "But she didn't seem pleased to see her. Their voices were sharp, unhappy, I would say, although I couldn't hear any actual words. Jenna went inside and they talked in the front room. She was in there for maybe half an hour."

"Was Jamie at home?" Dove asked.

"I didn't see him. He often works late now they've got the little one. They do seem such a nice couple," she repeated. "The curtains were open, you understand, so I could see Jenna and Caz arguing about something, waving their arms around. Jenna had given her the box and she took something out and looked at it for a while." Serena took the glass of water from the table again and sipped reflectively. "Then she put her head in her hands and sat down. Jenna went and sat next to her. I could only see their heads, and I thought whatever had happened they must have sorted it out. But the arguing must have started again because when Jenna came out, she had the box and she was crying, sobbing I would say. She drove off far too fast, poor girl."

Dove glanced at Steve before she smiled at Serena. "Are you happy to make a statement just covering what you've told us?"

"Of course," Serena said. "Are you sure you won't stay for a cup of tea?"

Steve rang DI Lincoln and sent Serena's statement to both DIs and DCI Franklin, while Dove leaned against the car door, breathing in the slightly cooler air. The sudden storm had cleared the dusty heat, leaving a salty freshness blowing straight off the sea.

The post-storm breeze was blowing litter down the street, mingling with the stench of dustbins and drains wafted down from further up the hill. The houses, as usual for this part of town, had their doors painted in bright colours — red, green, blue and even a bubblegum pink. Tall, narrow terraces going on and on towards the horizon, stacking neatly upwards until the junction with Framer's Way.

Dove glanced at her watch. It was gone five now, and it felt as if they were still uncovering more questions than answers. Had Jenna kept in touch with her former best friend's brother?

Steve finished his call as Dove glimpsed Caz at the upstairs window of her house, peering down at them. But the woman moved quickly away when she saw the police officers were still outside.

"So what now? Are we bringing Caz in again?"

Steve shook his head. "No, we leave her until the lab gets results on the bonfire and the rest of the house search. George said to go and see Jenna Essex now, before we check in on Jamie's parents. We can try and find out if she's part of the bigger picture, or if this is another chase down a rabbit hole."

"I looked her up. She teaches at her mum's dance studio on one of the industrial estates. She has classes all evening, with a half-hour break at five thirty."

"You drive, and I'll do some more paperwork," Steve suggested.

"Deal." Dove slammed her door and drove off with the windows wide open, wind in her hair. A sideways glance showed her Steve was rolling his eyes as he tapped rapidly on his iPad.

The sound of dance music drifted out of the open windows as they pulled up outside the Essex Dance Academy. It was a large warehouse, now converted into individual studios, and according to the large pink sign, also housed KD Martial Arts and Kerry's Toddler Trampolining.

The stick-thin girl on reception was chewing gum, and she blew a large bubble with a snap of her glossy red lips before cheerfully directing them to Studio Four. "She's just finished a class but she usually grabs a smoothie from the kitchen and sets up for the under-tens now."

The smell of sweaty feet reminded Dove of changing rooms after football. For a while she had pursued the game fiercely, playing for her university, but her love of the sea had won out, and she now found gyms boring and changing rooms claustrophobic.

Steve pushed open the door to Studio Four, and Dove saw a tall, slim, blonde girl arranging mats and benches. She looked up and smiled. She had the kind of icy teenage prettiness that sometimes comes with a heart-shaped face and candy-cute smile. Dove thought back to the photograph in the paper. Mickey's curly hair, big generous smile and snub nose contrasted with Jenna's slick perfection. A perfect match.

"Sorry to disturb you. DS Steve Parker and DC Dove Milson from the Major Crimes Team. Do you mind if we have a quick chat?"

Her professional smile faded into a blank stare, and she dropped the heavy blue mat she was holding. "Do I get a choice? Are you arresting me?"

"You are welcome to come down to the station with us if you prefer," Steve said cheerfully. "You aren't under arrest or anything. We're just pursuing our enquiries regarding the murders of Ellis Bravery, Dionne Radley, Aileen Jackson and Oscar Wilding."

"Who are they? I don't know anything about that," Jenna said, moistening her lips, and reaching for a smoothie in a plastic cup. She took a gulp and then chewed at the straw, watching them sideways under her lashes, her whole body tense.

"Jenna, can you tell us about Mickey Delaney?" Dove asked gently.

Jenna's look of surprise told them straight away she had not been expecting this, but she hastened to answer the question, words tumbling over one another in apparent relief. "She was my best friend, still is even though . . . well, she just is. Mickey was super-talented but sweet with it, you know?"

"Did it ever cause trouble with her teammates that she was so talented?" Dove asked casually. She had planned to try a different line of questioning, but decided to get the girl talking first. Steve sat down on one of the benches, stretching his long legs out, the glint in his eyes showing her he knew exactly what she was doing.

"Oh, people were jealous because I think she was probably the best of everyone." Jenna sighed. Leaning against the wall of the dance studio, long blonde hair piled on top of her head, dressed in a neon orange cropped T-shirt and shorts, she didn't look a day older than fifteen. But her eyes told a different story. Dove noticed whenever Mickey's name was mentioned she withdrew a little, dropping her gaze to her bare feet.

"Jenna, we do appreciate how awful it must be for Mickey's family and friends, especially Jamie and Caz, but we are trying to solve a multiple murder case," Dove said carefully.

"I always felt so guilty I didn't go with Mickey that night," Jenna said suddenly. "She was tired after the competition and sometimes we would both go down to the quarry and sit and talk. It was . . . peaceful down there." She looked up at Dove, her eyes filled with tears. "Everyone knew we used to go down there after a competition, so I guess that's another reason why everyone tried to blame me, to say I did it . . ."

"But surely everyone seems to have pinned the blame on Ellis Bravery? Jamie was certainly under the impression he was responsible, wasn't he?" Steve put in.

"Jamie was a classic older brother," Jenna explained. "He was very proud of her, and I know he also felt like he had failed her. In his eyes, she was a kid, and he was all grown up, so he thought the one time she needed him, he should have been by her side." She sniffed and wiped her eyes on her sleeve.

"And Ellis Bravery? You mentioned in your original statement you had seen him watching your group a few times . . ."

Jenna screwed up her nose. "I didn't take any notice, really. Hell, Mickey's dad used to give me that look occasionally, like when a bloke fancies you. At fourteen, I thought I was it, you know, and I'm sure I was a bit of a brat." She smiled sadly. "Mickey used to say we were both gymnastics brats."

Dove didn't get how the word brat was an endearment, but the memory seemed to please Jenna. "So you never felt Ellis was a threat?"

"No, I told the police back then. Jamie was convinced he'd done it because apparently Mickey had told him she'd seen him watching her in the garden."

Time to switch subjects. "Do you keep in touch with Jamie? With Caz?"

There was no mistaking Jenna's fear now. Her face paled. Her features suddenly seemed not pretty at all, but too pointed and sharp, and she was breathing fast. "I . . . Not really, no. They went travelling, but I still visit Mickey at the hospital, so I sometimes see them . . ."

"Have you visited their house recently?" Steve prodded.

"I . . ." Again the hesitation, as though she was weighing up options. "Yes, I did . . . I went to see Caz last week."

Dove flicked through the pages of her notebook. "When was this?"

"Um . . . the twenty-fourth, I guess . . . I went after I closed up here. I had a few late classes and then . . ." She put a hand to her chest and breathed deeply.

"It's okay, just tell us what happened," Dove said softly.

"Well, I'm moving out of my mum's place, into a rental flat of my own near the river. I was packing up boxes and you know, junk and stuff you keep for no reason." Her gaze was far away now, a half-smile on her face. "I found lots of Mickey's stuff. Presents she gave me, photos we had printed out for our bedroom walls, prizes and trophies we won as a duo." Her eyes filled with tears. "She always told me to keep them. Mickey knew my mum . . ." Jenna lowered her voice and flicked a glance towards the door. "My mum wanted me to win so much."

Steve smiled encouragingly at her. "My mum was like that with my sister and her acting — a proper stage-door mum!"

Jenna smiled weakly and continued. "She doesn't really want me to move out . . . But anyway that night I found . . . some other photos of Mickey and I thought Caz and Jamie might like them."

"So you popped over and gave them to Caz?" Steve suggested.

"Yes! I know it was late, but Caz has been up with the baby most nights. We, um . . . text sometimes."

"Was Jamie there when you visited?"

"No, Caz said he was working, but we arranged I should take the pictures over and she would show him the next day."

"What were the photos of?" Dove asked casually.

"Oh, nothing special, just some from us messing in the woods, by the quarry where we used to hang out after school . . . There were a few extra competition ones from our coach. I just thought they would like to have them . . ." Her voice trailed off again, before noise from the corridor outside made her snap back to the present. She squared her shoulders, blue eyes steady and hard now. "I really need to get on now, sorry."

The door opened, and two small girls dressed in leotards appeared. A woman in gym gear called over to Jenna. "Do you want me to get this lot started on the warm-up, if you're busy?" Her stare was curious.

"Yes, please, Angie."

There was a babble of voices and laughter as a group of kids were ushered past into the connecting studio by the other teacher, ponytails flying, faces bright with fun and exercise.

Jenna watched the kids go. "Just one thing I want to say before you go. Ellis Bravery killed Mickey. Everyone knows he finally caught up with her, and he attacked her."

"That's certainly what Jamie thought, isn't it?" Steve said.

She shot him a quick look and fidgeted with her phone in its pink sparkly cover, turning it around and around with shaking hands. "We all did."

Dove smiled reassuringly at her. "You aren't going to get into trouble, and we are not working on Mickey's case. We are working on a separate investigation that has links to Jamie Delaney and Ellis Bravery."

Jenna's face changed, her voice all at once passionate and filled with pain. "The filthy perv. My mum told me he looked at porn and the police once arrested him for it, but he got off."

"That wasn't exactly what happened," Steve commented mildly.

"No? Everyone knew about it. He was always spying on us from behind the hedge, or walking that ratty dog of his when we were playing up on the waste ground. I told the police all of this, and how Mickey said he watched her all the time . . . And my nan said he never had a proper job, was just creeping around like a loser. He was a right weirdo!"

Dove felt it was interesting how Jenna's mood seemed to have changed. Earlier in the conversation she had almost dismissed Ellis Bravery, and now, suddenly she was determined to pin Mickey's attack on him? It was almost like she had just remembered her lines . . . a bad actress who had dropped out of character and was desperate to regain the confidence of her audience.

"There was no evidence to show Ellis was even in the woods at the time Mickey died. You must know that. It would have been made clear at the time. He had an alibi, and even though he may have been cast as the perpetrator by your friends and family, we deal in facts. Ellis Bravery was not in Salthaven at the time of Mickey's attack," Dove said firmly. Jenna's account now echoed Caz's so neatly they might have been planned. Why *was* everyone so sure Ellis was guilty? "So unless one of you has rock solid evidence against Mr Bravery that you aren't sharing for some reason . . ."

"No! Of course not. It was just . . . Jamie said his alibi was a load of crap because his car was caught on the motor-way cameras, but anyone could have been driving." Jenna was getting agitated. "He was the only person who could have attacked Mickey."

"You were investigated too, weren't you?" Steve said casually, tapping a few notes into his iPad.

Surprisingly, Jenna laughed, but the sound was shrill and painful. "It was so wrong it was funny. We were crazy with worry about Mickey, and the police were asking if I hated her enough to beat her up and push her over the edge of the quarry. I was the last person to have seen her alive, and yes, I knew my mum was going to be mad because Mickey had been chosen to represent our area instead of me, but that's life. Things that matter so much when you're fourteen don't matter at all when you're older, do they?" Her voice softened. "I love Mickey, I would never hurt her."

"And Jamie never thought it was you?" Dove queried.

Jenna stared at her. "Of course not, nor her mum and dad." She was shaking with emotion and dropped the empty smoothie cup. Steve bent down to retrieve it for her.

"Do you really think Jamie killed Ellis and the others?" Jenna asked now. "Because I don't think he would do that." It sounded lame and mechanical, as though she felt she needed to add this into the conversation, or perhaps had been told to.

"And you haven't had any contact with Jamie recently?" Dove asked.

"No! I already told you. Why don't you go and catch whoever really did this and leave Mickey and Jamie alone?" Jenna stared at them defiantly.

"We are pursuing all leads at the moment," Steve told her gently. "You've been very helpful."

"I went to visit Mickey last week." Jenna had picked up the mat and turned to go, but seemed suddenly reluctant to leave the conversation. "I try and go every week and I just sit and talk or play music. I wonder what she would be like now, at eighteen, what kind of person she would have become . . . I think she would have got her Olympic gold, because for the rest of us it was just a dream. She was the only one who could have done it for real." Tears were spilling from her blue eyes now, leaving wet trails on her cheeks, and she scrubbed at them with her fingers. "Sorry."

"It's okay. If you do want to talk to us about anything at all, just call, okay?" Dove said, passing her a card. "Ring any time at all."

Jenna hesitated, opened her mouth as though to say something else, but instead gathered up her phone, and headed swiftly towards the laughter and the running feet without a backward glance.

CHAPTER THIRTY-FIVE

The rush-hour traffic slowed their progress back to the station for the evening briefing, and Dove, still the driver while Steve updated their notes, drummed her fingers on the wheel as they queued at the roadworks. "She's lying with that bullshit story about memorabilia. What could she possibly have taken over to Ship Street at that time of night?"

"Of course she is, but what if it wasn't just memorabilia. What if Jenna Essex found something in her old photos that showed Ellis Bravery, defying all odds and a solid alibi, did attack Mickey?"

Dove considered this, ignoring the driver to her left who flicked a V-sign even though it was her right of way. "Wanker," she muttered.

"Thanks."

She grinned at Steve, but her voice was sober. "Why not tell us, then, if that was the case? She seemed pretty certain Bravery was behind the attack, but even if she found evidence, and showed it to Caz who showed it to Jamie, how could they possibly have known the man himself would walk on to the pier as a client the very next evening?"

"No idea. The second problem is, as you just pointed out, why didn't she give us the evidence, if that's what it was?

All three, Jenna, Caz and Jamie seem to be so very sure it was Ellis Bravery who beat Mickey and pushed her into the quarry, and are quick to say the police investigation fucked everything up, but none of them have volunteered why. Maybe we need to ask all three why they are so very sure about this, and if, just maybe, they took matters into their own hands, taking out Ellis Bravery on home turf?" Steve suggested, as they finally reached the roundabout.

"Let's just stop by and rattle Caz's cage on the way to the station," Dove suggested.

"Why?"

"Just a thought."

After a quick detour, and turning left down Penny Lane, Steve obligingly waited outside while Dove ran across the road to Caz's and Jamie's house. She was grudgingly admitted and cursed her spontaneity when she saw Caz had company. Another mum and baby were sitting on the sofa.

"I just wanted to give you a quick update on how the investigation is going."

"I don't know what you're implying," Caz said, after Dove had told her a few select details. She shifted her sleeping baby to the other arm, casting a quick, anxious glance at the little face. But Lila remained fast asleep. "You're acting like Jamie and I are guilty, when you should be finding out who killed these people."

The other woman, who had been introduced as Emma, smiled supportively, if a little smugly. Her own baby was wide awake and sucking at a toy, held on her lap. "Caz told me what happened. I think it's shocking. I don't know why you haven't solved the case already. The police round here have always been shit."

Dove grimaced politely at her and silently wished she could boot mother and child out through the open back door. "There are several issues, as you know, Caz. The first being that both you and Jamie lied in your initial statements to us."

"We have to make money somehow, and this was a perfectly legitimate business transaction," Caz shot back.

"Then why lie about it?" Dove queried.

"Because we knew how it would look. Fantasy Play isn't something everyone would understand. I mean, these people are desperate and usually a bit pissed when they turn up," Caz explained.

"Desperate?"

"You know . . . To have to go on some hook-up site to find someone to have sex with. Jeez, if you want it, you just walk out and get it round here. There's enough bars and clubs around," Caz said, disdain seeping into her words.

Emma's eyes were enormous, and she was clearly drinking in every word, but Caz didn't seem to mind her friend hearing about Fantasy Play. Either that or she simply didn't care anymore.

Interesting, Dove thought. She spoke slowly and calmly. "Our issue at the moment is firstly that you both lied, and secondly you must see it seems a huge coincidence that Ellis Bravery happened to be one of the victims, given his historical connection with Jamie's family."

"Your colleague already said all this. Like we don't know, for Christ's sake." Caz scowled at Dove and opened her mouth to make another comment, but the baby woke up and started crying. "Just go, and get on with finding the real murderer, if there even is one. Maybe, like I told you, they did this to themselves."

As Emma's baby started crying too, Dove made a hasty exit. Steve had taken the wheel while she was inside. She slid into the passenger seat, shaking her head at his look of enquiry.

"Told you it was a waste of time. She wears the trousers in that relationship and she hates us," Steve said.

"Why do some people just hate us on principle?" Dove sighed, rummaging in her pocket for a snack.

"Do you really want an answer to that?"

"No, it would take all night and we've got visits to tick off." Dove tore open a packet of jelly sweets, tipping half into her mouth in one go, relishing the hit of sugar on her tongue. "Let's stop at McDonald's on the way through and grab a burger. We've got an hour."

Obligingly, Steve turned into Penny Lane, which took them through the one-way system and spat them out opposite North Point Hotel. "I was just thinking about Billy Jackson again . . . What if the Fantasy Play site was hacked? What if the victims' burn phones were hacked and somebody was tracking their movements?"

"I don't see Billy as a hacker," Dove said thoughtfully. "I agree he's still vaguely in the frame, though. Let's check in on the forensics on his electronic devices."

"I'll call Cybercrimes when we get back," Steve agreed.

They drove in silence for a moment before Dove said, "Hey, you know what I really want to do?"

"Visit Mickey Delaney." Steve looked at her.

"How did you know?"

"It's obvious you've got something else going on in the background, and this case has stung you, stirred something up," Steve explained.

Stung me. Dove sighed, and told Steve about the gymnast who had been at Ari's Bar around the same time Mickey had suffered her near-fatal fall. "It just got me right in the heart too. You know how some cases are. They stick with you and don't let you . . ."

"What happened to your prostitute?"

She shrugged. "She was tortured and murdered because they thought she was an informant."

"Shit."

"Exactly."

* * *

Greenview Hospital was on the outskirts of the town, a specialist facility mainly dealing with rehabilitation for patients recovering from strokes and head injuries.

Steve and Dove introduced themselves and were led down the cool, clean corridors to Mickey's room by a grey-haired consultant, wearing scarlet lipstick.

Dove stared down at the girl, looking so peaceful in her white sheets. She could have been asleep. *She is asleep*, she thought, but it was the deepest sleep anyone could imagine.

The fiery energy that had translated into her gymnastic performances had gone, and her face was closed, pale and blank, wiped clean by the injury to her body and brain, by the drugs and machines keeping her alive.

The room smelled faintly of lemons, and Dove noticed a candle on the window sill.

"Will she wake up?" Steve asked Mickey's consultant, as they concluded their visit with a quick chat in her bland, clinical office.

"It's hard to say. She is one of the exceptions in that we have detected very distinct patterns of brain activity, but after nearly five years, it would be a miracle."

"She yawned when we were in there," Dove said.

"Yes, that is perfectly normal for many coma patients. They sleep and wake as normal, but the waking stage is never what you would call waking. That is to say they are not in any way conscious or alert. But we know from other cases that people in comas do hear, and are often responsive to touch and hot and cold." She smiled. "It depends a lot on which part of the brain is damaged. For example if the visual cortex is badly damaged, visual dreams will be lost, and so on."

"So she might be able to understand what's happened to her?" Steve asked.

"Very unlikely, but I have read of patients experiencing a dream-like state while in a coma. Mickey has been with us here for three years now, and we are rather protective of her. Journalists often try to gain access, but the visitor list is short and security is maintained throughout the whole facility."

"Could we see the visitor list before we go, please?" Dove asked.

"Of course." The consultant printed off a sheet of paper. "Her parents, of course. Initially Caz, who I understand is her sister-in-law now. She doesn't visit very often. Her brother, Jamie, and her best friend, Jenna. Jenna comes every week, sometimes very late in the evening, but it seems to help her grieve for her friend, being with her, and hopefully it is helping Mickey."

"Do you think Mickey is aware of who visits her?" Steve pondered, studying a diagram of the brain on the wall.

"It's hard to say, but her brain activity indicates she does know on some level, even if it is just that she is able to register a familiar presence. We try our best for our patients, but you must understand the brain, even at full health, is very complex. There are some injuries we simply cannot fix."

* * *

Back at the station, Dove and Steve sorted through the statements in silence, updating their own paperwork, adding it to the online file system, emailing copies of relevant information to individuals. It was tedious but essential work.

"Feels like we're doing more on a cold case than on the actual investigation," Steve grumbled, yawning.

Lindsey heard him and called over, "Don't whinge, Parker. At least you've got some leads. All we've got are the poor spouses, who had no idea what their other halves were into in the evenings. It's such a crap thing to have to deal with: the grieving process, as well as the betrayal that comes with the discovery the victim had a whole other part of their life you knew nothing about."

Lindsey wasn't often sincere, preferring to hide behind sarcasm and briskness, so Dove could tell the case was getting to her.

By the time they got into the evening briefing, Dove was also feeling shattered, her head spinning and her injury throbbing. She touched the side of her head with gentle exploratory fingers before she saw Steve looking at her with concern and hastily dropped her hand.

DCI Franklin kicked off with a quick summary before he handed over to DI Blackman. DI Lincoln was still in the main office, talking urgently into his phone. He looked the most energetic Dove had ever seen him.

"We're just waiting on last results from the lab on the house search, but I'll start with well done for all your hard work." DI Blackman smiled round the room. "Jamie Delaney is still with us at the station, and we have a new statement from him. Caz Liffey has also as a consequence revised her initial statement. Both are claiming they did have the four murder victims as clients, but swear they were sent merrily on their way after an hour in Escape Room Six. There is no evidence to suggest any of them left the pier in between their initial visit and their deaths."

He looked down at his notes and clicked to bring an image up on screen. "This is footage showing someone swimming under the pier towards the outflow pipe of Escape Room Six on the night in question. As you can see, it isn't possible to ID who this was. Both Caz and Jamie were by their own admission up on the pier during this time."

DI Lincoln joined them, flushed and slightly sweaty, and DI Blackman immediately paused and nodded at him.

"Results from the house search. The bonfire in the backyard showed traces of a wetsuit and diving gloves, presumed to belong to Caz Liffey as hers are missing from both the house and office premises. We also recovered smashed glass from the recycling bin, which shows DNA matches to all four victims and, when examined closely, is the remains of a litre bottle of Smirnoff vodka and four shot glasses."

"Excellent," DCI Franklin said, as a murmur of approval and relief spread around the room. "So we now have additional evidence to nail Jamie and Caz."

"I think we have enough to arrest both of them!" DI Lincoln said.

"Jenna Essex definitely knows more than she's letting on, " Dove piped up, "and she was close to telling us more when we spoke to her today. Her excuse for visiting Caz was old photographs. What if she found evidence Bravery was responsible for Mickey's attack, and took it straight over to Ship Street? By her own and Caz's admissions, they hardly saw each other in the five years Mickey has been in a coma.

Why reach out now? Steve and I could bring her in for interview tomorrow to try and tie up loose ends."

"Are you two still going to talk to Jamie's parents?"

Steve nodded. "They're both home from work at seven, so we're going straight over now."

* * *

Dove slammed the car door— twice — so it actually closed properly, and followed Steve towards the houses. These were on the very edge of a large sprawling estate. She could see washing still fluttering on a line, an elderly man walking a dog, and a few teenagers gathered around a rusting white van with one wheel jacked up. There was wasteland to the right, grass dried yellow in the summer heat. Beyond that were the woods, and further to the west, the old quarry where Mickey's body had been found.

The aftermath of the earlier rainstorm lingered, lending a chill to the breeze. But the clouds were now thin, ragged streamers across the evening sky, promising the return of fine weather. In her thin shirtsleeves, Dove shivered. "I wonder why the parents didn't move?"

She turned to look in the direction of the woods. A group of kids were playing on a rusty old swing set, screaming with laughter as they swung on the ominously creaking metalwork. More kids were kicking a ball around near the hedge.

"I've seen it before. Either the family starts again somewhere new, or stays right where they have memories to keep alive," Steve said. "Come on, let's get this done. I'm starving and I was hoping to get back to do Grace's bath time tonight."

They stepped straight off the road into the front garden, and Dove noted the tall grass gone to seed, dandelion clocks nodding in the breeze. A rambler rose hung in long straggly loops from a rotting trellis. To the right of the front door, next to the hedge that divided the property from next door, was a shallow depression, the grass a different colour. Maybe a previous pond or perhaps a shed had stood there, she supposed, as Steve knocked briskly.

Minutes later, Dove could see Steve had been correct in his assumptions. Claire's and Russ's home was like a shrine to their daughter. In the living room, where they were offered tea and chocolate biscuits, one wall and almost every surface was covered in framed photographs of Mickey. Only in one corner of the mantel could Dove see any pictures of Jamie and his new family.

Shelves loaded with trophies added to the claustrophobic feel in the small room. Piles of newspapers and magazines surrounded the sofa. Peering into the kitchen area, Dove could see similar piles of recipe books, kitchen appliances and other clutter.

Steve politely took a biscuit and smiled at the nervous pair. "As I said on the phone, we'd just like you to take us through the events leading up to Mickey's attack." He paused, but the couple made no move to talk. "We appreciate this is very difficult for you, but it would be helpful in our current investigation."

Russ leaned forward, hands planted on his knees. His hair must once have been as red as his children's but now all that remained was a few grey wisps, and shaggy white eyebrows, flecked with ginger. "Jamie called us, of course."

"Of course," Dove nodded. "Then you'll know Jamie is also helping us with our investigation."

Claire spoke for the first time. She was hunched into an oversized pastel pink sweater with *KL Gym* inscribed across the front. Like her husband, her face looked older than her actual age, grief and loss scrawling harsh lines around her hazel eyes and drooping mouth. Dove could see from the photographs that her daughter, Mickey, had been her double. The snub-nosed, vivacious face, petite slender frame and rosebud mouth looked triumphantly down from the wall right behind the sofa, now a devastating contrast to her mother. "Jamie said Ellis Bravery was killed . . . But I don't understand." She glanced at her husband, and he took her hand, gently squeezing her fingers. "We don't understand why he would be at the escape rooms . . . Jamie's business. Was he threatening Jamie or something? There was some stuff about planning and permits when they first put in for permission, but I thought that was all sorted out . . ."

"That's one of the things we are trying to find out," Dove said. "Ellis Bravery was interviewed in connection with Mickey's death, wasn't he?"

"It was just routine because he was our neighbour. Everyone along this stretch of road gave statements, and all the kids who'd been playing on the waste ground," Russ said, rubbing his forehead with a pinched finger and thumb. "The gymnastics coach, Hawthorn, and Mickey's best friend, Jenna, seemed to be the main suspects. They were questioned again and again, and Hawthorn was actually arrested, but nothing ever came of it. Not enough evidence, the police said."

"In the end Ellis Bravery had an alibi for when Mickey was in the woods," Claire added. "The forestry workers heard a scream at half past eight, but by the time they got up to the quarry and found her . . . They never heard or saw anyone else."

"Any idea why Jamie is so absolutely sure Ellis was responsible?" Steve asked.

"There were rumours he had been involved in some child-porn ring at work, with another man. Initially we were worried, living next door with kids, but Ellis was never anything but polite and reserved."

"Jamie didn't like him," Claire said strongly, "and the kids all said he was watching them . . . I think he was just a bit of an oddball."

"We never saw any of it, and he was never funny with any of them that we saw," Russ said wearily. "We've given up being angry. It does no good. It won't bring Mickey back."

"I'm sorry," Dove said, flicking a glance at Steve.

"It wasn't your fault. You weren't there." Claire reached for her mug of tea, but instead of drinking she simply cradled the warm mug in her hands, tired eyes fixed on Dove's. "For a while after it happened we wondered if Ellis had fooled us all, but he had an alibi. Every year on the anniversary, we ask the police to reopen Mickey's case. It can't bring her back, but it would give us peace and closure to know who did it, to see justice done."

Dove's heart hurt for them, these sad, quiet parents who seemed to have lost the fight and fire they must have had. Budget cuts would have had a hand in refusing to reopen a cold case, but she guessed there had also been no new evidence linking Ellis to Mickey. Circumstantial simply didn't cut it.

"How did Jamie cope after Mickey's attack?" Steve asked.

"Badly, of course," Russ answered. "He adored his sister. He was the one who taught her to jump from the bars, to walk along the wall on the waste ground like it was a balance beam. We reckon that was what started all the gymnastics."

He was smiling fondly now, eyes distant as he recalled happier memories. "Jamie was so sure Ellis had hurt Mickey, and he used to rage and shout at the police when they came. He used to make diagrams of how Ellis could have driven back here to intercept Mickey. There was a very bad patch when he ran into Ellis one night, and threw a punch at him. Luckily Ellis never pressed charges, and Jamie agreed to get some counselling. Although I don't think he ever did . . ."

"He went travelling after he left school, and was away for a few years," Claire put in. "It seemed to help him come to terms with Mickey's attack, but he drifted between jobs until he became a diving instructor. Jamie has always . . ." She paused, as though trying to find the words. "Jamie has a very definite idea of things and once he gets an idea into his head as far as he is concerned that is what happened."

"And it was like that with Mickey's attack?" Steve asked.

Claire nodded, "We asked and asked the kids if they had any more evidence it was Ellis, but nobody had. It didn't matter to Jamie. It was like he was blind to any other suggestions."

"And he started a relationship with Caz while they were away travelling?" Dove said. She had been slowly letting her gaze drift around the room when she could, and so far had only clocked two photographs of Jamie. While Mickey, the shining star, the golden girl, leaped and stretched and posed around the walls, every picture a testimony to her brilliance. The two images of her brother were both school-photo headshots.

"Yes. Caz is a lovely girl, and they've known each other since they were kids. We were very happy when they opened the Beach Escape Rooms and had Lila. He seems to have settled down at last. He and Mickey were so close, despite the age gap . . ." Claire stopped abruptly, as though returning from her memories into a hostile and harsh reality.

"Where was Jamie when Mickey died?" Steve asked. "You said he blamed himself for not protecting her."

Russ rolled his eyes. "No more than I do. I was at the roadside strimming the verge, and saw Mickey walk off with Jenna." He paused, seeming to gather his thoughts before he could continue. "Jamie was playing football with his friends. They'd set up a pitch on the other side of the waste ground. Twenty or thirty of them used to gather there for matches every other night in the holidays."

"It was like one big party," Claire said. "Jamie has always blamed himself for not being with Mickey to protect her that evening. But I brought her home from a competition at eight, and she went off with Jenna to meet up with their usual group. Jenna said they went down the path that leads along the side of the woods." Claire took a deep breath, as though her thoughts were troubling her. "There's a big hedge of brambles and scrub. Jenna said they could hear the football match and she wanted to join the crowd, but Mickey said she was tired and she needed to be alone to go through the competition in her head."

Both her parents looked exhausted, Dove thought. They looked like they had been tired for a long time, and they must have been through the events before and after Mickey's death so many times.

"Has Jamie kept in touch with Jenna over the years?" Dove asked.

"I don't think so," Claire answered, looking doubtfully at her husband, who shook his head.

"No, he and Caz haven't had any contact with Jenna," Russ said firmly.

Dove glanced at Steve and saw he was thinking the same thing. Had Jamie or Caz warned them not to say anything about Jenna's late-night visit to Ship Street, or had Jamie not actually shared this with his parents?

"You must have read the reports, so you know who the suspects were," Russ said suddenly. "Are we helping Jamie by answering your questions, or are you trying to pin Bravery's murder on him?"

Steve shook his head. "We are following all lines of enquiry and at the moment nobody is accusing Jamie of anything, Mr Delaney. Three other people died on the twenty-fifth."

"I think . . ." Claire spoke with an effort. "I think it must be a coincidence that Ellis and his friends broke into Jamie's business, or perhaps they were drunk and intended to cause some damage . . ." She seemed to be aware how lame her words sounded, because she trailed off, still clinging to her untouched tea mug.

"Did Jenna Essex keep in touch with you?" Dove asked.

"Not really," Claire said. "She thought we blamed her, but we didn't. Mickey often went off on her own to clear her head. Jenna loved Mickey, despite their differences."

Russ swallowed hard and added, "Jenna visits Mickey every week at the hospital, sometimes more, and she stays for an hour or so, talks to her, sometimes sleeps in the chair next to Mickey's bed, holding her hand. I don't think there is anything else we can tell you that hasn't already been covered a thousand times."

"Thank you for your time." Dove stood up, closing her notebook. Steve did the same.

Claire showed them to the door. Suddenly she grabbed Dove's arm, her eyes desperate and pain-filled. "Please,

Detective, please find out what happened to Mickey. It's killing us, not knowing the truth."

Dove covered the woman's cold hand with her own warm fingers, a rush of sympathy strengthening her resolve. But her training led her to be cautious. No false promises. "Claire, if we can find out who is responsible during the course of our investigation, we will."

The woman nodded, slowly removed her hand and stepped back, the sudden energy and fire dying, shoulders hunching again as she opened the front door for them.

As they stepped out into the golden evening, Dove could see kids playing with a skipping rope on the waste ground, could hear their chant:

Down in the field where the summer grass grows,
There sat Janey
Sweet as a rose,
Along came Johnny
And kissed her on the cheek.
How many kisses
Did she get this week?
1, 2, 3, 4, 5, 6!

CHAPTER THIRTY-SIX

He should have gone right away, straight after Mickey's attack, after all the press interest. Someone must have leaked his past to the press, because we had reporters asking us if we thought he'd done it, read stories speculating the whole investigation was being blundered because the police didn't have enough officers to do it properly . . .

Each new article was like a fresh wound in my heart, and I know my parents felt exactly the same. "Not guilty, my arse!" Dad shouted, when the police told us Ellis had an alibi.

I was surprised it took him a few months to leave, but the For Sale *sign on his house was nothing but a relief to my parents. One of my mates got a job in a nursing home after school and he told me how Ellis would never come in and see his nan now, but everyone knew who she was.*

Ellis Bravery did a pretty good job of vanishing, and a pretty good job of reinventing himself, I'll give him that. From neighbourhood freak to loaded entrepreneur. Quite a journey.

Me and Jenna hooked up one night. I'm not sure what she was thinking, but she looked so sad, kept crying all the time. I told her I never believed she had anything to do with Mickey's death, got her drunk and slept with her. It was a one-time thing, both of us looking for comfort in the wrong places, I guess, and she crept out the next morning without waking me.

I suppose she was also terrified of what her mum would say, always scared of displeasing the dragon matriarch.

Caz and I had a bit of a thing going, but despite being such a support to me, we drifted apart, and she started seeing someone else. It didn't bother me. I went travelling straight after that, drifted through Europe, backpacked around Asia and wondered if I could settle somewhere where Mickey wasn't. Sometimes I swear I saw her, dancing on the sand on some remote beach, smiling down at me from a jagged clifftop, or I could conjure her face in the deep blue of the oceans I dived in.

There were a few times when I thought Mickey was actually back with me, and I had been wrong about everything. A girl was murdered on the beach near one of the backpacking hostels in Palawan, in the Philippines. We had been travelling in separate groups, but I had seen her around, talked to her, made her laugh on the ferry to El Nido. She had long red hair, and a laugh like Mickey's.

But one morning the police were on the beach and her photograph was everywhere, just like my sister's had been. Everyone was crying and I found myself sobbing, really sobbing at the candlelit vigil someone organised the next evening in her memory. I can't even remember the girl's name now, but I know she was special. I couldn't cry when I heard about Mickey, but this time I let my pain out in front of strangers.

Ellis stayed in my thoughts, but I was learning to let go, learning to live without my sister's presence in my life. By the time I met Caz again, I was still scarred, but at the same time as healed as I ever would be.

She wanted to come back to the UK, not me, but I didn't feel the same hatred for home as I once had, and Mickey haunted me less and less. My parents were happy to see us, and when we started the business just a few miles down the coast and Caz got pregnant, they almost seemed excited for us.

My mum even moved a few of Mickey's pictures and put up several of me, my family, and my baby. I felt Mickey was watching over us from her gallery in the living room.

And then I saw him again in the street. When he came into the escape rooms, my place, laughing with his sordid friends, dressed in an expensive suit and shoes, I couldn't stop myself.

The others went ahead, and he lingered a little, staring at me. That was when I said it, when I accused him outright of attacking Mickey, asked him how he could live with what he had done.

But this was five years on, and he didn't take it so well. He had power now, and I'd misjudged him, driven by my own rage and righteousness.

He leaned in close, eyes wary but disdainful. "Jamie, I think we both know exactly what happened that night. I let it go previously, but if you stir things up, well, who knows what might happen to you . . . and to your brand-new business venture. I have seen things, heard things, and as you probably knew back then, I was a watcher. Now I'm a player, so don't screw with me, Jamie. Don't even think about it."

He smirked, knowing he'd wrong-footed me, knowing the balance of power had shifted. I didn't say a word, but I could feel the rage and terror building in my chest, so I almost struggled to breathe. He took everything away once, and now thought he could do it again?

"I told the police about your hide in the woods, that you took photographs of us all," I blurted out, hating the fact my voice sounded childish and unsure.

"Jamie, a word of advice. Let this go or you will only damage yourself. Police only work on facts, on evidence, and if you have none of that, they can't act. Whatever you may have thought you saw, it was gone by the time they arrived, and to spell it out, I most definitely saw more than you did."

He smiled. Perfect unnaturally white teeth, strong cologne wafting from his hot body as he slipped off his suit jacket. "And don't flatter yourself. I was only interested in the pretty girls. You boys did nothing for me."

He was a good few inches taller than me, which also pissed me off.

The others called to him then, and the good-looking woman in the sexy black dress asked if he would rather sit this one out. She was laughing. They all were. Laughing and excited.

It was then I knew I'd lied to myself when I was a skinny teenager. I wasn't sorry I had attacked Ellis. I was just sorry I hadn't killed him.

CHAPTER THIRTY-SEVEN

There was no way, Dove thought, as she walked into the plush marble-tiled lobby of California Dreams that evening, that she was ever going to be happy at the sight of her niece writhing around a pole in front of an audience.

Colin, the manager, was setting up goodie bags for tonight's corporate event. It never failed to surprise Dove how many big businesses felt a strip club constituted a fun night out for the staff, or even how, in this enlightened day and age, they got away with it.

But Gaia had branched out and now ran pole-dancing fitness classes in the mornings, hosted hen parties in the afternoons, and still managed to keep her regulars happy at night.

"How's she doing?" Colin asked now.

"Fine. As you probably know, she's driving the hospital staff mad, but the X-ray showed there was some water in her lungs, so she had to stay in."

Colin grinned. "That will be why she yelled at me when I asked if she was okay. I'm only doing texts from now on. She must be the world's worst patient, but I'm just so relieved she's okay. How can I help you, anyway?"

"Just popped in to pick up Delta. We've got a dinner date at her mum's place. Sorry, I thought she finished at seven." Dove jangled her car keys in one hand, keen to make a quick getaway.

"She was supposed to, but Poppy never showed," Colin sighed. "It's so tough to get reliable staff in this industry. Delta's filling in for half an hour, but if you want to wait at the bar, I'll go and shout into the dressing room to get her to hurry up as soon as she's off stage."

"Thanks, Colin." Reluctantly, Dove made her way across the floor, weaving her way around tables, and seated herself at the bar, legs crossed.

She ordered a Coke and tried not to feel so uncomfortable in Gaia's club. Ren had always said she would never willingly set foot in the place, especially now her daughter was actually employed there.

Several girls were working the floor, chatting to the customers, serving drinks, flirting and laughing. Dove caught sight of Delta pulling off a particularly raunchy move and turned hastily away, almost choking on her drink.

As she did so, her arm caught a girl walking past with two champagne glasses, and the glasses fell to the floor. "Oh, I'm so sorry," Dove apologised, leaping to her feet.

The girl tottered on her high heels and stared at her like a frightened deer. She was very pretty in a delicate, elfin, blonde kind of way, and she had a distinctive and intricate tattoo on her bare shoulder. Dove's photographic memory recalled Delta's screensaver. "Abi, hi."

The barman was already coming round with a dustpan and brush to clear up the mess, and he addressed a few amused and sarcastic remarks to Abi about her clumsiness.

Abi just stared at Dove, before she cleared her throat. "You're Delta's aunt."

"Dove Milson. Nice to meet you properly. Delta's always telling me about how the two of you are saving up to go travelling." Dove smiled at her, noticing to her relief that her niece had been replaced on stage by another girl.

"Yeah . . . Yeah, we are." Abi's face was so milk-white, Dove worried she was about to faint. The pale blue eyes, lined with masses of black eyeliner and mascara, seemed huge, and emphasised her fragility. "You're a police detective. Delta talks about you a lot too."

"Well, I'll let you get on then," Dove said, as Abi just stood there staring at her. The girl was the total opposite of the sparkly, mischievous character Delta had always portrayed. Maybe she was just having a bad day.

"Yeah . . . See you." Abi swung away in apparent relief, and something about the movement caught Dove's attention. A half memory, the face in profile . . .

Watching Abi picking up another tray, serving fresh glasses of champagne, Dove was sure. Faces and facts were her thing, she had discovered early on. Sometimes it took a while to place things, but today it took mere seconds for her to be fairly sure where she recognised the girl from.

Abi had been the second attacker in the car park, where Alex Harbor had suffered a few broken bones and loss of dignity. Dove watched her thoughtfully as she sipped her drink. It was more of an impression than a memory, but the girl moved distinctively, lightly, like the dancer she was. She exchanged a couple of words with a performer in red lace lingerie sitting on the smaller stage, tossing her hair to one side as the woman laughed at something.

Dove drained her glass and set it down with a little thump, thinking hard. If the second person was Abi, who was the man?

As Dove considered grabbing Abi for a chat, Delta came out of one of the side doors, dressed now in loose tracksuit bottoms and a cropped yoga top, her hair tied up in a ponytail, make-up washed off.

"Delta!" Colin paused on his way past them. "I've told you before not to come through here when you aren't dressed."

"I am dressed," Delta said, but she held out a placating hand. "Okay, sorry, I know. I just forgot, and Dove's been waiting for me."

Delta waved to Abi as they left the club, and the other girl, preoccupied with customers, smiled back half-heartedly, her eyes straying to Dove once again.

"It's great of you to give me a lift," Delta said, chucking her bag in Dove's car.

"No worries."

Her niece shot her a knowing sideways glance, dark blue eyes narrowing. "But it clearly wasn't to save me getting the bus in the boiling heat. I don't need another lecture on my job choice."

Dove pulled her sunglasses on and considered which topic to tackle first. It was only a fifteen-minute drive to Ren's place, and she needed to probe the subject of Abi without getting her niece involved. She decided to switch gears. "I imagine you still keep in touch with your friends from that online vigilante set-up . . ."

Delta pulled out a packet of salt-and-vinegar crisps from her bag and ripped it open. "You want information." She sounded pleased, as Dove had known she would.

"I do. Ellis Bravery. Does the name ring any bells?"

"One of the men who was murdered at the escape rooms? Nope, but I've seen the pictures in the paper. He's never come up on our hit list. I mean . . ." she corrected herself quickly, "historically, I mean."

"Right." Dove waited. "What about the website Fantasy Play?"

"Mmmm . . . I have heard of them." Delta licked sticky fingers and hooked around in her crisp packet for the last crumbs. "I'm starving, do you have any sweets?"

Dove pulled open the glove compartment, and Delta swiped a couple of packets of multicoloured jelly sweets.

"They started in 2018 as an online pay-to-watch outfit, but last year they began to organise local hook-ups." Delta looked over at her aunt as they navigated a busy roundabout. "You know this."

"I do, but carry on."

"Right. They were legit when they were online only, and had a strict moderator, but word is since they started bringing their fantasy play time out on to the streets, it's become a go-to for prostitutes and their pimps."

"So?"

"So it's not just sad people who want sex their partner doesn't know about. It's become a lure for actual pay-to-play," Delta explained. "The Nicholls brothers apparently have a business interest."

"Why would they go from legit to doing business with those bastards?" Dove wondered aloud. She wasn't entirely surprised, but it would make it harder to investigate. The Nicholls were a local crime family, notorious for evading arrest, with a whole nest of criminal lawyers who got them off charge after charge. They had both done time in prison, but it made no difference to their business interests. Their families ran things while they were put away, and as soon as they were out, they took up the reins again.

Delta made the 'money' sign, rubbing her fingers and thumb together. "Some people have got some weird fantasies. The harder it is to make happen, the more they'll pay. As we know," she added carefully, as always mindful that her own father was currently serving time for, among other things, running a paedophile ring with the once notorious Glass Dolls Killer.

Dove leaned over and squeezed her hand, sensing where her thoughts had gone, her heart wrenching at the sick legacy her former brother-in-law had left his daughters. "Hey, have you just eaten four packets?"

"They're very small packets," Delta informed her. "And I'm still hungry. Did you get to talk to Abi?"

Indicating the coast road, which should have been a shortcut to Ren's house but was currently rammed with tourist traffic, Dove took the conversational gambit smoothly. "Not really. She was in a hurry. I did think she was very unlike your descriptions, though."

Delta was biting her nails now, long hair falling forwards to hide her expression. "Yeah . . . Hey, look, I can see Mum in the garden."

Cursing the sudden gap in the traffic and the bad timing, Dove pulled up outside her sister's house and waved.

Her eldest niece, Eden, was playing with her son in a paddling pool by the roses. His delighted giggles and splashes made Dove smile as she opened the gate.

"Any more news on Gaia?" Ren asked, after she had hugged her daughter and sister.

"I rang her this morning, and she said they were going to let her out tomorrow, but I'm guessing you probably spoke to her more recently than that?" Dove said. The sun had come out properly again, but the sizzling heat of the past few weeks had passed, and a light breeze rustled through the hedge. The clouds were light and drifting briskly across the blueness.

"She's got another phone now. Colin brought it in for her, apparently. You know, she must be more shaken up than she admits, or she would have walked out by now," Ren said, worry creasing her forehead. Her mop of glossy black curls was tied up in a red headscarf, and she was wearing a forties-style white summer dress, which showed off her curves.

"I agree, but at least we can be sure she's on the mend. She said she'd already booked in with her hairdresser, and she was going back to short hair to sort out the mess her stitches have made." Dove smiled fondly. Gaia was always perfectly groomed. She must be going nuts in her regulation hospital gown with half her head shaved and no make-up.

"And Uri and Colin have got her back at the club," Dove commented. She hesitated, a memory of Abi flitting through her mind, and quickly changed the subject. "You look amazing. How do you always look so gorgeous?"

"Natural talent," Ren winked. "Don't be stupid, I've been trying to diet all summer, but you know how much I love trifles and white wine . . . and . . ."

"Ren, for God's sake, you don't need to lose weight." Dove rolled her eyes, and picked up a strawberry tart from the wooden table in the centre of the front garden. It was a perfect suntrap, even in late evening, with the high hedges creating enough shade to sprawl on blankets tossed on the grass.

Today, as the lawn and garden furniture were wet, Ren had brought out a few chairs from her kitchen. Dove sank down on to a red-and-white-check cushion and stretched her legs out, closing her eyes briefly. "God, I'm so tired."

"I feel a bit like that too," Ren admitted. "I think it must be the worry about Gaia. Worse for you because you were actually there . . ." There was a note of concern in her voice.

Dove managed to smile at her sister. "It's okay, honestly. Now we know she's fine and coming out of hospital, I think about it a whole lot less."

While Delta and Eden played with the little boy, sailing boats in his paddling pool and getting far wetter than they needed to, the older women caught up with family news.

"I can't believe it's still this warm at nine o'clock, especially after the rain earlier," Dove said, gulping down her iced juice.

"Mmmm . . . Do you know who attacked Gaia yet?" Ren asked, returning once again to the subject that was clearly foremost in both their minds.

"Not my case, as you know, but I am keeping an eye on it." Dove was wondering how soon she could get Delta for a quick chat, or whether she should just see DI Rankin in the morning. Delta had been about to say something before they arrived. Oh shit, on top of everything else she was going to have to explain to Rankin she *thought* she *might* have identified one of the Claw Beach suspects based on an impression. In the dark.

"And you had *your* head bashed in fairly recently," Ren prodded, leaning closer to Dove.

"Wrong place, wrong time," Dove reassured her. "It was a robbery and I walked in on it." She could see how Abi might be able to lure men into meeting her through her job at the club. Presumably her accomplice lay in wait and then provided the violent aspect. It was a classic move. And he would be what? A boyfriend? Pimp? Did Abi do drugs?

"I don't want any more hassle," Ren said now. "I've got my family and my business as my rock and I need to keep it that way."

Beneath her air of maternal confidence, her generous hugs and smiles, Dove always hurt for her sister because she

223

could detect traces of the scars left by her ex-husband. In this spirit, and because it was an ongoing police investigation, she didn't feel she could share any of what was currently on her mind. She hastily searched for less sensitive topics. "Quinn and I have set a date."

"You have?" Ren glowed.

"Next summer. Twenty-sixth of July, and we're going to have a church service . . ."

"You hate all that stuff, and you aren't even a tiny bit religious."

"I don't hate it, I just feel a bit weird that the only time I go to church is for weddings and funerals. It feels hypocritical," Dove explained.

"Where are you having the reception?"

"On the beach if the weather is good, but we'll book a conference room at the hotel too. The patio opens right on to the shingle, so if it's raining we can all stay dry and just look at the beach longingly," Dove said, grinning.

"Sounds perfect." Ren beamed and leaned over for another quick hug.

Dove tried to speak to Delta on the way home, but her niece determinedly changed the subject. It was dark when they parked on the side of the road, and the air was cool.

A red van was parked just behind Dove's usual spot, and she had to inch her car in. There was a footpath on the left, cutting between two houses, winding through the back of the fish market and down to the beach. High hedges sheltered the path and as Dove turned to say something to her niece, she saw Delta was staring down the footpath, frozen.

Before she could say anything else, a hooded figure erupted from the hedge, running fast. The figure nearly ran right into Delta, put out his arms to steady her, muttered an apology, and ran on, trainers thudding on the pavement.

"Are you okay?" Dove was next to Delta, pulling her round to face her. The girl's eyes were wide and terrified, but she recovered quickly, shaking off Dove's hand and trying to smile. "Of course. Sorry, just freaked me out. I didn't hear him coming."

"Did you know him?" Dove's own heart rate was slowing now, but she kept glancing after the runner. It had seemed like an accident, and nobody had been hurt. So why was Delta so shaken?

"No! Of course not, how could I? Come on, I'm knackered and I just want to get to sleep," Delta said, leading the way in.

Quinn had made up a bed for Delta on the sofa, and left an ancient, almost-bald teddy bear, a relic from his own youth, on the pillow. Dove smiled. "He's such a goofball."

"You love him, though," Delta said, dumping her bag and rummaging for toiletries. Toothbrush in hand, she turned towards the kitchen.

"Of course. Delta? I'm not trying to pry or anything, but you would tell me if there was something wrong, wouldn't you?" Even as the words came out, Dove knew it was a pathetic attempt to reassure herself.

"Yup, and I'm fine. I'll just grab some water and go to sleep." Delta smiled at her aunt. "Stop being a detective for like five seconds and go and have sex with your fiancé or something!"

"Delta!"

"What? I will tell you if I need help, okay?" Delta's voice was sharp with irritation, and she was scowling at her aunt.

"Okay, okay." Dove gave up and left her to it, wearily walking barefoot upstairs.

CHAPTER THIRTY-EIGHT

Quinn woke up as Dove was leaving the next morning, but Delta lay snoring in her nest on the sofa.

"How long is she staying?" Quinn asked, taking the mug of steaming coffee Dove passed him.

"Just a couple of days, she said." Dove sighed, pushing her hair out of her eyes and yawning. "Something's going on with her, and it isn't just her row with Ren." She told him of her suspicions about Abi.

His green eyes were serious, despite the tousled morning hair and stubble. "Do you think Delta is in danger?"

"No . . . I mean, she's smart and I believe her when she says she would tell me if she needed help, but I think it might be more that she suspects Abi is up to something."

"If she knew her best friend was involved in attacking Gaia, there is no question she would tell you," Quinn stated.

"I know, which is why I think she's just concerned about Abi." Dove looked down at her phone. "Shit, I've got to go. See if Delta will go out on the boards with you this morning. She might tell you what's wrong. See you tonight."

"Will do. See you later, babe." He sat back against the pillows, smiling at her, coffee in his hands. "Shame you can't come back to bed for a bit."

At that moment there was a clatter and thump downstairs, and Dove grinned at her fiancé. "Couldn't do that anyway, sounds like the kids are up."

His responding smile made her heart glow. It wasn't too many months ago that she wouldn't have been able to joke about things that would never happen.

Dove found her niece in the kitchen, blearily making coffee. "Morning. I would have made you one earlier but I didn't want to wake you."

"Thanks. I might just watch some TV or something if that's okay? Quinn not up yet?" Delta yawned.

"Awake but nowhere near getting up," Dove smiled. "What time are you working today?"

"Not till eight, I'm on the late shift and there's another private party. Do you want me to get some shopping in later? I could go down to the store down the road and pick up dinner if you like?"

Dove stared at her. "Are you offering to cook us dinner?"

Delta huffed as she poured the coffee. "Don't sound so surprised, I'm quite a good cook actually, as long as you like steak and chips."

"I do, and sorry, I didn't mean to diss your culinary skills," Dove said. "That would be lovely. See you later."

"Bye. Oh, and Dove?"

"Yes?" She was halfway out of the door, keys in one hand and bag in the other.

"Do you think Gaia will definitely come out of hospital today?"

"I think she's got to wait for the doctor to give her the all-clear, but yes, she should be out this afternoon."

Relief in the dark blue eyes, and Dove got the impression the girl was about to say something else, but in the end she just smiled and turned towards the toaster.

* * *

Dove called DI Rankin as soon as she arrived at work. He was already out chasing up evidence on another case, so she quickly outlined her thoughts on Abi Fairchild, gave her home address and mentioned she worked at California Dreams.

"Thanks for this, we'll look into the club a little more," the DI said. "We think all of our victims have been in the club recently, but we were looking hard at the security team. Someone seems to have turned a blind eye during the robbery and attack on your sister."

"Someone?"

"Two fairly new recruits — both have criminal records, and one of the dancers was convicted of robbery in 2016. Leave it with me. You really can't be sure?"

"No," Dove said regretfully. "Sorry. It's just an impression and she was really off with me, like she was scared or something. It would make sense, because after she hit me with the rock she practically pulled him off me and they had this urgent conversation and just stared at me until they heard the sirens."

"So you think she recognised you on the night in question?"

"Maybe. She did say my niece, Delta, talks about me a lot, and I expect she's seen photos . . . Delta's always taking the kind of happy family snaps you see all over social media." Dove didn't add it would hardly take a psychiatrist to work out why.

She debated mentioning her car had been keyed, but dismissed it as being paranoid. There was enough going on without her jumping at shadows, and surely the perp wouldn't be stupid enough to be trying to freak out a known police officer?

Her mind flicked back to the night before, and the runner who had nearly knocked Delta flying as he emerged from the footpath.

Delta had seemed scared, defensive when Dove had asked if she knew anything about Abi, or needed help. Was it just normal shock, or was she hiding something?

CHAPTER THIRTY-NINE

Sometimes I sit with Mickey for hours, talking to her, watching her, willing her to wake up. The day I saw Ellis Bravery again in the street, for the first time in all these years, I felt like my sister was the only person who could anchor me to the earth, to prevent me from screaming and telling everyone what happened.

The nurse came in periodically to take her blood pressure, check her pulse, and adjust the bleeping machines. My eyes filled with tears and I just smiled faintly when he asked if I was okay. I know most of the nurses now, the different shift patterns. They go home, they live their lives, they come back. Would I have been an uncle? Would she have married? Would she have achieved her dream and won an Olympic gold medal?

I watched the rise and fall of her chest, willing her to keep breathing. Sometimes I put the back of my hand to her mouth, feeling her warm breath on my skin. She is okay, she is still here and safe in these four walls.

I think she would have travelled with me, my special, sparkly, vivacious little sister. I would have watched with pride as she won her Olympic medal, as I did when she took her first steps, won her first competitions, walked into her first day at school. So many firsts and I was there for all of them. The doctor came in, and I brushed a hand across my eyes, sniffing a little.

She nodded understandingly, and I rose from my seat, kissed my sister on her cheek, and squeezed her hand. Time to go, time to get back to my own life, my own family. If only she was coming with me. But I know she's safe there, and I kind of like that she always seems peaceful, cocooned in her white sheets and sometimes the blue blanket too. The smell of lemons, and the smell of her hair. I like to lean close and whisper in her ear, hoping on some level she can hear me.

Another part of my mind shouts, "But she shouldn't be here at all and that's his fault."

Now, I am alone and unable to prevent my mind spinning with horror as I recall our second recent meeting, the one where it all spiralled out of control. I thought I would never lose control again, and if I could take it back, I would. I sink to the ground and hug my knees, vividly transported in my head to the pier the night of the twenty-fifth.

Ellis Bravery left me standing in the darkness after our brief conversation, before strolling towards his companions, hands in pockets, laughing with the dark-haired woman, exchanging flirtatious remarks with his other two companions.

Part of me wanted to yell at him, to bunch a fist and take him out then and there, but the other part of me was too shocked to do anything but scurry after them, welcoming them as clients, smiling at the stupid curly-haired woman who asked if we had a condom machine on the pier, showing them to the room. I felt invisible, as though I was hiding my real self after Ellis's cutting words and his threat. A threat to me, to my family, to the business I have worked so hard to grow. I wanted to ask him what he meant, what he thought he knew . . .

Room Six is the lower room on the left of the pier. The Beach Escape Rooms are a radical design I pinched from something similar I once saw in Florida. The first architect I approached told me bluntly not to waste my time. But I was determined, and the next firm was half decent.

It's iconic, and the stuffy objectors have had to eat their words. The only thing is, we have a lot of loans to pay off, and although business is good, I want to get down to the serious business of making real money as quickly as possible. Now I have a daughter, a long-term partner, I want to provide for them.

That's why, when the first man approached me, I said yes. From their word-of-mouth and on the Fantasy Play website, anyone knows if they want a new place to have sex they can contact me, cash in hand, no questions asked.

Caz despises them. We both do. But we are both here to make money. We've even talked about trying to move Mickey somewhere else, paying for any kind of pioneering treatment that might help her. Caz loves my sister as much as I do, and it's one of the reasons I keep her close. She's loyal and never questions what I think or do. I am always right in Caz's eyes.

I was in a dark place after the night Mickey was attacked. I could barely walk, couldn't sleep or eat. I am not the same person I used to be, I'm sure of it. Eventually I came to accept that life isn't fair, that it was Ellis who altered the course of Mickey's life, stole her life even, and there was nothing I could do but keep watch over my sister, and live day by day.

And now there he was in Room Six, watching while I worked mechanically, carefully shutting the escape hatch after they were all safely down the ladder. He was so confident, careless, sure he had dealt with me. His expression said he had put the silly little boy in his place, I know it. Surely his threats were empty, but could I take the chance? He was in a position of power now.

Maybe if he hadn't been so desperate to get his rocks off, the sad git, he might have paused to consider the effect his words might have had on me, that they might have rekindled the rage I used to feel, and that the rage might be dangerous.

I walked back to the office to wait it out, trying to clear my head from the sheer terror that almost blinded me. I stumbled on the step as I pushed the door open and inhaled the smell of my own place. He was on my territory now. At least both women were of legal age. I'm very clear to anyone who wants to use the rooms that we don't have any underage shit going on.

Most people understand, and I don't think it's that kind of site anyway. These thoughts were not working as distractions, and the pain in my chest was suddenly so crushing I was terrified I was about to have a heart attack. I sat on the floor, knees to my chest.

I became a different person after Mickey's attack. The old Jamie was left behind somewhere next to the swing set on the waste ground next to our house. I shed a skin and became someone else.

231

Caz was an integral part of my transformation. I have come to see over the years that she is my soulmate, the one person who cares and who shows she cares by her actions. We feed each other's dreams, and each other's nightmares. When we talk about my sister, we talk about Ellis Bravery, about how evil he is and how he deserves to be punished. We agree on every single line of the story, every page of the book.

After Jenna showed up out of the blue, with her photographs, Caz called me and we agreed how we would deal with it. It seemed like fate, with the anniversary coming up. Jenna has a big mouth, but she won't say anything because of the part she has now played. I need to see her and speak with her to make sure if anyone puts pressure on her she keeps quiet. It can't be allowed to happen, not now.

Nobody will be allowed to tarnish Mickey's memory, to scrawl corrections across the pages I have written. It is done and it is over.

CHAPTER FORTY

Dove walked quickly up the stairs to the office, putting Gaia and the Claw Beach case firmly out of her mind. She grabbed her iPad and followed her colleagues into the incident room.

The general consensus during the briefing was that the team now had their prime suspects, Jamie Delaney and Caz Liffey, and it was all about building the case, 'brick by brick' as DI Blackman said, watching the video of the swimmer again and comparing it to photographs lifted from Caz's and Jamie's social media accounts.

"The build is right, and the suit is hers. They both state the victims were still alive when they left them, and the main gate was locked after them," DC Josh Conrad said.

"Which is bollocks, because either Caz or Jamie must have given them a drink, probably when they arrived, in which case it was Jamie, because at that point . . ." Lindsey paused and looked up at the timeline of stills lifted from the street cameras, ". . . at that point he was still on his own with the victims. Was there no trace of zopiclone in the house search?"

"None," DI Lincoln said. "Jess said it takes around an hour to work, but considering they had already consumed alcohol, and we assume the drug was taken with the vodka from the bottle discovered in the house search, it would have been quicker. Unlikely they were totally unconscious, but their ability to function would have certainly been impaired to the extent they might have struggled to find their way out of the escape room. I think it's on the lab report somewhere . . ." He was stroking his moustache again, frowning at the images of the street cam on screen. "Short timeline, but it's all possible."

"Perhaps the victims didn't realise the danger they were in?" Dove suggested.

Lindsey was reading from the lab report. "It's right here, boss; the tox results show the levels of zopiclone weren't high enough to completely sedate the victims, but combined with the alcohol, would have made them uncoordinated and confused."

"Good work. We need to separate them out now, check through everything again," the DI explained. "I think, with the evidence from the house search, we can now discount Billy Jackson. Right place, right time, he'd just been in helping to fix the broken overflow pipe with his mate, and the wetsuits are stacked in the back of the office, but he could hardly have offered our victims a few shots. Aileen would have freaked out."

"Maya, can you and Pete check to see if either Caz or Jamie have been issued with any medication and chase up any prescriptions?" DI Blackman said. "George, did you want to add anything else?"

"We only have Jamie's word he didn't know who was coming from Fantasy Play on the twenty-fifth. He says in his statement his only contact was Oscar Wilding, who would book in person so there was no trail. If Jamie for some reason *did* know or find out and Jenna Essex suddenly showed up with evidence that somehow reinforced their blinkered belief Ellis Bravery attacked Mickey Delaney, it would be a perfect storm," DI Lincoln informed him. "Especially if Jamie then seized the opportunity to confront him. If we could also prove the bolt cutters were on site at the Beach Escape Rooms previously, that would help. Pete?"

"On it, boss," Pete nodded, making a note on his iPad. "The photographs Jenna supposedly gave Caz haven't shown up either. There were fragments in the bonfire noted as photographic-quality flakes of paper, so maybe they burned the evidence after they acted on it?"

"Okay, thanks, we'll keep going. Oh, and DC Milson, DCI Franklin would like a quick word before you and Steve head off."

DCI Franklin, who was back behind his desk, asked them to shut the door. "I just wondered if you two got anything else from Jamie's parents? There is nothing I would like more than to solve Mickey's case at the same time as we wrap this one, but we simply do not have the resources to extend to all things, so it's just a case of whether our current investigation throws up any new evidence." He fixed them with a piercing blue stare. "Do you get my drift?"

"Yes, sir," Dove said, and Steve nodded too.

"As you will have seen from the notes we submitted yesterday, Claire and Russ Delaney admitted Jamie had called and told them he'd seen Ellis Bravery in Abberley, but they couldn't remember quite when he had seen him."

"They knew there had been contact," the DCI said thoughtfully. "I want you to see if Jenna Essex knows any more. She claims to have found these photographs, which seem to have potentially triggered off a chain of events leading to the murder of four people. I don't believe for a moment they were just happy snaps of Mickey."

"No, sir."

"Keep me updated. As I said, we are not a cold-case team, and the priority is to wrap this investigation up . . ." He sighed. "It still gets me every time I see a press article about Mickey Delaney. Her parents are good people, and for the first few months, I know they expected her to recover, were hoping she would just regain consciousness. Claire even told me she didn't care if we didn't catch who hurt her daughter, if she could just have her back, and Russ, he just couldn't get over the fact he had waved her off out of the garden gate."

He stood up and picked up a pile of paperwork. "Off you go, and remember, the slightest whisper of new evidence . . ."

Dove sat back down at her desk as DI Blackman, who was on the phone, signalled to both of them to wait a minute.

He was out of his office in under ten minutes, by which time Dove's phone was ringing. She answered quickly, turning to the window to talk, while Steve and the DI discussed Jamie's interview.

"It's Tracey. You know, from Camillo's?"

* * *

Tracey met them outside the industrial estate in a greasy-spoon café. She was huddled at a table in the back, stirring her plastic cup of tea with a spoon.

"Hi Tracey, what's up?" Steve said kindly, and she jumped. Weak tea sloshed on to the scratched off-white tabletop.

"Thank you for calling in," Dove said to her, as they joined her at the table. There were several other customers attacking huge plates of burgers and chips or pancakes soaked in syrup. She felt a twinge of hunger.

"I don't want anyone to know I saw you," Tracey said nervously. Her baseball cap was pulled down low over her face, straggling grey hair falling over one skinny shoulder. She wore a faded red T-shirt and jeans.

"Was it something about Dionne?" Dove asked encouragingly.

"Yes. I . . . I was worried about her, I told you, and after we'd finished our last job I took the bus home. I live in one of the flats opposite the pier, and she told me that's where she was going that night."

"Wait, she told you she was going to the escape rooms?"

"Sorry, I was scared to tell you in case I got into trouble, but then I seen in the papers it wasn't anything to do with Dionne or Camillo's. It was that paedophile Ellis Bravery, wasn't it? I read Jamie Delaney killed him because he attacked

236

his sister, so it wasn't anything to do with Dionne. She died by accident, didn't she?"

"I wouldn't quite agree with all that. The papers don't always tell the exact truth, do they?" Steve suggested.

"No, but Dionne was an innocent victim, wasn't she?"

Unable to see what Tracey was driving at, Dove agreed. "Wrong place, wrong time, maybe."

"Yes! That's exactly it." Tracey looked relieved. "I went across to the pier at half past one, just to see . . . I couldn't see any lights on, so I thought they must have done what they wanted and all gone home, but then this woman came out. She never saw me, but she spoke to someone behind her. She said, 'Go down by the beach steps and take her home.' I could hear a baby crying, and a man's voice answered, but I couldn't hear what he said."

"What happened then?"

"I was a bit worried but I couldn't move or she would have seen me, so I waited. She did too, but when he was gone, she reached up and smashed the CCTV by the gate. Then she clipped the padlock and chain with bolt cutters. She had blonde hair and she was wearing gloves. After she had done that she walked away and I slipped out. I wasn't sure what to do, because Dionne told me having sex in all these different places was illegal and I didn't want to get her in trouble. I thought maybe the man and woman were part of the whole game."

* * *

"Going back to the night in question, you say in your revised statement that you left the Beach Escape Rooms with Caz Liffey and your baby at half past one, after Caz let the four victims out of the main gate," Steve said, turning a page in his folder. He and Dove now sat across from Jamie and his solicitor in the cramped, sour-smelling interview room.

"Yes, that's right." Jamie eyed them warily. He was sitting still, not fidgeting, hands clasped neatly in front of him again.

"We have a witness statement that says you left first with Lila, leaving Caz on the pier while the victims were still in Room Six," Steve told him.

"What? That's crap." His hands were gripping the table now, eyes blazing. "What the hell are you trying to pull?"

"The victims never left Room Six, did they, Jamie?" Dove said.

"You had just come face to face with the man you believe attacked your sister, and Caz had come over to help you deal with things. Did her dealing with things go a little too far, or did you agree between you what needed to be done?" Steve prodded. "You must have been devastated, grieving for your sister, wanting to see justice done . . ."

"All those things." Jamie glared at him. "Mickey was a little angel and do you honestly think I haven't gone over and over how I should have been there that night, should have said yes when she wanted to come to the football with me after training, instead of brushing her off all the time?" Tears brightened his eyes. He dashed them away angrily. "She was my sister and I failed her. I've had to live with that ever since. But that doesn't mean either me or Caz killed those Fantasy Play people."

"Jenna Essex brought some photos over to show Caz, didn't she? Where are those pictures now?"

"I don't know."

"What was in the pictures? Was it something else that made you sure Ellis Bravery was your man?"

"No! Of course not. They were just pictures of Mickey she thought we might like to have. I don't know where they are." Jamie sat back in his chair, eyes wet, and he scrubbed at his cheeks. "I can't believe it. And of course we didn't say we were going to kill Ellis. Caz loved Mickey too, but I can't believe . . ." He slumped forward, head in hands, the picture of misery.

"What did you do with the photographs Jenna brought over?"

"I don't know, I think Caz put them somewhere. It was too painful to look at them in the end. She may have even put them on the bonfire."

Dove laid out the timeline of events, ending with Tracey's witness statement. "We also know that you were prescribed zopiclone after Mickey's attack, so perhaps you had a packet lying around somewhere. You offered the Fantasy Play clients a drink at some point, drugged them and disabled the shut-off valve. One of you swam out to put the bung in the outflow pipe. You left before Caz, and she cleaned up, staging the break-in and leaving four innocent people to die."

"Do you have anything to say, Jamie?"

His face was shuttered and eyes hard now. "No comment. I want to talk to my solicitor."

"Of course."

As Dove stopped the recording, and they all stood up, Jamie said suddenly, "She hasn't been well since Lila was born, you know. She's been so emotional." He seemed to be stronger now, latching on to the idea, which Dove could see would be used by the defence.

Dove watched as several ideas seemed to fall into place, reflected first in Jamie's face and then his solicitor's. A perfect storm. This was going to be interesting. *Is he really going to say it was Caz's idea to kill Ellis Bravery?*

CHAPTER FORTY-ONE

Steve and Dove waited until the pair had been escorted from the interview room, before gathering the paperwork from the table, and heading back upstairs.

DI Blackman met them on the stairs. "Caz has admitted it, but says she doesn't really remember what she was doing. She was just, I quote, an emotional mess and desperate to save Jamie from having another breakdown. We just need to take a formal confession for the recording."

"Defence team are going to use that for sure, and Jamie says Caz has been struggling with her mental health since Lila was born," Dove said, as they reached the coffee machine.

"I'd like to change up a bit, and have Steve and George do Jamie's next interview," DI Blackman said. "Dove, you and I will move on to Caz Liffey in Interview Room Two. If you need a break, get your caffeine now. Point to note, Caz insisted on using the duty solicitor, not hers and Jamie's, which makes it easier for us now . . ."

Ten minutes later, Dove and DI Blackman moved on to Caz's interview.

Caz was defiant, wild-haired and snappy, like a cornered animal.

DI Blackman explained the procedure and started the recording, introducing everyone in the room. Dove noted that Caz's new solicitor didn't look at all happy with his client and barely spoke during the introductions. Interesting she had apparently insisted on using the duty solicitor. Did she suspect her husband might be going to pin the blame on her?

"On the night of the twenty-fifth of July, you persuaded Jamie to go home, telling him you would lock up after the victims left?"

"Yes. It was easier than I thought. I wasn't quite sure how I was going to do it, but I couldn't let Ellis ruin our lives again."

"Was there any kind of conversation between Jamie and Ellis?" Dove asked.

"You keep on about that, and I keep saying no!" Caz shot back.

"Okay, carry on." Dove made a note. Caz and Jamie insisted nothing had been said, but it still made no sense. Jenna's photographs alone might have been enough of a trigger, and if Ellis had laughed at Jamie when he was confronted . . .

"I remembered there had been a problem with the shut-off valve in Room Six recently. I was there when they fixed it and I paid attention. It was easy to reverse the fix and make sure it didn't kick in. Then I pulled on the wetsuit and gloves, took one of the rubber bungs we use when we are cleaning out the overflow pipes and dived down to secure it."

"You blocked the pipe?"

"I've had plenty of practice training myself to hold my breath for a long time. It's a fiddly job and normally only done at low tide when the pipes are exposed, but the opportunity was there and I took it." Caz fiddled with her sleeve thoughtfully. "It seemed like fate, and once I realised what I had to do, so many things dropped into place. The zopiclone Jamie had been prescribed, for instance. He thought I didn't know, but he always makes sure he has it with him, like a kind of . . . a comfort blanket. He hasn't taken any for a while, but he still carries it to and from work. That night, he had it stashed in his desk drawer as usual, so I slipped it in my pocket before he and Lila left."

"And the vodka?" Dove asked.

"We had a couple of bottles of spirits from grateful clients, and kept forgetting to take them home. It was in the cupboard, and of course the shot glasses were all displayed on the shelves. I crushed the pills with a hammer from the toolbox, and mixed them with the vodka," Caz told them.

"Did you realise you would be killing all four of those people?"

"All I could think about was getting rid of Ellis before Jamie could talk to him, could start his obsession going again. I didn't think about the others. You don't understand what Jamie was like after Mickey was attacked." She sighed, "There was this thing that happened while Jamie was travelling too . . . He, he sees things differently to the rest of us and he took it really badly."

"What happened while he was travelling?"

"He said he kept seeing Mickey, which was impossible of course. And one time he told me he was actually talking to her on the beach one night, and when he woke up, there was blood all over his clothes. It was in the Philippines somewhere . . ."

"Go on."

Caz rubbed her eyes wearily, "I assumed he was just drunk, but then I heard that a girl had been murdered. I looked online, and she had long red hair, just like Mickey."

"Do you think Jamie killed this girl?" DI Blackman made quick notes, his face grim. "Do you remember anything else about the incident? Dates? Exact location?"

"No! I don't know . . . All I know is he seemed better after that. He started saying he felt he had been able to grieve properly, and was ready to move on. Move on with me. He was planning our future together." Caz stared at Dove, "If he had just killed that girl, he wouldn't have been ready to move on. He would have gone crazy, wouldn't he?"

"Why?"

"Because of Mickey of course. You don't understand. Travelling put him in a better place. Before, he was so depressed I worried he would kill himself or something. I didn't think of anything that night except keeping Jamie and Lila safe."

"So what happened once you had mixed the zopiclone with the vodka?" Dove asked, trying to keep track of these revelations. It was obvious Caz was in a terrible state, half realising what kind of person Jamie might be, half clinging to her obsessive love, her almost idolising of him. Maybe she had been fighting her true thoughts for a long time.

"After the drug was mixed with the vodka, I screwed the cap back on, put the glasses, bottle and a little tray from the desk into a bag and took them out to the clients. I'd checked on the screen and I was lucky. They were just talking and laughing, because Oscar knew Jamie would set the alarm off. It's just a red flashing light in the centre of the rooms that signals the beginning of the games."

"So you went down into Room Six?" DI Blackman asked, making another note.

"As soon as I could, because I wasn't sure how long the drugs would take to work. I told them this was an extra freebie, part of our super service or something equally crap, and handed round the shots. I made a thing out of it and I kept pouring until the bottle was empty." She frowned. "One of the women started singing and waving her arms like she was off her head. It was annoying, but I was focused on Ellis. Part of me was fascinated to be so close to him after all these years. Obviously he never recognised me, had no idea what my name was, even. He was all over the shorter woman. It was vile."

"So you left them inside, presumably locking the bolt as you went back to the office, to wait for the inevitable. Did you watch them die?" the DI asked.

"Of course not! I didn't get off on it, if that's what you're implying," Caz snapped. "I knew from the monitors when

243

the room was full, so all I had to do was wait and silence the two automatic alarms. It was all over in an hour."

"Then what did you do?" Dove queried. She was thinking as a last-minute murder plan, it had depended on so many factors. As Caz said, luck had been on the murderer's side. If the tides hadn't been favourable, if the drugs and alcohol hadn't been there, if her victims hadn't already drunk a fair amount of alcohol, she could never have achieved her aim.

"I took the bolt cutters from the toolbox, made it look as though we had a break-in, scrubbed the CCTV and smashed the screens, threw the bolt cutters over the end of the pier." Caz shrugged. "It seemed barely five minutes since Jamie had called me from home, but so much had happened. I gathered up my wetsuit, the bottle and shot glasses, locked up and went home by the ladder down the pier."

"So you admit to the murder of Oscar Wilding, Dionne Radley, Aileen Jackson and Ellis Bravery?"

"I didn't want to kill them all. I already told you that, but I had to protect Jamie and our life with Lila," Caz repeated slowly, like she was talking to a child. She was twisting her hair, winding it and unwinding it between shaky fingers. "You didn't see what he was like after Mickey was attacked. He was so depressed, and he used to get drunk and say over and over how he should have been there, should have protected her. I was afraid he might do something stupid. I couldn't let him go through that again."

"What about the photographs Jenna brought over?" DI Blackman asked.

"Why do you keep going on about them? They were just pictures of Mickey. If you want the truth, I burned them. Jamie didn't see them. He didn't need another reminder of how Mickey had been, how she should be now. The anniversary is always hard." She stopped and started to draw patterns on the table with her fingers, before continuing with her monologue, picking her words slowly and carefully. "Last year he didn't speak all day and spent the night sleeping next to Mickey's bed at the hospital. Don't you see? He knows, and his poor parents know — sooner or later she'll die, and the last hope will be gone." Caz's eyes were wet with tears, her voice cracking with apparently genuine emotion.

"Who do you think attacked Mickey, Caz?" Dove asked.

"It was Ellis!" She was angry again now, afraid.

"We know you, Jamie and Jenna believe that, but I think the photographs Jenna found might have in some way showed how Mickey was attacked," the DI said.

"No comment."

"Did *you* hurt Mickey, Caz?" the DI said suddenly, and Dove glanced at him.

"No! I loved Mickey. Of course we were rivals! It was competitive gymnastics, not a little hobby. Places on the team were limited. You had to be the best," Caz said harshly. "I was at the football match on the waste ground that night. It was Jenna who nobody saw for a good half an hour. The police questioned *her.*"

"Mickey was the best at gymnastics?" Dove suggested.

"At that time, that month, that summer. She could have been just a flash in the pan, one of those girls who comes and goes. I trained harder than her, but Coach Hawthorn just went on and on about her talent," Caz said bitterly. "It's not talent that makes an elite athlete. It's bloody hard repetitive work, training until your body hurts and you are so exhausted you want to lie down and never get up. But you never do, because you see that Olympic medal in your dreams every fucking night."

"You gave up gymnastics six months after Mickey's assault," Dove commented.

"I aged out. Too big, and too old to make the top level, so that was it. There was no point after that. I accepted I'd given it my all and not made it." Caz glared at them and added spitefully, "I'm not some wet blanket like Jenna, *I'd* never be happy teaching little kids how to turn cartwheels."

"I don't think Ellis did attack Mickey, Caz. I think you did." The DI spoke slowly, clearly, watching her face intently.

Her eyes flashed with fear, and Dove could see the words hammering home, like nails into her heart. "Of course I bloody didn't! You have no proof at all, and I've got an alibi. I already confessed to killing Ellis Bravery. This is a whole different thing . . ."

Finally, Caz's solicitor came to her rescue. "My client has given her statement, is extremely distressed and, as she has mentioned, you have no reason to suggest she may have been involved in the attack on her sister-in-law."

"Jamie loves me. He always did, and I would do anything for him," Caz interjected, calmly, mechanically. Her eyes were dull, her shoulders drooping.

"Do you think Jamie would want you to lie for him?" Dove asked. Caz had put Jamie on such a high pedestal, she must have realised it would only be a matter of time before he came crashing down. Tracey's witness statement was enough to show both Caz and Jamie had been trying to cover up the murders.

"I'm not lying. I've already told you what happened. It was me, me who killed Ellis and the others, and Jamie had no idea," Caz stated. "I have nothing else to say."

"What about your baby?"

Just for a moment, pain clouded her face, softening her eyes, making her mouth droop slightly at the corners. "She'll be fine. And Jamie knows I did this for him, and for Mickey. We are on the same page, always."

"Which means you would also lie for him?"

"No comment."

Nothing they said could dent her version of events, and eventually Dove and the DI finished the interview, leaving Caz with her solicitor, waiting to be taken into custody, before they walked wearily back up the stairs.

Dove stopped at the coffee machine, then shoved some coins into the snack machine for her favourite sweets as they passed. "She's not going to give him up, is she?"

The DI shook his head, evidently still mulling it over. "I'll send the Philippines incident information straight over to Interpol and see if we can get an idea of what happened and if they found their perpetrator."

"I suppose either Jamie was involved or maybe read about it, enough to make up a sort of fantasy about his part in the girl's murder, based on his own experiences?"

"I know which version I'm betting on."

Dove nodded. "And what was all that stuff about Mickey? Do you really think Caz was responsible for the attack as well?"

"I was trying to find out what was in the damn photos Jenna took over more than anything, but she could have been the one. There's a lot of anger and jealousy. I honestly think she's obsessed with him and would have done anything to protect him, or to keep his attention," DI Blackman explained.

"But if Caz was responsible for attacking Mickey, thus in her mind, disposing of the only real rival for Jamie's affections, and Jamie found out, he would kill her for sure," Dove said soberly. "That's some tightrope to live on."

CHAPTER FORTY-TWO

I can smell the dwarf lemon trees in the garden. Mum grows them in a sunny spot by the front door, and they come indoors in the winter to the conservatory at the back of the house. A miniature lemon grove, she calls it.

The sun is hot on my head, as I breathe in the scent in my bright cocoon. I watch. He watches. They all see different things, don't they?

He was watching me again today. I saw him across in the garden while we were playing by the swings. Caz and I were doing cartwheels and roundoffs, and Jenna was doing handstands. She was wearing that frilly pink skirt, and you could see her knickers every time she did a handstand, but as usual she didn't care.

As soon as he saw me watching, he just gave that smile and moved away, like it was nothing. Should I say something? Should I tell Mum or Dad? But I can't even begin to think how I'd say it. It's not a crime, to watch someone, is it? Jenna says he fancies her, and Caz just giggles, like she does when we hang out with the boys' trampoline squad at the gym.

They train around the same times we do, and I've seen a few of the older boys at the bus stop down the road, logo hoodies and wet hair after training, high-fiving before they head home. So confident and casual in their team tracksuits. So normal.

It makes me feel cold and sick, though, like spiders are crawling across my bare skin. And it's getting worse. Wherever we are, he is too.

Maybe I could get Jenna to wear leggings.

*I wonder where he will be in ten years' time . . . In jail probably.
The thought gives me a tiny knot of fear, right in my stomach. But
that's okay, because I'll be an Olympic gymnast, and he won't be able
to get near me. I'll move away, get a swanky apartment in London or
New York and have security guards.*

*I can hear the beep of security alarms now, the thud of running
feet . . .*

*I wonder where I'll be when I'm forty? I hope I look back and
be proud of everything I've achieved. That's not being arrogant, is it?
It's being hopeful. But most of all, now more than all of my Olympic
dreams, I hope I am free of him.*

*The beeps of my security alarms are getting faster and my heart
speeds up, my breathing laboured. The desert heat is back, and all I
want is a drink. I am being attacked, but even as I scream and struggle,
I know it will be like last time and nobody will hear me.*

Beep
Beep
Beep
Beep
Beep
Beep . . .

CHAPTER FORTY-THREE

Dove's phone buzzed next to her ear and she stretched out a hand, fumbling for it. She blinked at the digital alarm clock, confused. It was 1 a.m. Next to her Quinn groaned and turned over.

Mindful of his day off tomorrow, Dove crawled out of bed and stumbled to the bathroom as she answered.

"Hello?"

"Dove, it's me." Delta's voice, quick and panicky.

Dove woke up properly. "What's wrong? Where are you? At work still?"

"Back at the flat. I came here after work to sort a few things out. Dove, Abi's boyfriend just turned up, and he's taken her away with him."

"What do you mean? He's abducted her?" Dove leaned against the wall, mind flickering over possibilities, fully awake and heart pounding.

"I . . . no, she just sort of went with him when he told her to. He didn't drag her away or anything." Delta was slightly breathless. "She told me not to call the police, said she'd be fine and *he* said I was an interfering little . . . Anyway, that's why I called you instead of 999, because I don't know what to do."

"It's okay. Can you lock the doors from the inside?" Dove asked, thinking rapidly.

"Yes, there are security bolts."

"Do the bolts and wait for me. Don't open the door to anyone else, okay?"

"I won't. It's number 289."

"I remember." Dove ended the call and slipped her clothes on, padding back into the bedroom. Quinn was fast asleep again. He adored Delta. Should she wake him? In the end, she fudged it and scribbled a quick note. They were so used to each other's night-time comings and goings for work, and Dove felt this definitely counted as work. She could always call him if she needed to.

Dove found the town-centre apartment block easily. It was next to another block of cut-price student accommodation. The walkways were grimy. The stairwell stank. There was no way she was trusting the rusty lift.

She jogged up the stairs, taking shallow breaths because of the smell, but on her guard as she rounded each corner. A rough sleeper, curled in a grey, mouldy duvet, peered blearily at her on the third-floor landing.

Dove could see a light on at number 289, and as she knocked she saw Delta's worried face appear at the window in the kitchen, peering through the net curtains.

"It's okay, Delta, tell me what happened," Dove said as soon as she was inside. The flat, though littered with the detritus of two teenage girls, was clean enough. Magazines, clothes and make-up were heaped on the two slightly grubby sofas, a pile of takeaway cartons had taken over the kitchen counter, and a string of fairy lights was hung around the window.

"Abi's been weird the past few months." Delta's words rushed out, far from her usual cool, sardonic self. "About two weeks after he started working at Gaia's, she started dating Leo Caper. I reckon he came by California Dreams a few times with his mates before he landed the job, but he's one of the security team."

"He works at the club?" Dove swore under her breath. "And Leo is the one she went off with tonight?"

"Yeah. She started off saying he was just doing the security job to save money for a house, and that he was going back to university to study law. Lots of crap, basically," said pragmatic Delta. "He was always spoiling her — like buying her bottles of champagne and clothes and jewellery. But then he changed and started telling her what to do on her days off. He doesn't like me at all and he even told her they should move in together, but she said it was too soon."

"Has he ever been violent towards her?" Dove asked.

"No, not that I've seen . . . I mean, tonight he was arguing with her but he doesn't really shout. He just speaks really calmly, and it's what he says that seems to get her."

"Would you say she was afraid of him?"

"Yes . . . I would, but she won't admit it. He's so controlling, but most of the time she says she would never end it because he's such a great guy. She gets really defensive when I ask about him."

"All right. Delta, I'm going to call it in, okay?"

Delta looked at her for a moment and then nodded, the fire back behind her eyes. "You think there's something else too, don't you? You've got that detective look going on."

"I do not have a look," Dove told her, picking up her phone.

"So do. Dove? Thanks for coming."

"It's okay. Where does he live?"

"Downstairs in Flat 8."

Dove selected DI Rankin's number and called him. He answered after a couple of rings, and she explained everything Delta had told her. "Well, you did say to call you if I remembered anything else."

"Funny," he replied. "We actually went over to the club tonight to arrest Leo Caper. We got some results from the lab — DNA samples from three of the scenes, including Neil Ockley's, are a match, and one of the other dancers has given a statement to the effect that he bribed her to say he was

252

working on the floor during the time the robbery and assault at the club took place."

"He was supposed to be working tonight?"

"He was, but he hasn't shown up. I sent a car round to his home address but the house is empty." He gave her an address across town.

"That's because he's at Flat 8, on the Highcourt estate." Dove explained the rest as rapidly as she could.

"On our way."

Now she knew Delta was safe, Dove was worried about Abi, and also keen to keep eyes on the man responsible for attacking her sister. She went quickly and quietly down the filthy stairwell, located Flat 8 and stood, listening carefully. Just as before at the beach, she heard a scream, then sounds of a scuffle, the slap of a hand across someone's face, and then crying.

She knocked on the door, unsure of what she could do, but focusing on the fact she might be able to distract Leo before Abi was too badly hurt. Back-up would be here soon, and she couldn't let a teenage girl be beaten while she stood by and did nothing.

Leo himself opened the door, shock and then amusement on his face. "Oh, look, it's Auntie Dove, the copper. I suppose Delta called you. Come in, Auntie Dove." He swung the door wide, and Dove could see Abi half-sitting half-lying on the dirty couch, a red weal across her face, and blood on the corner of her lip. Her bare arms were bruised at the wrist.

"Leo Caper, I presume, and no thanks, I'm just here to take Abi home," Dove told him firmly.

He leaned against the door, considering her. He stank of weed and booze, but clearly fancied himself as the hard man. "You gonna tell me police are gonna waste their time on a domestic? Nothing wrong with Abi, as you can see, is there, darling?"

Abi shook her head, her hair falling forward across her face. She reached over and pulled a cardigan on, covering her bruises. Dove remembered Delta mentioning a few months

253

ago that Abi preferred waiting the tables at the club to dancing. Was it because she could hide her bruises better with
more clothes on?

"Nothing to see here, Auntie Dove." Leo grinned again,
showing a dimple in his left cheek as he smoothed his hair
back.

"Yeah, she looks the picture of health," Dove agreed sarcastically. "Of course, I called for back-up, and it's on the way."

"But here you are by yourself." He leered at her. "You
sleep naked sometimes, don't you, Detective? Nice. Ha! Yes,
I've been to your place a couple of times, and I know where
you go and what you do. Shame about your car, wasn't it?
These things happen, though . . . You like to play around at
night on your own. It's dangerous on the beaches after dark.
You should be more careful."

Dove couldn't believe he was stupid enough to threaten
her.

"Don't you have enough things to do without hanging
around after me?" Her voice was calm but she was fuming.
The movement in the shadows and the presence she had felt
were not ghosts from the past, but this muscular drugged-up
idiot trying to warn her off.

They could both see the arrival of two squad cars, blue
lights flashing, but Leo shrugged casually. "I've been here
before. You lot couldn't care shit about some teenage stripper
girl. It'll go down as a domestic, and you'll keep your mouth
shut because you've got two pretty nieces who you wouldn't
want me taking out on the town."

Dove was blown away by his arrogance. "That's where
you're wrong, Leo. Because we do take domestic violence
seriously, and it doesn't matter who the victim is, or what
gender they are. Plus, there's the other matter of five robber-
ies, GBH, attempted murder of Gaia Minton-Smith, and
the actual murder of Neil Ockley. I think that's plenty to be
getting on with, don't you?"

He paled in the harsh light of the passageway. "You got
nothing on me about that, and Abi won't say nothing." He

shot an arm out and grabbed at Dove's wrist, but she slipped it neatly away. She could hear a team of uniformed offices in the stairwell. Sharp commands, the fast-moving thud of boots.

"Your DNA is all over at least three of the scenes. You should have been more careful with those men you lured into your honey trap," Dove told him, stepping aside as her uniformed colleagues took over the scene. "See you down at the station, Leo."

Abi stayed where she was on the sofa until Dove and a PC managed to calm her down enough for medics to treat her. The wounds were superficial, but Dove feared the scars underneath were far deeper than that.

She laid a gentle hand on the girl's arm. "It's okay now, Abi."

From the shadows outside another figure appeared at the door. Delta, seeing it was safe, had come to check on her friend. With a cry, Abi tore herself from the medics and flung herself into her friend's arms, sobbing. "I'm sorry, Delta, I'm so sorry."

Delta closed her arms tightly around Abi, and met Dove's eyes over her friend's shoulder. The dark blue eyes were steady. Although she was still pale and shocked, she held Abi with strong arms.

Thank you, Delta mouthed to her aunt.

CHAPTER FORTY-FOUR

Dove smiled reassuringly at Abi. The girl was a mess, her face bruised and her hair extensions greasy rat-tails. She was hardly recognisable as the fragile beauty from California Dreams. "It's okay, you're safe now."

Abi's pale blue eyes filled with tears. She had insisted she would only speak to Dove, and Dove, keen to hear what she had to say, had agreed that one of the duty officers, Marion, would sit in on the interview while Abi made her statement.

The girl sniffed, biting her lip, before she said, "He'll come after me as soon as he gets out. He already told me however long it takes, he'll always find me."

"Abi, I promise you Leo will not be coming anywhere near you, or even outside the prison gates, for a long time." Dove paused and glanced at the other officer, who stayed silent, but nodded in agreement. "You need to tell the truth about what happened, because I only know what Delta said when she called me for help."

There was a long silence, but Dove let her think. Delta had said Abi was swayed by the money, but also her infatuation for the man. "Did you love him?"

Abi laughed, but it was a bitter, harsh sound. "I thought I did. Delta tried to tell me he was an arsehole, so many times, but she . . . Delta's so strong and so focused with what she wants to do with her life. Me, I was saving so we could go travelling, sure, but I hadn't got a clue what I was going to do afterwards. My parents were so disappointed when I got a job at the club, and my sisters won't speak to me."

"To be fair, not many of us have a five-year plan," Dove confided. "Did you meet Leo at California Dreams?"

"Yeah, he would come in with a group of friends, gave me great tips, always singled me out, telling me how cute I looked. I'm not stupid, and I was wary, because, I mean, he's thirty and I'm nineteen . . ." Her voice trailed off. "Then he got a job as part of the security team, and I thought if Gaia had checked him out, he must be okay."

"Did you date?"

"He took me to some flash places, a few clubs and bars. We got in the VIP lounges. It was . . . different to what I was used to. Leo started saying why was I wasting my time going backpacking and living like a student, when I could be out with him every night, shopping designer and maybe doing some modelling."

Dove felt a twinge of pity. It was a classic grooming story, and victims were always picked carefully. Leo had sussed Abi out, and no doubt she had soon told him about her college-drop-out history, her rows with her mum and dad, feeling the rest of her old schoolfriends and siblings had turned against her because she worked as a dancer at the club.

"One night he asked me to target a particular client at California Dreams. He told me his name, gave me photographs . . ."

"What was his name?" Dove asked, showing the girl a photo of their supposed first victim, but the girl shook her head.

"Arthur, Arthur Andrews. This was back in May. I got him to meet me in a car park next to the old leisure centre."

Dove frowned at the thought that, as they had suspected, there were more victims who had been too afraid to come forward. "How badly was he hurt?"

"Oh, not badly at all," Abi assured her, chewing her lip again. "Leo only threatened to hit him and he was crying and handing over all his stuff. Leo gave him a slap at the end just because he said he was a wimp and deserved it."

"Charming. What about these people?" Dove flipped the iPad round and showed Abi the line-up of the five other men, including Alex Harbor, Neil Ockley and, just for fun, Gaia.

"All of them. I asked why to start with, but he just said get friendly with them and get them to meet me somewhere after work." She paused again. "I told him no way. Gaia's really strict about that, and Leo was saying you know, prom- ise them sex, or a date or whatever. I freaked when he said sex. I'm not a bloody prostitute!"

"What happened when you refused?"

"Leo was quite nice about it, just said okay, but later that day, he came back to our flat, and started telling me he was in a lot of debt. All the places he had taken me, the clothes and jewellery he had bought to make me feel special, had used up all his spare cash."

"He made you feel guilty?" Dove's colleague asked.

"Of course, and then he broke down and cried, said he wanted us to be together properly but he didn't deserve me and he was worried about the age gap." Abi straightened and pulled her shoulders back, a little bit of confidence in her eyes. "Okay, I know how dumb it sounds that I fell for it, but he was pulling my strings. I can see that now."

"It's okay, he's probably used the same routine on a lot of girls." Dove decided not to bring up the fact Leo was a both a pimp and a drug dealer just yet, but Abi surprised her.

"I know, and me and Delta asked around. People know he's bad news. But after we did the first scam on Andrews, I was trapped. I promise I never knew he was going to beat them up. He just said I should distract them and he would come in and steal the wallet, or watch or whatever was there. He said they would never tell the police because we only chose men who had good jobs, married with kids and a lot to lose. They were never going to tell the police they arranged to meet a nineteen-year-old stripper for a date, were they?"

"I guess not," Dove agreed. "But then you arranged to meet Alex Harbor at Claw Beach on the night of July twenty-fifth?"

"Yeah. He was a big one, always flashing a lot of cash in his wallet, expensive watch, lots of jewellery for a man . . . Leo said we might have enough for us to set up with a place together after we did him, but by then I was scared, in too deep and scared. I really wasn't sure "

"Abi, are you sure you don't want a solicitor present?" Marion, Dove's colleague, interjected, but once again Abi shook her head firmly.

"Did Leo give you drugs?" Dove asked.

"Pills. I think it was just Ecstasy, but it gave me a buzz and carried me through the dates." Her gaze faltered. "I felt like Leo was letting it go on too long. It was my job to get them to meet me, and drive to somewhere remote — Leo would tail us from a distance. My phone's got a tracker and he always used a different car. But he was supposed to come in and steal stuff before I had to do anything . . . I didn't want to actually have to have sex with them, but I felt like that's what he wanted. He was getting a kick out of it."

"But that night, I was at the beach," Dove said, feeling her healed ribs twinge at the memory.

"Leo had just beat up the man and I'd thrown his stuff in the van. My job then was to be lookout while Leo finished taking watches or whatever. They almost all put up a fight, which is crazy when you look at Leo. I would have just given up the valuables if it was me."

"So you were lookout and saw me coming up the beach."

"I didn't know until I saw your face later that it was you, I swear, but I told Leo there was someone coming." She pulled a face. "He was in a crazy mood and just kept hitting the man, even though we had the stuff. I never hit anyone."

"Except me," Dove pointed out.

"I honestly didn't mean to hit you. I was still high and just threw the rock in between both of you to try and break up the fight."

Dove sensed she was lying, but she didn't care. They had enough. Leo would go down, and Abi would be able to take steps to rebuild her own life away from an abusive partner.

"What about Neil Ockley?"

She winced and wrapped her arms around her body, shivering. "It was horrible. I went in to meet him, and he kept trying to kiss me. Leo was already in there, hiding in the opposite cubicle along. I knew he was watching everything, and I was waiting for him to come out . . . But he kept leaving it later and later, letting me struggle with keeping the men interested, and stopping short of like actually having sex with them." A flash of anger made Abi sit up straighter. "He was enjoying it wasn't he?"

"Probably," Dove commented.

"The man didn't try and fight, but Leo hit him anyway. He, the man, swung the bottle, and it broke against the wall, but his arm kept on swinging. Instead of hitting Leo, he cut himself, here." She indicated on her own neck.

"He cut himself?" Dove checked.

"It was an accident. He just swung and it happened. It was just crazy. I think Leo was high that night. I screamed at him to stop, but he hit me too. Then suddenly, the man wasn't moving, just crouched there bleeding everywhere, all surprised. His hand against his neck to try and stop the blood, but it went in an arc right up to the ceiling. It missed us, but later I found I had some fine spray on my top . . . That's when Leo took his suit jacket hanging from the door because he said we could get some cash for that too, then said we got what we wanted and we had to get out of there."

"So you left him to die?" Dove said shortly.

"We didn't mean to! Well, I didn't, anyway. He was still breathing when we left him and staggering around, I swear he was!"

"Did you see a bag in the corner of the cubicle?" Dove asked, estimating how long the man would have taken to bleed out — seconds rather than minutes, which meant it was rather unlikely the victim had been alive when Abi and Leo left the building.

"Yeah, a white one. Leo took a quick look before we left, but he said it was just some shitty clothes and a make-up bag, nothing of any value. Why?"

That explained why Dionne's bag had still been in situ when Dove had discovered the body, she thought. Perhaps the mobile phone had been in a hidden pocket. If Leo was high, and the bag was covered in blood, he wouldn't have wanted to hang around. "Why didn't you make an anonymous call to the ambulance service?"

"I wanted to," Abi whispered. "But I couldn't do it right away because Leo took me off in the car, drove for miles, kept putting his foot down. He was wired and crazy, and he wouldn't let me out. Finally, we drove back into town and he shoved me out next to the kebab place on Reever Street. That was when I was going to make the call, but my phone was out of charge . . . It was too late by then, wasn't it?"

"Yes, far too late," Dove said.

"When he did Gaia I was going to tell you, honestly, and get out. This was different to what he'd been doing, and we knew Gaia. She was always good to us, but he hit her really hard and enjoyed it." Abi shivered. "He's really evil sometimes, but then he changes back to being so nice and saying he's sorry for everything. I didn't know what to do. I'm an idiot, aren't I?"

"No," Dove said. "You got sucked into a situation and couldn't find a way out. It's what you do from now on that matters the most."

"Will I go to prison?"

Dove frowned. "That will depend on the CPS, but as you were forced into being an accessory, and the only time you hurt someone was when you chucked a rock at my head, you should be okay. This isn't my case, so I really can't say anything for sure."

"Leo will, though, won't he?"

"Yes."

"If he's inside, he won't be able to hurt anyone," she said softly. "But what about when he comes out?"

"Abi, I really don't think you realise how serious the charges are — multiple assaults, robbery, the list goes on and on. Leo Caper is going down for a long time," Dove told her. "There is help available for you, you just need to be willing to take it."

"Delta told me to get rid of him," Abi said, as they finally left the interview room. "She stood up to him too, told him to get lost, and he didn't like that at all. The night she left the first time around, to stay at yours, she'd had a row with Leo the night before and he slapped her face. She slapped him back, and he was so shocked, but she said at work she was going to stay with you for a bit, until I sorted my head out."

"And Leo heard that." She hadn't been losing it after all. Leo had been trying to make sure she knew someone was in the shadows, waiting, but not daring to make himself known, instead content with scaring a couple of teenage girls.

CHAPTER FORTY-FIVE

Having got home at five that morning, rung DI Blackman and explained she was going to grab an hour of sleep and a shower, Dove sank gratefully into bed. She woke two hours later, and started to get ready for work, texting Steve to ask what was happening. The case was pretty much wrapped up now, with Caz's confession in the bag.

Delta and Quinn were downstairs, drinking coffee and watching a travel piece on the news. Delta made no mention of the night's events, but went straight in with, "Hey, Dove, check out this travelogue. It's Japan, so cool! I might add it to my list."

Dove rubbed her eyes and stared at the chirpy reporter pointing at the iconic Tokyo skyline. It took a while to focus, and she was struggling with waves of tiredness, which were making her movements clumsy and uncoordinated. "So you know exactly where you're going, then?"

"Yeah." The girl smiled confidently. "Quinn said I should think about what I want to do, make some choices, rather than dwell on what happened with Abi and Leo."

Quinn looked slightly uncomfortable as Dove raised an eyebrow at him. "You know what she's like, and now she wants to go travelling next month."

"Hello? I am still in the room," Delta told him. "And before you start about me going on my own, I might not be exactly on my own."

Dove made a mug of coffee, bringing it to her nose, inhaling the fragrance. "Surely not with Abi?"

"Hell no. She wouldn't get a visa with her criminal record anyway. But more than that, she was a flaky friend and she hooked up with Leo without telling me. It's a trust thing. If you're travelling round the world you need someone you can trust . . ." Her cheeks coloured slightly and she tossed her hair out of her face.

The new style suited her, Dove thought, emphasising her blue eyes and Ren's perfect forties bow lips. "I meant to say last night — but there was quite a lot going on — I like your new hair. When did you get it done?"

"After work. Kelly's a hairdresser in the daytime, dancer at night. She does everyone, so I stayed on last night and we used the changing room as a hair salon." Delta smoothed her fringe. She looked older, but in a good way. "That was before Abi phoned and I decided to go back to the flat and collect some more of my stuff . . ."

Dove grinned at her niece. "Well going back to the subject of trusting who you travel with, I don't suppose Bollo, your rather gorgeous boyfriend, will blow you out for a pimp."

"How did you know?" Delta demanded, glass halfway to her mouth, eyes wide.

"She's sneaky like that," Quinn informed her. "That's why she's a detective."

Dove threw a towel at him, and he stretched out a hand and caught it lazily, laughing at her.

"I think Abi will be okay," Delta said suddenly, her face serious. "And to be fair, Leo was dead convincing. She believed the whole story about stealing money for them to buy a flat and to get Abi a decent car . . . What? What did I say?"

Dove leaning wearily against the countertop, thoughts racing around her brain, drained her coffee and looked at her watch. *What if?* It was a cop question, and something she asked herself at least a dozen times a day when she was on a case, trying to figure out how someone's mind worked.

"Why do you need to go in today?" Quinn asked, clocking her exhaustion, green eyes concerned. "I thought you said you know who did it?"

Dove picked up her bag and keys. "We do, but it's complicated."

"Always," Delta muttered, pulling a half-empty bag of Doritos towards her and dipping in.

"I'll pick up some groceries on the way home," Dove added. "See you later."

"I'm going back to stay with Mum and Eden for a bit while I get my plans sorted out," Delta said. "You guys are amazing, but I can't stay dossing on your couch for ever, can I?"

* * *

Dove pulled into work at midday, turned off the engine and briefly closed her eyes, her head back against the headrest. Funny, normally she felt good after they had the perpetrators, but she had this niggling feeling about Jamie and Caz. Caz had confessed. The evidence was there, incriminating both of them. So what was wrong?

DI Blackman greeted Dove as she walked into the office. "You didn't need to come in, you know."

Steve was less reserved. "You look like shit. Why don't you leave it till tomorrow?"

She shrugged and muttered something about needing to tie up loose ends.

DI Blackman had moved over to talk to Lindsey, who was pointing to her computer screen, so Steve updated her. "Caz is adamant Jamie left, even when we said Tracey heard a baby crying, and a man's voice — says she must have been mistaken." Steve rolled his eyes. "She's determined to take the fall on this one, but I don't know if she's thought any further than confessing and what it will mean for her daughter."

"She was desperate for Jamie not to fall back into depression, wasn't she? Tunnel vision?" Dove suggested.

"Yes. So they will both be charged and it'll be up to the CPS to sort it out," Steve finished. "There you go, case solved, so you can go and get some sleep now. But before you go, tell me what happened last night."

She yawned, saw the DCI was watching her from his office and hastily turned it into a cough. "I think I might need more coffee quite soon." But she went rapidly back over the events of the night.

"Bet DI Rankin is pleased to have his case solved," Steve commented.

"He'd already solved it," Dove said. "He was on his way to arrest Leo yesterday evening. They thought he'd done a runner, but he was staying at a friend's flat."

She should be feeling pleased, looking forward to some time off. But she wasn't. "Fancy a short drive?"

He narrowed his eyes. "Where?"

She lowered her voice. "I want to visit Mickey again. It's Wednesday, and when we were there last time, I noticed in the visitor's log Jenna Essex always goes on a Wednesday morning. If we hurry, we can catch her just before she comes out."

"Okay." Steve glanced round. Both DIs were back in their offices, and the DCI had just gone out of the door, clutching a stack of files to his chest.

* * *

Dove looked from the unconscious girl in the bed to the sleeping girl in the chair.

"She comes here on a regular basis." The nurse smiled at Dove. "Spends a couple of hours in Mickey's room, chatting away to her. Sometimes she plays music."

"We'll hang around for a bit, if that's okay?" Dove said.

"Sure, just make sure you sign out at the main desk when you go, please." The nurse gathered up her clipboard and walked quickly out of the room.

"You want coffee?" Steve asked softly

"Sure. It's okay I'll get it. You stay here in case she wakes up."

He nodded and pulled out his iPad, settling into one of the other chairs in the room. Dove checked Jenna was still sleeping and then wandered down to the coffee machine. It was far superior to the one at the station, and she fixed them two lattes with cinnamon, before approaching the reception desk.

The woman behind the desk smiled. "Have you finished visiting?"

"No, not yet. I just wondered if I could have a look at Mickey's visitors in the past six months," Dove said, still not quite sure why she was pushing this so much. Was it guilt and her memory of a girl she hadn't been able to save? The hospital was clean and peaceful, all white-painted walls and big panels of glass looking out on to neatly mown lawns.

Patients were walking outside, some with walking frames, others with nurses beside them. A raised vegetable bed had several wheelchair-users gathered around it, their gardening forks and trowels busy turning over the damp earth.

Five years next week. Was it too much to hope for a miracle for Mickey Delaney?

Back in Mickey's room, Jenna had woken up and was sitting, holding Mickey's pale hand, stroking it.

Steve accepted his coffee with thanks. "I was just saying to Jenna, I'm sorry I startled her," he added, smiling easily at the girl opposite them.

"Hi, Jenna," Dove said.

Her face registered shock, eyes wide. "What are you doing here?"

"Just visiting," Dove told her.

Steve took up the conversational thread. "I don't know much about people in a coma, but how is she doing?"

"I've read up on it ever since they said Mickey might never come round," Jenna said fiercely. "And there's a chance she could still wake up any time and be okay. They don't know how much damage was done in the fall, so she might not have use of her legs or something but she could still be alive!"

Dove knew from her own reading that Mickey's was a rare case and she was unlikely to wake up, but she smiled as if she believed in miracles too — and hell, the job she was in, maybe part of her did.

"She had a fever last month, and the doctors were worried in case it turned into pneumonia, but she fought it off. She's still strong, even like this!"

"We believe you," Steve said gently. "And we can see how strong Mickey is. She was an athlete, and she survived being attacked, that drop into the quarry. She's tough, isn't she?"

Jenna studied them. "Why are you here? I saw on social media Jamie and Caz are being charged with the murders, so that's it, isn't it?"

"You don't seem surprised," Dove observed.

Jenna's cheeks flushed pink. "Oh, but I was. I never thought it was them, but when I saw it, I guess it just made sense. I'm not saying they should have done, but everyone knows what Ellis did . . ."

"Three other people died too," Dove reminded her. "And actually, as I seem to keep reminding you, there is a high probability Ellis didn't attack Mickey."

Jenna said nothing, rummaged in her bag and pulled out her phone.

"I saw in the visitor's log you come every week on Wednesday morning."

Jenna nodded, her curtain of blonde hair hiding her face now as she bent over her friend. "Sometimes I have to work and need to go after twenty minutes, but when that happens I always pop back in the evening to spend a decent amount of time with her. Her parents and a few other friends visit too. Lots of people came to start with, and sometimes journalists do a piece on her. They even did a reconstruction of what might have happened that night for a Crimewatch programme."

"But nobody appears to know what really did happen," Steve said softly.

"It was Ellis," Jenna said obstinately. "You know, Russ — Mickey's dad — won't even look at her properly because he feels so guilty about what happened. He told me he almost told her to stay in after the competition and rest." She looked down at her watch and got up quickly. "I've got to teach a class at two. Gotta go."

She grabbed her bag and almost ran from the room. Dove looked after her, and then back at the girl in the bed. One of the many photos around the room showed the three girls, Mickey, Jenna and Caz, posing in school uniform, laughing at the camera. Their hair was flying out in the wind, and they looked carefree and so young.

Dove picked up the framed photo and studied it, then passed it to Steve. The girls in the picture were all laughing, but was Caz's expression slightly off? Less genuine than the others? Dove shook her head, and Steve placed it carefully back on the bedside cabinet. The niggle was still there, deep in her belly.

"Something still isn't right with this lot, is it?" Steve said, watching Mickey as her chest rose and fell in a steady rhythm, and the monitors bleeped with her heart beat.

Dove was watching Mickey too. "I wonder if she can hear our voices?"

As she spoke, a stray beam of sunlight shone out through the scudding grey clouds, lighting a path to Mickey's bed, highlighting the girl's quiet face. Dove almost held her breath, but nothing happened, and the sunbeam was gone as quickly as it had arrived.

CHAPTER FORTY-SIX

'Are you scared, Mickey?'

It was the first thing I heard after I fell, that whisper in my ear. I can't feel much now. I drift along wrapped in a snuggly white blanket, cocooned and safe, but the whispered words make my heart race.

Machinery bleeps and I hear other voices now, raised in worry.

There were sharp concerned voices as I lay broken and helpless at the bottom of the quarry. They asked me to open my eyes, they asked me what happened, who did this to me.

I tried to tell them, but speaking was beyond me.

I could feel my eyelids flutter, and then the noises became distant, as though I was in a tunnel. When I woke again I was warm and safe, still in the light-filled tunnel. New voices came and went.

I can't open my eyes. I can't speak. I can't move. I'm always drifting through my tunnel, observing as far as I can with my eyes shut, but never taking part. Just the one voice has the power to terrify me, even now.

'Are you scared, Mickey?'

CHAPTER FORTY-SEVEN

Dove was in the garden, She'd just laid out her yoga mat in the shade, when her phone rang. She didn't recognise the number.

"Is that DC Dove Milson? It's Jenna Essex, from the dance academy . . ."

"Hello, Jenna. Are you okay?"

"No . . ." There was a sob and a scuffling sound. "Sorry, but I'm in the car park at Greenview Hospital. Mickey died . . . She actually died. I can't bear it."

"All right, Jenna, I'm so sorry. Is someone with you? Mickey's parents?" Dove was devastated for the family. Another blow after Caz's murder charge. And how would Jamie take this? Whatever their thoughts on collusion, the evidence showed Caz alone was the perpetrator — she had carried out the murders. He had lost his partner, his baby's mother and now his sister. It was a horrific sequence of events for anyone to bear.

"I need you to meet me . . . I . . . I want to show you something," Jenna said unexpectedly, grief and pain raw in her voice, tears still clogging her words. "Can you meet me at the waste ground by the Delaneys' house?"

"Yes. Give me twenty minutes to drive out there. Or do you want me to pick you up? Are you all right to drive?"

"I'm fine." A note of steel had crept into Jenna's voice. "I'm really fine."

She ended the call, but Dove was already thinking about the fastest route. Layla had stretched happily out on her yoga mat, narrowed eyes daring Dove to move her, so she abandoned the mat and pulled her shoes on.

Jenna was waiting on the swings. She must have broken all the speed limits to get up here so quickly, Dove thought, as she jogged towards her.

The girl's face was streaked with tears, her hair pulled back in a messy knot, but she held up a hand as Dove opened her mouth to say again how sorry she was. "Please don't, or I'll lose it. Just come with me."

Dove slid her hand over her phone in her tracksuit pocket, and followed as Jenna led her through a gap in the hedge and into the woods. "Am I allowed to ask where we're going?" Dove enquired. The shadows were lengthening into evening, and the smells of hot baked earth and dusty greenery filled the air.

It was cooler under the trees, and Jenna led the way to the quarry, paused, gave a stifled sob and turned left. Puzzled, Dove followed her. They carried on for another ten minutes before they came to an old bomb shelter. It was an ugly concrete structure, set half in the ground, half above. Covered in tangled ivy and brambles, the roof was hardly visible from the path.

Jenna stopped. "This was our secret place, mine and Mickey's when we were kids. Nobody else knew about it, or if they did, they could never get in. The only way is to swing down from that tree and climb in through the broken roof . . ." She pointed to a long-branched ash, which trailed green and grey lichened fingers across the derelict shelter. "We found it by accident one day . . ."

Dove wasn't quite sure what she meant, but without warning, she dumped her bag, sprang lightly on to an ancient fallen oak and jumped, catching the tree branch as though it was one of the uneven bars. She hung there for a second, before swinging to gain momentum, launching on to the barely visible roof, and disappearing inside.

"Hey, be careful!" Dove found her palms were sweating. Oh God, what was in this place? If Jenna got hurt, she would be screwed for not calling this in. Just as she was wondering whether to follow the girl, and try to find another way in, Jenna emerged, pulling herself out of the crack in the roof with both hands, bending back to retrieve something.

She threw it deftly towards Dove. "Catch!"

Dove retrieved the plastic container, as Jenna reversed her swing and jumped, landing lightly on flattened weeds, her long hair catching the light, her face fierce.

She reached out, took the box carefully from Dove, and prised it open. With a sound like a gunshot, the plastic, brittle with age, cracked right across the lid. They both jumped, then Jenna reached inside and took out a slim notebook. The once glossy pink cover was mildewed, but the pages rustled with secrets, protected by the box. "This is Mickey's diary," Jenna said.

* * *

Jenna sat in the interview room, back very straight, face composed. DCI Franklin started the recording, but Dove hardly had time to ask any questions before Jenna began speaking. Clearly this was something she had been holding on to for years, and the relief she felt at finally releasing the secrets was evident from her body language. As she spoke, her shoulders began to sag, and exhaustion showed in her face.

"Jamie always hated Mickey. Everyone thought he adored her, but the truth was he was jealous. Mickey always said he told her he wanted to be an only child. That stupid story about him starting her gymnastics career by hanging her up on the bars? It was bollocks. He hung her up there to scare her, and he was pissed when she was stronger than he thought."

"Did he ever hurt her physically?"

273

"Yes, lots of times, but he was so clever nobody saw what was going on. He would give her Chinese burns or pinch her to make her cry. She was terrified of him, and she said gymnastics gave her a chance to forget. He couldn't hurt her in the gym, and she trained harder to stay away from home. It was getting worse around the time she had her accident. Mickey said he watched her all the time, stole her stuff to freak her out, but never in a temper, you know? I never once saw Jamie lose it. It's like he doesn't have any proper emotions. He's so cold all the time. He never cries properly because he's sad or angry, although he's a bloody good actor and can turn it on when people are watching."

"Why didn't Mickey tell anyone what was happening?" Dove asked.

Jenna shook her head. "You don't understand. Jamie told her he would kill her, would ruin her career, and she was so scared. Don't forget she had been suffering this her whole life, and by the end she had lost track of what was real."

"But she told you?"

"I found out by accident," Jenna said. "I went to her house to see if she wanted to hang out, and her mum said go on up." She paused. "They were in Mickey's bedroom, she and Jamie. She was lying on the bed and he had his hand right here," Jenna indicated high up on her own thigh. "He wasn't doing anything, but I could tell Mickey was scared."

"What happened then?"

"He laughed it off and gave her a hug, turned on the charm with me. He's so good-looking and like I said, he's an actor, but I've always been good at reading people . . ."

"So Mickey told you?"

"She said he had been terrorising her for years," Jenna frowned. "After that, she would tell me when he hurt her. It wasn't just physical. It was mind games. That was one of the reasons she said she couldn't tell anyone else. She said she never had a black eye or anything, so who would believe her own brother hated her so much? She was ashamed, too, like she had done something to deserve it."

"Was it sexual?"

"No . . ." Jenna considered this. "No, because I don't think Jamie felt that way about anyone. Caz, Izzy, Mae all slept with him when they were teenagers. Caz has been so in love with him for forever . . . I wasn't surprised they had hooked up together, but kind of shocked when they had a baby. It didn't fit. But then I thought he was just blending in, doing what was expected. The escape rooms was perfect for him. He likes to see people afraid, maybe because he can't experience it himself?"

Dove sat back and flashed a glance at her superior. He looked as drained as she felt. "So what did you take to Caz's house the night before the murders? Not the diary, surely?"

"Of course not," Jenna said scornfully. "I promised Mickey I would hide it away, and I kept my promise. I heard Jamie and Caz had a baby, and I was kind of worried . . . Nobody else knows what Jamie is, you see. Even if I showed Caz the diary, she would say it was just Mickey hating her brother, and full of crap. But it's true I was looking at old photos and I found some from the night Mickey was attacked. I was kind of into photography then and I'd borrowed my uncle's old camera. I had piles and piles of film I never bothered to get developed, not till recently. Now I'm moving out, I kind of wanted to put the past to rest, as much as I could."

"Even though you took photos on the night Mickey was attacked, you didn't bother to get the film developed?" Dove queried.

"It didn't seem important, and everyone had their phones anyway. The police got us all to show them any photos and videos we took, checked through our social media. There were over twenty kids at the football, and me trying to get artistic shots with an old camera didn't seem relevant. I still didn't think it was, even when I finally got them all developed and shoved them in a folder. I never saw anything wrong. Until the night I was packing up my stuff." Jenna pointed at the photos that lay before them on the table, now displayed in tagged folders. "They're timestamped, which always annoyed me because I figured it ruins a good photograph."

Dove and DCI Franklin let her push the photos into order, even though they had already been through them. Jenna had been smart enough not to part with the originals to Caz. She had copied the relevant ones on a home printer and stashed the real ones away.

"Here at half nine, Jamie is playing. He's in the red top. I'd only just arrived because I was hanging out with Mickey, before she said she was tired and walked off into the woods."

Jenna tapped the next two photos. "Jamie had finished his game. The next team came on and he was drinking with Nathan and Oliver." There were a few pictures of the next match, more of bystanders laughing and smoking. Cans of lager were stacked by the hedge. A few kids were dancing. Dove could almost feel the heat of a carefree summer evening.

"This is the last one Jamie is in. It was taken by Izzy, and it's me, Becky and a few more from gymnastics. You can only just see it, but . . ." She broke off and bit her lip.

Behind the pouting, posing girls, a back view of Jamie in his red top, slipping through the gap in the hedge, heading towards the woods.

"Did you mention to Jamie that was where Mickey had gone?" DCI Franklin asked.

Jenna nodded her head miserably. "Yes. I was annoyed she wouldn't come to the game with me and hang out. When he asked where she was, I said she had gone off into the woods. He would have known she was heading down to the quarry. It's where we went to smoke or party sometimes. Whether Mickey lost or won a competition, she liked to just sit there, on the edge of the quarry, going over every move she had made during the event. She told me once it was what made her good. She could correct any mistakes in her mind before the next training session."

"You must have suspected it was Jamie who attacked Mickey?" Dove said flatly.

"Of course, but I thought he was there, at the game, partying with us. Everyone said so, and there was footage to prove it," Jenna said. "I was terrified of Jamie afterwards, because of the diary, and he came looking for me, found me on my own by the swings. He . . . he was so convincing when he said it was Ellis, so intense and . . . I suppose I wanted to believe him, didn't want it to be Mickey's own brother. Even though he had been a bastard to her, she was kind of obsessed with him. Anyway, why would he suddenly want her dead?"

"Maybe they had a row?" DCI Franklin suggested.

"No . . ." Jenna hesitated. "Mickey was holding out for this letter. She's gone for a scholarship at an elite training academy in Yorkshire. It would have meant being at boarding school, training and touring during the holidays. She'd gone through all the selection process and she was waiting to hear. Every day she'd text me to say the mail had come and the letter hadn't."

"Did Jamie know about this?"

"No. She made me promise not to say anything."

"Her parents didn't tell Jamie? It's a big thing to hide from him if they didn't?" DCI Franklin mused.

"Mickey said Jamie didn't know," Jenna told them.

"Okay, leave that for now." The DCI made a note and moved on. "What happened when you realised Jamie was implicated in the photos you developed?"

"When I saw the photos, I felt sick. Eventually I called Caz on her business phone. Her mobile number is on the website, hers and Jamie's. I didn't know who else to tell, and suddenly it seemed important to speak to the only other person still involved, who had been there with us. It was a massive mistake, wasn't it?" Jenna's eyes filled with tears. "I made it worse."

"You couldn't possibly have predicted what would happen, so please don't beat yourself up about it," DCI Franklin said kindly. "Thank you, Jenna, for being so honest with us, and I can promise you Jamie will not be walking free from this one."

CHAPTER FORTY-EIGHT

"Mickey!"

Jenna is calling me, and I shout back. She's crying, saying something about a letter. My letter. My whole life could change with that letter.

"Mickey!"

I am running down the stairs, hearing the thump of letters on the mat, my fingers fumbling to see the names on the envelopes. Nothing. I sink on to the bottom stair, and my phone beeps with a message. Jenna wants to know if today is the day. I reply with a sad emoji.

I don't remember when it started. I've lived with this my whole life. It sounds stupid, but I wouldn't even know how to begin telling anyone what happens behind closed doors.

My brother has always hated me. He's kept up a string of little cruelties since I was a young child, probably even since I was a baby. He thinks I'm the favoured one, the one given a chance to pursue my dreams. He never misses a chance to tell me I'm nothing, pathetic and weak.

From stolen toys to the time he burned my cuddly toy bunny with a cigarette lighter, right in front of me in the garden. I was eight, and he said I was too old for soft toys. He watched me constantly, and I know from the outside looking in he was the devoted brother, but the hugs and hand-holding people saw came with pinches and squeezes that left me breathless and hurting.

He tried not to leave bruises, although these were always explained away by my active nature, my clumsiness, and then my gymnastics training.

Jamie teamed up with Caz, although he told me she was pathetic too. He used her to hide my kit, steal my lucky mascot, a pocket-sized plastic pig. Just before try-outs I would find my possessions missing, catch a group of girls whispering and laughing behind their hands.

My brother would feed Caz little bits of gossip — how I still slept with the light on, how I wet the bed, how I cuddled up to an old brown bear at night. Little cruelties. The kids at school devoured it all, and my handsome big brother indulged them. He made his way through the lot of them, telling me the intimate details of his sex life, how the girls were boring or pathetic.

Only Caz seemed to remain in his good books. He was still disdainful of her, but he told me she was different. She liked to be scared, and he liked to be worshipped, so I suppose they were a match made in heaven. Or hell, depending on how you look at things.

* * *

I was almost at the quarry when I heard him coming. A twig cracked under his feet, and when I swung around I spotted the red of his football shirt. Exhausted from the competition, relieved to be almost free of him, I walked a little faster. I could turn left at the fork in the path, and hide down by the old bunker until he went away again.

But he called my name softly, and I knew then. The smell of dust and dense greenery filled my senses as I paused in panic, before I started to run.

I could hear the drumbeat of his running feet, following me steadily, the hunter after its prey. When I stopped at last, bursting from the overhanging branches into the dappled late-evening sunlight, I whirled round to confront him.

I was exhausted, terrified beyond my worst nightmares, body hurting, sweat sticky on my face. I saw in his face what he was going to do. It was what he'd wanted to do all along.

The thrill of the chase, maybe . . . He moved quickly towards me as I threw up my hands to ward him off, opened my mouth to say *something, anything. His hands were on my arms, long fingers cruel and pinching my skin. The pale blue eyes, so much like mine, but faded somehow, colder, without any fire and passion.*

He was like an automaton, moving towards his goal. I noticed then that he was wearing those plastic gloves Dad keeps in the shed for when he does the weedkiller. Thin, blue surgical-type gloves that Mum jokes make him look like a serial killer.

"Why do you hate me so much?" I rasped finally, my throat dry and dusty, finding the courage to confront him, here in this private place. "Why can't you leave me alone?"

He smiled, slowly, contemplatively. "Are you scared, Mickey?"

"Why? Do you want me to be? You do, don't you? It's all you've ever wanted, to make sure I live my life being scared of you and what you might do to me." I was astonished at my own bravery. Even though I felt so small and fragile against his superior height and physical strength, I was still strong.

Jenna's words stayed with me when I told her about the scholarship, gave her my diary. "Soon he won't be able to hurt you ever again." I could still feel her arms around me, her soft hair on my face, our cheeks touching. My one true friend, and I loved her so much.

He didn't answer, just pulled me close, forcing my chin up so our eyes met. "You can't just leave me, you know. Did you really think you could get away with not telling me?"

"What do you mean?" I genuinely had no idea what he was talking about.

"The letter, Mickey, I saw the fucking letter!"

"I honestly don't know what you mean!"

"Farley College, the gymnastics scholarship? Elite training scheme? You thinking you can just piss off and live in Yorkshire . . . Ring any bells?"

"I haven't got it yet, and even if I do get offered a place, I haven't decided whether to go or not."

He could tell I was lying, and his face contorted with rage. "You little bitch. All these years I've supported you, hell, I made you what you are today. You'd never be so focused, so good if I hadn't trained you. It was all me! Not Mum and Dad with their precious little gymnast, giving you all of the chances I never had."

I saw it then, as I'd never done before, had missed in my terror, in my childish blindness. My own brother was broken. His version of our childhood, so different from my own memories. Did Mum and Dad see it too? Was this the real reason for the secrecy about the training scholarships? All that stuff about not hurting Jamie's feelings . . . Were they just trying to get me away safely?

Jamie has no feelings, no real ones anyway. He has rage, and impulses, I suppose, and he enjoys fear, but those are just useless emotions. He has no love, no compassion, no loyalty and tenderness, none of the things that make us truly human.

He started to hit me then, methodically beating every part of my body, pinning me down so I couldn't escape. I tried to scream, but he shoved a balled-up football sock in my mouth. It made me gag, even as I tried to fight him off. My body felt like it was on fire. The reason for the gloves became clear. He had come prepared.

I could feel blood on my face, the fiery bursts of pain as he hit me again and again. I rolled away, trying to protect myself, pushing his hands away, but each blow was measured and controlled, and each blow broke me a little more.

As one hand moved for my throat, I felt the ground beneath my desperately scrabbling hands. Our fight had brought us close to the edge of the quarry. The long drop to rocks and water was so very near. My eyes were so swollen, I could hardly see, but flashes of light showed me the sun was nearly gone, the shadows were calling, feeling the rush of air, the freedom. My fingers scrabbled harder, nails tearing, pulling at the earth, trying to jackknife my body — and then I started to fall.

I think he would have killed me slowly, but this way I was finally free of him, and at the very last moment I was in control.

It seemed a long time before I hit the ground, the rocks sharp and vicious, surrounding the oily water like sharks' teeth, sinking into my body. He made no sound as I fell. No yells of horror, no screams for help floated down after me. I cried out just once, my voice echoing around the quarry.

For me, it was as though I was truly flying, leaving everything behind. The pain, the fear, the humiliation — I left it all in the quiet woods.

It was him all the time. Did he want me to die or had he planned to keep torturing me? Perhaps he would go home and pretend it never happened, that he never had a sister at all.

281

I wonder what he will be doing in five, twenty, or thirty years' time? Perhaps he too will be dead. Or maybe he will be living his life, daring to pretend I never existed.

It seemed a long time before anyone came to help me, as I lay broken and bleeding in the quarry, and in my head I started to count — 1, 2, 3, 4, 5 . . . I knew if I made it to 6 I would live.

But everything was too bright, too jumbled, and the voices, when they came, were too loud. I retreated into another place, a more comfortable version of my world.

CHAPTER FORTY-NINE

"Mickey Delaney passed away earlier this evening." DCI Franklin started the meeting with this sombre announcement, genuine sorrow in his voice.

There was a murmur of shock and speculation from the team, as they waited for him to continue. Most of them had been looking forward to going home early for once, Dove thought, watching their faces. There would be weeks spent building on the evidence they had already accumulated, preparing for the court cases, but the initial pressure was off. They had a result.

"According to the hospital, Mickey passed away peacefully, and her family have been informed." He sighed. "Given the nature of our current investigation, and the interest from the press, we will proceed with caution. However, certain new evidence has come to light regarding Mickey's initial attack, which means we have been given the green light to re-examine the case." He smiled grimly. "You will see from the email I sent that Jenna Essex came forward with information after Mickey died." He clicked the mouse on the desk.

Dove bit her lip as images of Mickey's diary, that sad, battered pink notebook, followed by Jenna's photographs, appeared on screen. Why hadn't she ever told anyone what was going on?

"As far as I can see we still have the same problem as we had with the Beach Escape Room murders. Granted, the new evidence shows Jamie Delaney in a whole different light, and if he was abusing his sister he must be a prime suspect, but Caz is up there too. And we know she is also capable of murder," Josh said. "What about the murder in the Philippines? Did Interpol get back?"

DCI Franklin nodded. "It's going to take a while, but early signs are good. A local barman was arrested but later released without charge, and there are a couple of witness statements stating they saw a man with blood-stained clothing running from the beach on a track down to the road. The physical description does match Jamie's. Just to note, we have evidence Caz was definitely not present during that incident."

"And don't forget Caz was at the football match during the time frame we have for Mickey's attack," Steve added, "So she is only in the frame for the escape-room murders."

Dove was staring at the timestamp on the photographs. "Mickey and Jenna arrived on the waste ground at eight. According to her original statement she said Mickey wanted to be on her own and walked away into the woods, using their usual path." She pointed at the second photograph. "Any of the kids near the hedge line, which is exactly where Jamie was standing, could have looked over and seen her heading for the trees. Jenna said they all frequently used that path to get to the quarry, but only she and Mickey knew about the old bunker, where the diary was later hidden."

"But why was he mad at her this particular evening?" DI Blackman asked thoughtfully. "If he'd been abusing her for years, what suddenly triggered the urge to kill her?" He looked down at his notes. "According to the doctors' reports, the beating she sustained was extensive, and the fall into the quarry should have killed her outright."

Mickey's smiling face appeared back on the screen, flanked by Jenna and Caz, and again Dove felt a little catch in her heart. "Jenna mentioned in her interview Mickey had gone for a scholarship at a boarding school. She seemed to think Jamie was kept in the dark about it, and Mickey was waiting for a letter that she hoped would offer her a place. Perhaps their parents decided to tell him after all, or he found out?"

"The forestry workers heard a scream at 8.30 p.m., and when they arrived at the scene there was no sign of anyone else," Lindsey said. She looked up from her iPad. "Are we going to interview Jamie about this new development tonight?"

"No, tomorrow morning," DCI Franklin said. "The Chief Super was very clear that with the extra budget we follow exactly where the new evidence is pointing, so evidence from the scene will be retested, but at this stage we will not be re-interviewing unless we find any anomalies in the witness statements. I'm confident we can lay this to rest within the week, but we need more to be confident the case is watertight."

Dove could tell by her colleagues' faces they too thought this was a little optimistic.

"We aren't a cold-case unit, though, so shouldn't they be dealing with this?" DS Pete Wyndham was clearly not impressed with the added workload. "I just mean they are better equipped than us for this kind of reinvestigation," he added hastily, as DCI Franklin turned a frosty gaze on him.

"Because we have already charged Jamie and Caz, we are involved, and this case, I shouldn't really have to point out, will also be relevant to the Beach Escape Rooms murders when our perpetrators come to stand trial," the DCI said icily, his cool blue gaze sweeping the room. "I understand you are all exhausted, and appreciate your efforts, but we are a team. I want us to pull together until we are finished. Any questions?"

There were mutterings of "No, sir," and the team moved back out into the main office area.

Dove lingered for a moment, still focused on the photographs. "Boss, I was just thinking . . . What if Ellis Bravery was watching the kids when Jamie snuck out into the woods? Perhaps he saw him head after Mickey."

DI Blackman nodded. "Go on."

"So if Jamie has convinced himself and everyone else that Ellis was responsible for Mickey's attack, basically rewriting history, as he has possibly also done with the murder in the Philippines, maybe he was worried by Ellis. Could Ellis have threatened him? Or maybe not even that, it could just have been a comment Jamie took as a threat."

Steve, halfway to the door, had heard her suggestion. "But if he saw Jamie the night Mickey was attacked, why did he never speak out at the time?"

DCI Franklin was frowning. "Maybe he didn't see anything at all, but when Jamie confronted him that night at the escape rooms, Ellis said enough to rile him and make him think that after all this time, Ellis might be going to reveal who was actually responsible. It would ruin Jamie's whole life."

CHAPTER FIFTY

Two days later, the DCI was waiting impatiently as they filed into the briefing room. "Firstly, thank you for your time on this one. We are not a cold-case team, but obviously our investigations have led us to this stage, and we were lucky to receive the funding to reopen Mickey Delaney's case. It was not easy, but as you know, with a key witness and further evidence presenting itself, I took a chance. A big chance. You have all pulled it out of the bag to get to this very satisfactory result."

Dove waited, almost holding her breath. The final piece of Mickey's puzzle, and justice for the girl that had been so long coming.

"If you would like to look at the screen, you can see we had the evidence from the original scene retested. It was a huge site, stretching from the quarry to the path through the woods, and the site was challenging regarding access and egress." He paused to take a mouthful of coffee as he clicked the mouse, bringing up a timeline they were all now extremely familiar with.

"This close-up is Jamie Delaney leaving the match through the gap in the hedge. As you can see, although it isn't great quality, he is wearing two gold earrings in his left ear. DI Lincoln?"

George pulled several plastic bags from the box on the table next to him. "The earring in this bag, recovered from the quarry floor, next to Mickey's body, was assumed to be hers. She was missing an earring, and this gold stud is similar enough for the assumption to have been made. This is not an excuse, but I can see how it happened. We are all human," he added sternly. "Retesting, and lab analysis of the photograph, has shown us firstly the earring Mickey had in her right ear was a gold flower. Jenna has told us the girls often wore just the one earring at that time." He looked baffled at this but continued with grim pleasure. "Secondly, the DNA match for a second earring recovered at the top of the quarry, at the scene of the attack, and buried in crushed grass and weeds, is Jamie Delaney's."

The DCI took over again. "There is a ninety-eight per cent probability the piece of jewellery doesn't belong to Mickey, but to her brother. Coupled with our witness, the diary and the photographs showing Jamie at the match wearing an earring, and then leaving through the gap in the hedge, lead us to the conclusion he was responsible for the attempted murder of his sister. Clearly it will be up to the CPS, but now that she has died, he will likely be charged with murder. Following an exchange of information with our colleagues in the Philippines, it also looks like Jamie will be charged with the murder of Elsa Murphy, a nineteen-year-old backpacker from Wales."

Up on the screen, photos of Mickey and Elsa smiled down at the assembled team. The girls were similar in looks, with both having striking red hair.

* * *

"You have no reason to question me again! Haven't you already wrecked our family?" Jamie said angrily.

"We will be making a formal complaint regarding this harassment," his solicitor added. "My client is suffering considerable emotional stress, and is also grieving for his sister."

DCI Franklin laid all the evidence out methodically and succinctly. After a few furious protests, Jamie grew cold and silent, hands clasped neatly in front of him, pale bony face composed and cruel.

In answer to all the questions, he merely stated, "No comment."

Once DCI Franklin had finished, he looked long and hard at the young man. "You will be formally charged with the attempted murder of Mickey Delaney. And as I mentioned, our colleagues will want to interview you regarding the murder of Elsa Murphy."

Jamie looked coolly round the room and smiled so thinly it barely touched his lips. His hazel eyes were icy. "It wasn't me, you know. It was someone else who hurt Mickey and Elsa. It wasn't me."

"Do you want to explain?"

"No, but it was a different person, not me at all. I always get the blame, and it wasn't my fault." He sighed. "You don't understand."

"You could try to explain?" the DCI suggested.

"No point," Jamie shrugged. "Police are all bastards. You managed to clear up a few cases by pinning the blame on me. Congratulations."

After the interview, Dove followed the DCI upstairs to his office. He sat down behind his desk and indicated the seat opposite. She felt completely drained, exhaustion coming in waves, but she forced herself to sit upright in her chair, shoulders back, feet together.

Dove waited, unsure what he was going to say, feeling a bit like a kid in detention at school, despite the good result.

But he finally smiled, relief in his pale blue eyes. "You got lucky with Jenna Essex."

Dove nodded. "I'm glad Jenna found the courage to finally come forward. I'm just sad Mickey died. I was kind of hoping for a miracle."

"I think we all were, but fairy-tale endings rarely happen. Mickey's case was one that stuck with me, you know — you always get ones you can't solve, and you feel maybe you failed in some way. So this result is extremely satisfying."

He watched her. "Just remember we won't be able to solve everything, and injustices will still occur sometimes. Even though we might have all our evidence, sometimes it just doesn't pan out."

"Understood, sir."

He frowned at her. "I spoke to Chris earlier today."

Dove blinked at him, shocked. Her old boss. "You did?"

"He was saying how much he wanted you back now Rose has left."

"Rose has left? She never told me," Dove said. She and her ex-colleague didn't have the easiest of relationships, but she was surprised and a little hurt Rose hadn't shared the news. "I thought she was in it for the long haul."

"Would you ever go back to source handling?" he countered.

Dove shook her head. "No. It was an experience, but I'm happy with the MCT. I feel like I've learned a lot and put down some roots now."

"I'm glad to hear that Chris won't be able to lure you away, because I feel you are correct. You do fit right in here." He smiled at her. "Now go home and get some rest, or go surfing or whatever you do to relax."

"Yes, sir." Dove walked back through the office smiling to herself. He was right. She couldn't solve every injustice, but — her smile deepened — she could have a damn good go at trying.

Steve was waiting at the door, coffee in each hand. "Ready to go, partner?"

"I'm ready." Dove led the way down the corridor.

CHAPTER FIFTY-ONE

Dove sat cross-legged on the edge of the quarry, the rough stones hot from the midday sun under her hands. Far below, a number of sharp rocks had been left exposed by the summer drought. The same ones Mickey had seen as she fell that sweaty summer's evening five years ago.

The emerald-green water, with its slick of oily dust, gleamed as the sunlight dazzled through the trees, and paused to dance on pointed toes — the star of the show, the prima donna — right in the centre of the quarry.

"Dove? You know, when you said a little car ride, I didn't realise you were coming out here." Delta scrambled down next to her, long bare legs in cut-off denim shorts, red-spotted top tied at her midriff, her short brown hair framing her serious expression.

"Neither did I!" Gaia sat down carefully on Dove's other side, wincing slightly. She wore her usual black trousers and black silk top. Her make-up was perfect, and her hair was cropped and smooth.

"I just thought it was kind of fitting. You know, closure maybe," Dove said. "I'm so glad you're okay, Gaia."

"So you thought you'd treat me to a ride to an old quarry," Gaia sighed, "Gotcha. Most people send flowers. Uri gave a voucher for a spa day . . ."

"That's a bit cheapskate for Uri," Delta said slyly, and giggled as her aunt reached out to slap her arm.

"It's a spa in Monte Carlo, and he's flying me there in his helicopter. We're staying for the weekend," Gaia continued.

"Better," Delta grinned. She wriggled round until she was comfortable, one leg up, chin on her knee, fingers linked. Her expression changed as she looked down into the quarry again. "Jamie nearly got away with it, didn't he?"

"He won't now. The evidence will convict him, I'm sure of it," Dove said. "I just wish she had survived — been, I don't know, a medical miracle. It's sad it was only after her death Jenna felt able to come forward. She said she had a bargain with fate, that she wouldn't tell on Jamie and Mickey would be okay."

Delta shot her a look, blue eyes narrowed against the sun. "I wonder what Mickey would be like now, if it had never happened? She'd be eighteen, if she'd lived. A year younger than me."

"She would be."

"I guess we won't ever really know exactly what happened, why he killed her. If Jamie won't tell, Mickey is dead and nobody else witnessed it," Delta said, throwing a small handful of pebbles down into the quarry. They fell, landing far down with the faintest of sounds.

"Mickey's parents, Russ and Claire, confirmed Mickey had just been awarded a scholarship to some elite sports college in Yorkshire. They said they got the letter the day she was attacked, but the mail was late that day and Mickey had already left for school. They intended to tell both the kids the next day, apparently. Perhaps Jamie saw it, realised she would be leaving, and he just lost control. The psych evaluation suggests Jamie displays all the traits of antisocial personality disorder, which makes it easier to understand his reasoning. People with these traits are often manipulative, charming, very controlling and have little or no conscience." Dove pushed her hair back. "He must have worn gloves to beat Mickey — his DNA wasn't on her body — although they were never found, which shows forward planning, again typical of his type of personality disorder."

"I've worked with people like that," Gaia said. "Their perception of the world, and their place in it, is different. In their heads, they are never to blame for anything. And they are often deceitful and reckless."

Her sister and niece stared at her, until she said, slightly irritably, "An ex of mine, okay? I just know, and I did some study into personality disorders when I removed myself from the relationship."

"I'm leaving California Dreams next month," Delta told her suddenly. "I handed in my notice. It's on your desk right now."

Gaia studied her, assessing, "Your choice. I always said it was your choice, Delta."

"Did you quit because of Abi?" Dove said sympathetically.

Her niece shrugged. "Kind of."

"So what are you going to do now, or have you just got as far as buying that plane ticket?" Gaia queried, swinging her legs over the drop. She picked up a handful of stones in immaculate manicured hands and threw them over the edge.

All three sat in silence as the stones finally dropped with a tiny splash into the pool of water, barely even ruffling the surface.

Delta kept her gaze on the quarry. "Oh, I'll think of something. But you just know in your heart when it's time to move on, don't you?"

"I suppose you do." Dove regarded her thoughtfully. "Come on, I checked, and the tide's perfect, weather's gorgeous, and Quinn and I are taking the boards over to Claw Beach. Want to come? Gaia, I've got beer in the cooler in the car boot. You can sit on the beach and be glamorous."

Gaia rolled her eyes at her sister, and impatiently pushed her proffered hand away, "I can get up by myself, you know."

They walked slowly away, Delta linking arms with Gaia, Dove leading the way back to the car. She could hear her sister and niece laughing as she took in the sunlit woods, the narrow track, the brambles catching at their legs, absorbing the peace, the memories, and the pain of what had happened here. As the path forked, Dove took one last look back at the place and blinked hard. A cloud threw shadows over the quarry. The sunbeam had moved on, to dance somewhere else.

EPILOGUE

'Are you scared, Mickey?'

He's alone with me now, I think. There are no other voices. I can feel the pressure of a hand on mine, fingers closing around mine. I would love to jerk my hand away but suddenly I realise he isn't going to hurt me any more. He is happy with me as I am.

I don't want to wake up, to face him. I want to keep drifting along, warm and safe in the light.

But he keeps coming. Sometimes there seems to be a long time between his visits, although I don't really have much concept of time, of night and day. I dream I have feeling in my hands, just across the palms and around my thumbs, and I can hear my own breathing, deep and slow, like I'm underwater.

Voices, I recognise, and some voices I don't. Music, I like to hear. The smell of lemons, and of perfume, heady and sweet with the tang of summer. Caz for a while and now it's just Jenna. My best friend for ever, her words, her tears soothe me further. Her love, my parents' love, reaches my dream world, wraps me in warm velvet, and sends me drifting faster and further away. If I could talk to them all, I would say there was nothing she could have done, because it's true. It was all about me and him, nobody else.

The final scenes replay over and over in my head, and my body aches as though it is again under attack, but the fear is gone. I can't move, but the panic has long since faded, and my emotions are not a part of me anymore.

It is a different feeling to my fear of the man next door and so very far from my terror of the boy in my house. The boy I grew up with.

It's a blessing I can't see his cold, hard eyes, but even when he asks the same question again and again, he can't touch me. The lightness in my broken body, the gentle warmth enveloping my soul makes me drift off for longer and longer periods. Sometimes I am surprised I wake. Sometimes I don't want to.

I think he comes one final time, holding my hand, his voice echoing through my head. But as the warmth and light wrap me closely, and I turn towards them, away from him, I wonder, was he ever there at all?

'Are you scared, Mickey?'

Finally, I am not.

THE END

AUTHOR'S NOTE

This was a tough book to write, a bit of a milestone for me. My second novel written during a lockdown, my tenth book in all, and my sixth for wonderful Joffe Books. I am so grateful to be working with such an enthusiastic and professional team.

Many thanks are due to the whole team at Joffe Books, including Jasper (of course!), Emma, Nina, Elodie, Rudi and Annie. I have been lucky enough also to work with some amazing literary agents: thank you Lina Langlee at the North Literary Agency, and Kate Nash and her team at the Kate Nash Literary Agency.

Of course huge amounts of thanks and applause for all they do to the bloggers, the book reviewers, the tour organisers and the wonderful readers. Without you my books would never venture so far into the world, or be read by so many. To Jill, Bev, Tracy, Meg, Alan, Debs, Zoe and everyone in my Readers Club Newsletter.

To my wonderfully supportive groups of fellow authors and creatives — not only do we celebrate together and commiserate together but you provide me with a never-ending TBR pile!

You are all amazing.

Finally, thank you to my long-suffering family — my boys who are so used to me thumping out books on my ancient laptop, muttering plotlines and scrawling character notes on random scraps of paper.

I hope you enjoy Detective Dove Milson's third outing.

Best wishes,

D.E. White

If you have been, or are currently affected by any of the issues in this book, including domestic violence, you can call these numbers for non-judgemental, confidential information and support:

UK
Freephone National Domestic Abuse
Helpline 0808 2000 247

USA
0808 200 0247

In an emergency call 999 (UK) OR 911 (USA)

ALSO BY D.E. WHITE

DETECTIVE DOVE MILSON MYSTERIES
Book 1: GLASS DOLLS
Book 2: THE ICE DAUGHTERS
Book 3: THE ABBERLEY BEACH MURDERS

RUBY BAKER MYSTERIES
written as Daisy White
Book 1: BEFORE I LEFT
Book 2: BEFORE I FOUND YOU
Book 3: BEFORE I TRUST YOU

Thank you for reading this book.

If you enjoyed it please leave feedback on Amazon or Goodreads, and if there is anything we missed or you have a question about, then please get in touch. We appreciate you choosing our book.

Founded in 2014 in Shoreditch, London, we at Joffe Books pride ourselves on our history of innovative publishing. We were thrilled to be shortlisted for Independent Publisher of the Year at the British Book Awards.

www.joffebooks.com

We're very grateful to eagle-eyed readers who take the time to contact us. Please send any errors you find to corrections@joffebooks.com. We'll get them fixed ASAP.